Goodnight, Irene

— Jan Burke —

—— Simon & Schuster ——
New York   London   Toronto   Sydney   Tokyo   Singapore

SIMON & SCHUSTER
Simon & Schuster Building
Rockefeller Center
1230 Avenue of the Americas
New York, New York 10020

SIMON & SCHUSTER and colophon are registered
trademarks of Simon & Schuster Inc.

Designed by Songhee Kim
Manufactured in the United States of America

1   3   5   7   9   10   8   6   4   2

Library of Congress Cataloging-in Publication Data
Burke, Jan.
Goodnight, Irene/Jan Burke.
p.   cm.
I. Title.
PS3552.U72326G66   1993
813'.54—dc20   92–30745
                                 CIP

ISBN 0-671-78200-2

To

Antonia Adamo Fischer

Velda Kuntz Fischer

Eileen Stillman

Martha Burke and

Martha Otis

in gratitude for their faith

Author's Note

Naturally occurring high levels of fluoride can be found in the ground water of a number of areas of the United States, including some places in Arizona. However, the Arizona town used as one of the settings for this story was chosen because of its proximity to both the California border and Phoenix, not because of its water. I never came across the "five old crabs" when I visited there.

Acknowledgments

Deep appreciation is given to the many people who helped me with the research for this book, especially Debbie Arrington, of the *Long Beach Press Telegram;* Bob Flynn, retired *Evansville Press* political reporter, Don Smith, National City Police Department; Sergeant John Conely, Maricopa County Sheriff's Department; the Cypress, California, Police Department; Liz Martin-Snow of the California Dental Association; Skip Langley, for his expertise on fire and explosive gases; Garry Dougan of the Southern California Gas Department; Gary Wuchner of the Orange County Fire Department; Jacqueline Prebich, R.N.; Mark Prebich, R.R.T.; Ed Dohring, M.D.; Kelly Dohring, R.N.; Enda Brennan, Public Defender extraordinaire; Tonya Pearsley, Sandra Cvar, Paul Blevins, Peggy Lausin, Vera and Laurie Speake, and Sharon Weissman. A great deal of help in researching the book was given to me by the librarians at the Long Beach Public Library, the Angelo M. Iacoboni Library, and California State University, Long Beach Library. My thanks also to my friends and family, who were so supportive of this effort.

I am especially grateful to my father, John Fischer, who told me a story that led to writing this one, and to my husband, Timothy Burke, who encouraged me to write, shared the computer, read the drafts again and again and was supportive in a number of other ways.

While I acknowledge the help I've received from these and many other people, the errors are my own.

1

He loved to watch fat women dance. I guess O'Connor's last night on the planet was a happy one because that night he had an eyeful of the full-figured.

We had gone out that Saturday night for a drink at Banyon's, and somehow an honest-to-God bevy of bulging beauties had ended up in the same place. O'Connor never got up and danced with any of these women himself; I'm not sure he really would have enjoyed being the dancer as much as he did just watching them swing and sway with amazing grace. I don't think he heard a word I said all evening, which is just as well, since I was only grousing on a well-worn set of subjects. He just sat there, with an expression crossbred between reverence and desire, whenever some big old gal got up to shake and shimmy.

O'Connor and I had managed to remain friends through one of the ugliest divorces in the state of California—the divorce of his son, Kenny, and my older sister, Barbara. We were friends before their romance started and we both thought it was doomed from the word go. My sister has been a glutton for lousy relationships for years, so no surprise there. But I'm still mystified about how a great-hearted guy like O'Connor could have had anything to do with the gene pool of a nasty little bastard like Kenny.

My guess was that O'Connor's ex-wife was a real harpy, even though he never talked about her to me. Barbara told me they had split up when Kenny was a baby. Kenny had lived with his mother until he was fourteen, at which time she had packed him up like worn out clothing and sent him to live with O'Connor—no note, no warning, just a call saying the kid was coming in on a flight from Phoenix that afternoon. She had taken off for parts unknown—no one had heard from her for years.

The dancing ladies called it a night, and we decided to do the same. As I drove him home, he started telling Irish jokes, a sure sign he'd had a few too many. The jokes were old, but O'Connor could make me laugh just by laughing this ridiculous laugh of his. It started as a kind of noiseless shaking, then guffawing, on to tears, and he ended by taking out his handkerchief and blowing his big nose. I could never watch this performance with a straight face—by the time the handkerchief came out, I was a goner.

Kenny's red Corvette was parked in the driveway, so I pulled up at the curb. O'Connor climbed slowly out of the car. "You're dear to me, Irene," he said with a wink and little drunken bow.

"O'Connor, please don't sing it. It's one o'clock in the morning. People are trying to sleep."

I should have known better; he was going to sing it anyway, and my plea only made him relish doing so all the more. He laughed as he turned and took his bearings on the front door, heaved his big shoulders back as he took a deep breath and began to belt out "Goodnight, Irene" at the top of his lungs as he shambled up to the darkened house. This was old hat to me and his neighbors, but next door Mrs. Keene felt honor-bound to turn on her porch light to register annoyance. O'Connor grinned and went on in, waving as he closed the door.

The morning after our night at Banyon's, somebody left a package on O'Connor's front porch. Mrs. Keene was out watering her lawn and later she said she saw him come padding out in his bare feet and bathrobe to pick up the paper. He was a little hung over, I guess, because she said that he didn't see the package until the return trip. She was a little embarrassed to see him in his robe, so she didn't call out a "good morning" or anything, but she's a nosy bird and she was curious about the package.

Nobody knows exactly what happened after that, except that the explosion knocked Mrs. Keene on her keister and sent little pieces of O'Connor just about everywhere they could go.

I was at home, having a lazy morning, hanging around in an old pair of pj's and reading the paper with the supervision of my big gray tomcat, Wild Bill Cody, when the phone rang. It was Lydia Ames, an old pal of mine over at the newspaper where I used to work, the *Las Piernas News Express*.

"Irene! Does O'Connor live on Randall Avenue?"

"Who wants to know?" I asked, wary of her tone.

"Shit, Irene!"

Now Lydia has only cussed one other time in her life that I know of, and that was when Alicia Penderson showed up at our high school prom in a gown identical to Lydia's—a strapless affair, only on Alicia it seemed to be working harder to defy gravity.

So all of a sudden here's Lydia on a Sunday morning, talking blue and sounding like she was about to cry. I told her O'Connor's address. She didn't say anything for about four hours, or so it seemed, but I guess it was really about half a minute.

"Lydia, what the hell is going on?"

"Shit, Irene . . ." Now she *was* crying. "Irene, I think you better get over to O'Connor's place. We just got a report that there's been some kind of explosion—Baker's on his way to cover it."

The whole time I was getting dressed and driving over to O'Connor's, I kept telling myself that Lydia was pretty hysterical and that I didn't really know that anything had happened to O'Connor. Maybe just his house, maybe not O'Connor but someone else, maybe some other house.

That all started to change when I saw the rising smoke from half a mile away. A slow, cold numbing started in my throat and eventually froze me in place on the sidewalk across the street from his house. Clusters of firemen formed tense huddles with cops. The place was surrounded by fire trucks, police cars, the bomb-squad van, the coroner's ambulance. The house was smashed as if it were nothing more than an egg; a yolk of mud and debris was spilling out of its broken shell. I wanted to find O'Connor. I felt certain that if they would just let me look, just let someone who had cared about him look, I'd find him.

I sometimes hear about people knowing right away that someone they loved has died, that they feel the dead person's spirit leave or something. O'Connor stuck around.

I heard someone yell "Kelly!" and turned to see a tall black man walking toward me. It was Mark Baker, the reporter sent out by the *Express*. "Oh, God, Irene, I'm so sorry," he said in a shaky voice. I wasn't ready for sympathy, and looked away. He understood and stopped talking, just put one of his burly arms around my shoulders and guided me away from the crowd. Mark took me over to where Frank Harriman was trying to get some sense out of Mrs. Keene, then left to talk to one of the guys from the bomb squad.

Frank and I had met when he was a rookie cop in Bakersfield and I was on my first crime beat as a fledgling reporter. Now he was a homicide detective with the Las Piernas Police Department. I hadn't seen him for a long time, since before I quit the paper, but this wasn't the time to renew old acquaintances.

As I stood to one side, Frank noticed me and gave me one of those very protective "are-you-okay?" looks. I tried to avoid his eyes, and turned away from him, but to my horror looked up to see a coroner's assistant bagging a little piece of something soft.

Thank God I'm not a fainter. I must have looked bad, though, because Frank took me gently by the elbow and said, "Go home, Irene." I just stared at him.

"You still live in the same place?" he asked.

I nodded, because I didn't trust my voice. I was also busy with a tug-of-war—one minute I was trying to take it all in, the next, trying to shut it all out. I heard Frank say something about wanting to ask me some questions, later. I figured Mrs. Keene had told him about the previous night's serenade, but I was past caring. I heard the camera shutters of the forensic team, and out of the corner of my eye kept seeing the coroner's assistants with their goddamned plastic bags and forceps. I felt sick and weird . . . disconnected.

Frank was quiet for a minute; then he asked a cop to drive me home, but I shook it off and told him I could manage. I made sure he had my address, then left. I could feel him watching me as I walked to my car. I didn't look back at Frank or the house as I drove off.

As I rounded the corner I saw Kenny's red Corvette heading toward the house. For the one-millionth time, I felt sorry for him. He wasn't equipped for everyday life, let alone something like this. And for the two-millionth time, I knew I couldn't do anything about it.

It was a long time before I asked myself what had made Kenny get up and at'em so early on a Sunday morning.

2

Frank almost waited too long to come over. I was damned restless by late that afternoon.

Most of the time from when I left O'Connor's house until Frank came over I spent stewing and pacing. I'm not good at sitting around, and it was a hot day. As the afternoon wore on, the Santa Ana winds began to blow, making my house a regular oven. Like most southern Californians, I can only take so much of those desert winds before I go a little nuts anyway. I live a couple of miles from the beach in Las Piernas, which is on the coast, just south of L.A. Usually by late afternoon, there's cool air off the ocean. But even with nothing but the front and back screen doors to slow down any little breeze that might come along, the old house was hot. It's a little 1930s bungalow down in a section of town that can't decide how to gentrify.

So I paced around, sat and tried to cry, but couldn't. Got up and paced around again. Cody sat watching me, twitching his fat tail nervously. At one point I felt so wound up, I took off my shoes and hurled them as hard as I could against the wall. I didn't pitch them anywhere near Cody, but he decided he'd had enough and took off through his cat door—converted from an old ice-delivery slot in the kitchen.

It was hard to find anything worth thinking about. If I thought about the past, I mourned the end of days with O'Connor. If I thought about the future, it was to cancel plans. Nothingness, sharp as a knife. I paced barefooted.

I knew that the time would come when I could really indulge in this feeling-sorry-for-myself stuff, but now wasn't the time. If I could just get myself pointed in some direction, maybe I could find whoever did this to O'Connor. And kill them. Slowly.

In the midst of these thoughts I heard someone on the front porch. The silhouetted figure of a tall man stood looking in at me from my front door, shading his eyes with his hand against the screen.

"Irene?"

"Jesus, Frank. You startled me. How long have you been out there?"

"How about letting me in? It's hotter than hell out here."

I took off the latch and opened the door for him. I flopped down on the couch and gestured toward my big old-fashioned armchair, but he waved it off and leaned up against a table instead.

"You okay?" he asked.

"I'll get there. You know me."

He smiled a little and said, "Yeah, I guess I do." He was quiet for a minute, then he stood up straight. He was studying me, and I felt uncomfortable. I decided to watch my toes for a while.

He started over. "Look, I know you're tough, but I also have some idea of what O'Connor meant to you. Nobody could see what you saw today and walk off whistling. So you don't have to talk about this now if you don't want to."

I glanced up at him. He had a funny kind of concerned look on his face. It scared me or I probably would have started crying after all. Something in his sympathy moved my feelings to the surface. There he was, big, handsome, and a mere four feet away, looking concerned. But there was no room in me at that moment for old history or rekindled anything.

"Have a seat, Frank."

He sat down. Tall as he is—somewhere in the neighborhood of six-three or six-four, I'd guess—the back of the chair was still taller. I love that big old chair. Nobody since my grandfather had looked that good in it.

"Go ahead," I told him. "Take out your notebook. Ask questions. It'll be good for me. At least I'll be doing something. Maybe I can help somehow."

He just sat there for a minute, still quiet, as if undecided. Then he reached into his inside pocket and pulled out a notebook.

"Why don't you take that jacket off? I'm not so formal here with my shoes off."

"Thanks," he said, standing up again for a moment. He took off his suit jacket and folded it neatly over the back of the chair. Even in the long-sleeved shirt and shoulder holster, he looked a lot more comfortable. He sat back down, loosened his tie and flipped his notebook open to a clean page. I felt nervous again.

"Look, how about something cold to drink?"

He gave me that questioning look again. "Sure," he said.

Hell's bells, I thought. I've got to stop acting like an idiot. I realized that every time one of us was on the verge of discussing what had happened to O'Connor, we fumbled around and stalled.

I poured a couple of glasses of iced tea and brought them into the living room.

Outside the big picture window, the heat waves made the street look like a river. A big dark-blue car ferried its way past the window. I could see Cody stretched out in the sun on the lawn.

I handed Frank his iced tea and sat down again. "Sorry—I should have thought of offering you something sooner. I'm a little distracted, I guess. What do you want to know?"

"It's okay. I guess I'm distracted too. Anyway, you saw O'Connor last night?"

"Yeah, we went out to Banyon's. He was in a festive mood, you might say. He did quite a bit of drinking, but I was driving, so I quit after a Guinness. He was thoroughly enjoying himself." I thought about O'Connor and the dancers. I stopped the story for a minute and looked outside. Cody had moved into the shade. I took a deep breath and went on.

"Anyway, we talked and watched people dance, and left sometime after midnight, probably about twelve-thirty. I drove him home. Got there around one. He got out of the car, sang 'Goodnight, Irene' to me on his way in. He likes to—he liked to sing that to me."

Why was it so hard to tell something that I'd been thinking about all day? I looked out the window again—the blue car, a Lincoln, I noticed—was going slowly back up the street.

"Did you walk up to the house with him?" Frank asked.

"No, but I watched him go up the porch steps—he wasn't too steady on his feet. There wasn't any package there. Kenny was already home—at least, his car was in the driveway."

"What was O'Connor working on?"

"The paper wouldn't tell you?"

"Haven't been over there yet—figured you'd know more about what he was really up to than that jackass Wrigley."

I had to smile at that. "You're not just trying to get on my good side by saying that about the esteemed editor of the *Express*, are you?"

"No, I decided he was a jerk long before Mark Baker told me why you left the paper. That just confirmed it."

"Well, he is a jackass. But maybe it was a mistake to leave the paper. I probably shouldn't have let him get to me. O'Connor was always pushing me to go back, said I'd let my Irish get the better of me. He was a real old-school newspaperman. The genuine article. 'Duty to the public,' and all of that. He wasn't naive in any way about anybody or anything, but he hadn't soured on the world like some do."

"Same thing happens to cops," Frank said.

"I know. We all get to see the underside of the rock, I guess. Hard to remember there's anything else sometimes. Of course, in the line I'm in now it's all sunshine and lollipops. God, I hate public relations work. I spent most of last night bitching about it to O'Connor. Anyway, he believed in what he was doing. I don't believe in what I'm doing right now and it's turning me into a real cynic."

"You'll do what you need to do."

"You sound like O'Connor. Anyway, you asked what he was working on. Well, let's see. He was spending time on a campaign-funding story—mayor's office. That took most of his energy lately."

"I didn't really know him," he said. "Just met him once or twice. Saw him around City Hall now and then, used to catch his column once in a while. One or two of the old-timers in the department told me O'Connor had some pet story about an unsolved homicide?"

"Oh, you mean Hannah. Yes, there was always Hannah. That wasn't her name, that was just sick newspaper humor. Pretty gruesome story, really. Young woman, about twenty years old. Found her in the sand down under the pier. Somebody didn't ever want her identified. Bashed in her face and cut off her hands and feet. Some wag in the newsroom named her 'Handless Hannah.' The autopsy showed she was about two months pregnant at the time. That was in the summer of 1955. O'Connor was about twenty-seven, I guess.

"Well, ten years earlier, O'Connor's older sister went missing. She was about the same age as Hannah, about eighteen or nineteen. They found her body about five years later but never figured out who killed her. She had disappeared in the spring of '45, just before the end of the war—on her way home from a defense plant. Didn't find her until 1950. So that was only about five years before Hannah showed up on the beach.

"When he talked to me about his sister, he told about how it had driven his mother crazy; it was hard on the whole family, not knowing for those five years. He was really close to this sister. I guess he usually walked her home from work, but he had a hot date that night. Lots of guilt over what happened. On top of everything else, the date stood him up."

"So because of his sister, he got caught up in the story of this Jane Doe without the hands?"

"Right. The old bulldog kept trying to figure out who she was. It was an obsession, really. When the coroner's office got tired of holding her in the morgue, O'Connor spent his own money to arrange for a decent burial and a tombstone for her.

"He would even use his vacations to try to figure out where she had come from, what she might have been doing here. Every year, on the anniversary of the day they found her, he'd write his famous 'Who Is Hannah?' story. He wrote about her case and any recent Jane or John Does lying around in the morgue. Sometimes the story would get picked up by out-of-town papers. He actually helped to get the identification on a couple of bodies. But nobody ever claimed Hannah. Every year someone looking for a missing daughter or sister or wife would contact him, but it wouldn't turn out to be Hannah. Now and then he'd tell me he thought he had a lead on it, but I don't think he ever really learned much.

" 'Irene,' he'd say, 'somebody misses that girl. Every night they go past her room and wonder if she might still be alive, if maybe she has amnesia, if she secretly hated them and ran away, if she has been tortured or treated cruelly. They miss her. And somewhere some black-hearted bastard knows he killed her, knows where her hands and feet are buried. I aim to make him feel a little worried.' "

Frank stretched and sighed. "Thirty-five years ago. The killer may not even be alive now, let alone worried." He stood up and walked around a little. "I guess O'Connor ruffled a few feathers along the way."

"I've thought about that," I said, standing up too. "This town's so thick with potential enemies, you can't stir 'em with a stick. Lots of people who didn't like what he had to say about them, people with power to do something about it. He got death threats occasionally. Didn't mention any lately, though."

There was a knock at the front screen door. We turned to look, and it appeared that no one was there.

"Cody. Wild Bill Cody, my cat," I explained. "He's got a cat door, but this way he can make a nuisance of himself." I opened the door and let him in. He pranced over to sniff Frank's shoes—shoes must be to cats what crotches are to dogs, although cats are more delicate about it—and Frank bent down and picked him up. Cody is a sucker for affection, and even with the heat he was happy to be scratched between the ears. Frank stood there holding Cody and looking out the window. He seemed to be staring at something, when suddenly he dived toward me and knocked me to the floor, landing on top of me and knocking my breath out. Cody went tearing out from between us just as three gunshots blew out the window.

3

Frank lifted his head and I saw blood on his face. I started to cry out, but he put his hand over my mouth. He was listening for something. We heard the car drive off. He scrambled up off me and pulled out his gun, looking outside quickly before going out the front door. I got up a little more slowly. There was glass all over the place and a gaping hole in the back of my armchair. That really pissed me off. Trying not to step on any glass, I went out to the front porch.

The gunshots had been loud enough to draw a few of my neighbors out for a little rubbernecking. "Frank, get in here, you're scaring the neighbors." Not every day they saw a bloodied man with a gun standing out on my lawn. "Nothing to worry about, folks, he's a cop."

"You're a real laugh riot. I guess that means you're not hurt."

"Thanks to you, I'm not."

He managed a quick smile and said, "All in the line of duty."

He was looking out at the street in front of the house next door. Suddenly, I saw what he was staring at. A red Corvette.

"That your neighbor's?" he asked.

"No," I said in disbelief, "but it looks just like Kenny O'Connor's."

"Yeah, that's what I was thinking." He walked over to it, took a quick look through the windshield that apparently didn't reveal anything special, and came back to my house. "Let's go back inside," he said.

He made a phone call to headquarters while I went to get something to clean up his face.

"Yeah, dark blue, late model Lincoln, no front plate. Probably headed up Ocean Boulevard. Also, check out the registration of an

'87 Corvette, license 3RVE070. Yeah. No, we're all right. Okay, thanks." He hung up.

I sat him down at the kitchen table and then pulled a chair up facing him, and started to sponge the blood off his face with a warm washcloth. He winced a little, and I realized that he hadn't been cut by glass or shot—he had a lovely deep set of Cody's claw marks on the right side of his face.

"Cody got you good, didn't he?"

"Not his fault, I scared him. Where is he?"

"Ran off—if my closet door is open, he's up on the top shelf. Otherwise, ten to one he's hiding under my bed."

I had some antibiotic ointment and tried to be tender as I put it on the scratches. He was watching me with those beautiful gray-green eyes. He reached up and touched my hair.

"You've got little pieces of glass in your hair," he said, and gently pulled a bead of it from near my ear.

"So do you," I said, and reached into his soft brown hair to retrieve one of them. We took care of each other like a couple of parrots for a few minutes. We were interrupted by a knock at the door by something bigger than a cat and parted, both looking a little sheepish.

"Detective Harriman?"

"Yeah, be right with you," Frank answered.

He stood up, shook his head, and squared his shoulders, trying to get into his Detective Harriman mode again.

The young, pink-faced, uniformed officer who came in the door looked as if the heat was about to do him in.

"Bob Williams, sir. We picked up a call to come over on a drive-by. They said to contact you."

He noticed the scratches on Frank's face and gave me a look.

A fleeting grin crossed Frank's face. "Officer Williams, this is Miss Irene Kelly. You're in her home." Williams nodded toward me and then looked around. He got wide-eyed when he saw the chair, and I noticed for the first time that Frank's coat, once so neatly folded, had been blown to shreds.

"I hope you weren't sitting there, sir."

"Not when it mattered. Anything on the Lincoln?"

"No, sir, not a sign. We can ask around the neighborhood if you'd like. Forensics will be here anytime now. Also, the Corvette is registered to a Kenneth O'Connor, 803 Randall Avenue."

Frank and I exchanged looks.

"Is that helpful, sir?" Williams asked.

"Yes," Frank said, "I think it is. Please try to discover where Mr. O'Connor is now." He pulled out the notebook and flipped to one of its pages. "When I spoke with him this morning, he told me he planned on staying at the Vista del Mar Hotel down on Shoreline Drive. Find out if he's been there yet today and if he's visiting anyone here in the neighborhood. If not, ask if anybody saw him leave the car."

Williams noted all of this with care. He looked up and eyed the scratches on Frank's face again. "Do you need anyone else here with you?"

"No, we're fine. Let me know if anyone noticed anything unusual going on. Besides windows being blown out."

The young man headed out the door.

"Officer Williams?" I called to him.

"Yes, Miss Kelly?"

"The scratches? From a cat."

"Yes, of course, ma'am." He blushed and left without looking at either one of us.

Frank and I cracked up as soon as the kid was out of earshot.

"We shouldn't laugh," I said. "I remember when you were just a rookie yourself."

"And I remember a fairly-wet-behind-the-ears reporter."

"Yeah. Green as they come."

We stood there in silence for a while, remembering. I thought of that spark of attraction between us all those years ago. We were much younger then, not so much in years—Frank and I are about the same age, nearing the final approach to forty, landing gear down—as in experience.

I thought back to Bakersfield, to the nights when we'd go for coffee and long four-in-the-morning talks at the end of our respective shifts. God, we were both so full of confidence in our ability to change the world.

Of course, we saw that world from different perspectives. My job was to get the story, Frank's was to enforce the law. On some level, we were wary of each other then, as we were both trained to be by our employers. Sooner or later, every cop is burned by some reporter who misquotes or coaxes out too much information. And sooner or later every reporter is given a bum steer by some cop.

And yet, over time, I suppose we both learned it isn't always that way; plenty of people manage to maintain a certain professional distance and still be friends with one another. Somehow Frank and I stayed friends. I guess we both had that ideal of doing the public some good.

I tried to figure out how long ago all that had been. It was about twelve years ago that the *Express* had offered me the job in Las Piernas, and I had moved back to my hometown from Bakersfield, Frank's hometown. Seven of those twelve years passed before he got transferred down here; by then we were both seeing other people. He got in touch with me once when he first moved to Las Piernas, but other than hearing word of each other from other cops or reporters every now and again, our lives had stayed separate. The last I had heard of him had been a year or so ago, when Mark Baker told me that Frank had asked him about me, and about why I had left the paper. I wondered if Frank was still seeing the same woman he had been with five years ago. Or any other woman.

There was another knock on the screen and Frank let the forensics team in. While they talked to him, I walked back to the bedroom to look for Cody. A quick search of the closet revealed nothing, but when I got down on the floor and looked under the bed, I saw a pair of almond-shaped eyes reflecting back from the farthest corner near the wall, out of arm's reach and harm's way. I tried coaxing him, but no luck. I got a flashlight and tried to see if he was hurt, and couldn't see any damage—just irritation and fright. I left him there, thinking that it was better to let him come out on his own time, when he felt safe again.

I walked back out and watched as the very reserved and professional Detective Harriman started winding things up with the lab guys. It hadn't taken them long.

As they left, I realized that I was seething with anger at the folks in the blue car. I walked back to the kitchen and got a broom and started sweeping up the glass to try and work some of it off.

"Let me do that; you'll cut your feet."

"What will Officer Williams think when he comes back to report?"

"I'll tell him it's a time-proven evidence-gathering method. Officer Williams will never be the same after today anyway."

"That makes two of us," I said, looking for my shoes.

"No, three," he said.

I watched him for a moment, then my thoughts turned back to

O'Connor. "Frank, it's the same people, isn't it? But why? Why would anybody take a shot at me? Or at my house, anyway."

"Hard to say. Somebody was probably watching O'Connor's house last night before they delivered the package. They may have followed you from there. They may have been watching today, may have seen you talking to me at the scene and figured you were going to tell us too much. They could have followed you from Banyon's. They may have already known you and O'Connor were close friends and figured they'd call on you just in case he had told you something. Maybe they saw the Corvette and thought Kenny was here."

He looked over at the chair and the remains of his suit coat. "If they hadn't hit so low, and risked it the middle of the day, I'd think this was just a warning, but maybe they didn't care whether they killed you or not. They can obviously do it if they want to. They succeeded once already and came close to being two for two."

I felt a little sick to my stomach. Frank saw the look on my face and set the broom down and came over to me. "Sorry," he said, "I'm so used to you being a reporter, I wasn't phrasing things the way I should." He put an arm around my shoulders. "Got any coffee? Let's go into the kitchen and I'll call somebody to board up the window. Getting the glass replaced on a Sunday would cost you a fortune."

While we waited for the board-up crew, I made some coffee and poured a couple of cups. We sat back down at the table.

"Before we were so rudely interrupted by gunfire," I said, "we were talking about O'Connor. What did you learn from Kenny? Like I said, his car was there last night. This morning, as I was leaving . . . after the explosion, I mean . . ."

I heard my own voice trailing off, as if it belonged to someone else. I could suddenly see the destruction before me again, feel the numbing chill of realizing that it was impossible for O'Connor to have survived it, knowing that he was gone, would never be around again. No more listening or laughing or talking or anything at all.

Again that need to wail like a lost child was welling up within me, that longing to cry and cry. But nothing happened.

Frank was waiting for me to pull it together, trying not to make me feel self-conscious. He got up to refill his coffee cup. I took a few deep breaths and went on.

"Anyway, Kenny's car was parked in front of the house last night, but not this morning. He doesn't usually get out of bed before he has to—one of the things that drove my sister Barbara nuts when they were married. But he was safely out of the house this morning before the explosion, got back there after you guys were already on the scene. Now his car just happens to mysteriously appear near my house on the same afternoon I'm shot at, and he's nowhere around."

"Yeah, it's odd, all right, and I'm anxious to talk to him. But he has a legitimate reason for being gone this morning and it checks out . . . Yes, I checked it myself," he added, seeing my look of disbelief.

"Where was he?" I asked.

"You know I can't tell you that."

I was furious. "Frank Harriman, you've got a hell of a nerve coming in here and asking questions and then refusing to give me information in return!"

"Don't give me that crap, Irene! This isn't some goddamned newspaper story. You're not a reporter anymore and we're not just involved in an exchange of information. An old man was blown to kingdom come this morning. I've been shot at, I've had my face scratched by your cat and my best suit coat blown to shreds. All the same I've tried to protect you from harm and from what would probably be a much less considerate style of questioning. I don't . . ." He stopped.

I was finally starting to cry.

4

"**Irene**. Irene, I'm sorry . . . "

I held up a hand. When I could talk again I said, "Not your fault. Not a good day for either of us. I'm sorry. Excuse me for a moment . . . "

I got up without looking him in the face and went back to the bedroom. I closed the door, flopped down on the bed and indulged myself with a good cry. Cody came out from under the bed and crawled up next to me, licked my face and gave little mews of consolation. I was angry with myself for breaking down in front of Frank, felt awkward about the idea of going out red-nosed and froggy-eyed from crying. How embarrassing. But I knew I couldn't just leave the guy standing out there in my living room.

I heard Williams come back by, but I couldn't make out anything they were saying. He left and all was quiet again. A couple of times I heard Frank start down the hall, then hesitate and go back toward the front of the house.

The doorbell rang. I could overhear him talking to the board-up crew and was relieved to have him occupied. I went into the bathroom, blew my nose and splashed a lot of cold water on my face. My blue eyes were puffy and red-rimmed. For a distraction, I twisted my dark hair up off my shoulders and pinned it. My neck was cooler, but a glance in the mirror convinced me I looked like a schoolmarm, so I let my hair down again. I brushed it; the action calmed me. I didn't look great, but at least I had stopped crying.

There was a soft knock at the bedroom door, and Cody ran back under the bed.

"Irene?"

"Yeah, Frank—I'll be right out."

I opened the door, and he backed up a couple of paces, as if he was afraid of what I might do next. Couldn't blame him. I didn't know either.

It was getting dark, and looking out the back screen door, I could see a bright-red sunset. He leaned against the hallway and watched me. In the background, I could hear the board-up crew break out the remaining glass in the window.

"You okay?" he asked.

"Yes, I think so. Actually, you've been a help. I've been trying to cry all day."

"Glad it made one of us feel better."

"Don't feel bad, Frank. I know the rules. I've covered crime beats and I know better. I'm just . . . not quite myself right now. I'm so damned angry. Sorry I took it out on you."

"Normal to be angry."

"God, don't start telling me I'm normal. I've had all the bad news I can handle for one day."

He smiled. "You're not as off-beat as you think you are."

The crew was hammering the boards in place, making a hell of a racket.

"Let's sit out back," I suggested. We brushed off a couple of chairs on the back porch and sat down. The winds had died down to a breeze. Crickets had started to sing and the air was laced with the fragrance of jasmine from my neighbor's backyard.

"Irene, look, I've been thinking about it, and I can let you in on a few things under certain conditions. And, well, I've got an idea that might work out for both of us. If you're willing to try it."

"Go on, I'm listening."

"You can help me in two ways. I figure the intended target of the bombing may have been O'Connor himself, or his son. Any other possibilities became a lot less likely this afternoon when those shots blasted through your window.

"I think you can help me learn more about O'Connor and his son. In exchange, I'll tell you whatever I can, on the condition that you do not try to pursue this on your own—that you keep working with me and let the police deal with these people." He paused. "I mean that, Irene. Whoever they are, they're dangerous and they mean business. I don't want your blood on my hands."

"What are the 'two ways'?" I asked.

"Promise me you won't try to play Nancy Drew."

"Frank, I'm the curious sort. Too many years of reporting to say I won't snoop into things. But I promise to tell you whatever I learn, and that I won't intentionally place myself in personal danger."

He sat there thinking for a while, unconsciously reaching up and touching the scratch marks. "I might as well face it; even this morning I knew you'd start digging around on your own, no matter what I said. You're about as hardheaded as they come. Maybe if you'll work with me, we can keep that stubbornness from getting you killed."

"I'll be careful. Tell me how I can be of help."

"I need for you to try to get your job back at the paper. You'll have to eat humble pie, kiss Wrigley's behind and tell him that O'Connor told you all about the mayor's problems and every other story he was working on. Offer to take up where O'Connor left off."

I nodded. I had been thinking about doing it anyway. It was the only way I could learn more than I already knew about the things O'Connor was working on. Working with Wrigley would be hell on earth, but if I knew him at all, he had already started to worry about what he was going to do with the mayor's story. I was also pretty sure I could manage getting my job back without too much groveling. Wrigley had already made overtures, which until now I had turned down.

One of the workers made his way back to say they were finished, and I went inside to pay them. I thanked them and closed and bolted the front door after they left.

"Okay," I said to Frank as I came out back again, "I'm with you as far as the paper goes."

"Great. I'm afraid the next item involves telling you something that's not going to make you happy."

I waited. What could make this day any worse?

"Williams came by a little while ago," he said. "He told me that Kenny had not checked into the Vista del Mar. He asked the lady across the street from you about the Corvette, she said she saw Kenny pull up and park; shortly after that a tall redhead that she's seen over here before pulled up behind him; said she thought the woman was your sister."

"Barbara?!"

"I couldn't remember if your sister was a redhead from back when you used to talk to me about her. So you think it's her?"

I nodded.

"Your neighbor said the woman acted like she was going to come to your front door but that the man stopped her, and then they got into her car and drove off."

I was stunned. Kenny had gone middle-aged-crazy at forty, bought the Corvette and started hopping from bed to bed like crab lice. When Barbara was finally forced to confront him about it, he gave her the "It's all your fault" baloney and worse. He said things to her that boys in a high school locker room would blush to hear.

"Jesus, Frank. I've heard of gluttons for punishment, but this is like volunteering for the Spanish Inquisition. How can my own sister have such low self-esteem? I'm calling her. I'm calling her right now."

"Hold it, Irene. Barbara's not a child. Your older sister, as I recall. She can see anybody she wants to."

"It won't work. God, he is *such* a user! She'll mother him."

He didn't say anything.

"You're right," I said, calming down a little. "You're right. I've got to stay out of it."

"Well, actually, what I had in mind was a little different. I need you to be sympathetic to her. We've got to find out what, if anything, would make someone want to kill Kenny."

"You'd better arrest me."

"You know what I mean. From what I can tell at this point, all three of you may be targets. Kenny must be pretty sure he's a target, or he wouldn't have left his car here. He may not have wanted to leave it in an unfamiliar neighborhood, or maybe he was trying to draw attention to you, I don't know. Anyway, I'm going to have it towed in, so you should have some satisfaction."

I must admit it cheered me to imagine Kenny's face when he found his most prized possession missing.

"Meanwhile," Frank went on, "for obvious reasons, I don't think you should stay here. At least not until we get a better handle on things. They probably won't come around here again until they're sure cops aren't going to keep dropping by, but you need to watch your back. Anybody you can stay with?"

I thought about it. It wasn't a problem of being willing to leave— I wasn't really feeling comfortable in the house, and even the nuisance of living away from it for a few days didn't seem like much compared to being on edge in my own home. Barbara's house was out of the question. There was a limit to what I could stand in the way of watching her sacrifice herself to Kenny.

"Let me try Lydia Ames. We've been friends since grade school."

I called Lydia, and angel that she is, when I explained what had happened, she urged me to bring Cody along.

I lured Cody out of hiding with a piece of chicken, then felt very mean as I stuffed him into the cat carrier. He yowled his protests while I packed a few things. Frank went around latching my remaining windows. I gave Lydia's number to Frank, and he gave me his work and home numbers.

"I'll follow you over there," he said. "I just want to make sure you're not tailed."

I didn't object. I stuffed the cat carrier and my other belongings into the front seat of my Karmann Ghia.

"I can't believe you still have this car," Frank said.

I smiled at that and climbed into my faded-blue, '71 ragtop. The odometer had flipped more times than a circus acrobat, and the defroster didn't work right, but the old car was still reliable transportation.

Twenty minutes later we were on the other side of town, in front of Lydia's place. Frank got out of his car and helped me carry Cody up to the door. I looked at his tired face and realized that he probably still had to go in and write up reports tonight.

I took his hand. "Thanks, Frank. Thanks for—well, thanks for lots of things."

"Goodnight, Irene. I've been thinking about getting back in touch with you again, just sorry it had to be under these circumstances."

We shook hands awkwardly, then he walked back to his car. He stood waiting for me to get safely inside. I rang the bell, then waved good-bye to him as Lydia let me in.

5

Lydia was solicitous in the extreme. I was all for it at that point. After letting Cody out of his carrier to slink around exploring his new environs, she asked me if I was hungry. It dawned on me that I hadn't eaten all day, and that I was quite hungry indeed. She sat me down at her kitchen counter and mixed a nice stiff Myers's and OJ for me, then set about warming up some homemade lasagna, making garlic bread and tossing a salad. I offered to help.

"Oh, no, you just relax, kiddo. You've had a terrible day. You leave everything to me."

The room was soon redolent with the aroma of honest-to-God Italian cooking. She still went by her ex-husband's last name, but Lydia's maiden name had been Pastorini. Mr. Ames had not left her because of her cooking.

I downed the drink a little faster than was probably advisable, and soon was feeling a slight buzz, my empty stomach transporting the good news straight to my brain.

Lydia paused in her salad-making dervish and looked up at me. "You know, Irene, this is the first time in a long time that you've let me do anything for you. I mean, I've done things for you, but you never turn to me when you need somebody. It makes me feel good that you called."

I thought about this. It was probably true. O'Connor had long been my refuge.

"Well, Lydia, then I just didn't know what I was missing. You're the first friend who came to mind."

She seemed immensely pleased by this. She cheerfully put a place setting before me and served the salad. It was a great mixture of vegetables—cucumbers, carrots, radishes, sprouts, Romaine lettuce, tomatoes, green peppers and more. Once again I was reminded that Lydia never did anything halfway. She poured a couple of glasses of a wonderful dry red wine and then pulled up a chair next to me and sat down.

"Glad to see you settle for a minute."

She laughed. "Oh, I'm turning into my mother. You hardly get Cody out of his cat carrier and I'm telling you, *'Mangia!'* "

"No complaints here."

We clinked wineglasses in an unspoken toast to one another and drank a few sips in silence.

A few minutes later I was eating as if I still thought I'd grow taller. I paused just long enough between mouthfuls to ask Lydia how her own day had been.

"Well, I didn't think it was so great until I talked to you about yours." She stopped smiling for a moment, and I knew she was thinking about O'Connor. "Of course, you know how it began."

I nodded.

"That creep Wrigley had no sympathy for anyone. We were all upset. His only concern was getting it into the headlines. Then he began to moan and groan about what was going to happen to *'his* story'—can you believe it? He was running around yelling, 'What about *my* mayor's race story?' I loved old man Wrigley, but some days I wish to God that some outsider had bought the paper when he died. His son is such a loser."

"So Wrigley's worried about O'Connor's stories?"

"Yeah. He's going nuts about it."

"Great!" I said. "Look, Lydia—I've got another favor to ask of you. I need you to drop a lot of hints to Wrigley about how I knew all about what O'Connor was working on. Then tell him I'm thinking about going to work for the *Sacramento Bee*. It's all bullshit, but he won't figure that out. If he gets nosy, I've got a friend at the *Bee* who'll make it sound good. Anyway, don't let him know I'm staying at your place, just tell him you might be seeing me tomorrow night. Make it sound like I'm dying to get back to reporting, but that I didn't think I'd be welcomed at the *Express*, after our little, er, misunderstanding."

At this Lydia hooted. "Misunderstanding!" She refilled our glasses, then asked, "You're not seriously thinking of coming back to the *Express,* are you? I'd love it, but I figured you'd never come back. Not after the way he treated you."

"Lydia, for a good enough reason, I'll chew a little crow now and again."

She studied me. "This is about O'Connor, isn't it? You're going to look through his papers and try to figure out who killed him."

"Guilty," I said. "But nobody can know."

"It seems to me somebody already knows, Irene. That somebody who blasted out your window this afternoon."

"Maybe. But my only chance of not living with the sensation that somebody is following me everywhere I go, or to be ducking under a table every time a car slows down in front of my house, is to find these people and figure out what, if anything, O'Connor had on them."

We drank in silence for a while.

"You're right," she sighed. "But it still scares me."

"It scares me, too. Are you really okay with my staying here? I mean, I'm obviously some sort of target."

"Get real. As I said, I'm glad you turned to me. Besides, no one knows you're here, and no one is going to learn it from me."

Cody had relaxed and was walking around in the kitchen sniffing in the air. Lydia gave him a little lasagna and he devoured it in nothing flat. I helped her clean up, over protests, and then went back to her guest room to unpack my bag. In the meantime she had actually drawn a hot bubble bath for me.

"Lydia, I can't stay here if you're going to play Jeeves the whole time."

"Don't expect this treatment every day. But I think you'll find this will help you sleep better."

It was too tempting to pass up, so I wished her goodnight. I undressed and studied myself in the mirror before stepping into the tub. Not bad, I decided, and then felt embarrassed at my lack of modesty. The bath was great. Lydia had even put some magazines next to the tub. I picked up a *Cosmo* for the first time since Lydia and I had bought them in college to take the sex quizzes.

Eventually, fully pruned and getting cold, I made myself get out of the tub. I dried off, put on my pajamas, and crawled under the clean sheets. Lydia used a better fabric softener than I did. Cody climbed up next to me, and fell asleep purring. I felt good, like maybe things would come together from here.

All night I dreamed of breaking glass and O'Connor picking up packages.

6

I woke up startled by my surroundings, then remembered where I was and why. I was tired even after eight hours of sleep. The morning sun was shining in through the bedroom window, and I heard the sound of Lydia's car starting up and pulling out of the drive. I had that weird feeling I get sometimes when I sleep at other people's houses: The bed was oriented differently from my own at home, so I had the sensation of having slept with my head at the foot of the bed.

Cody stretched and yawned and I followed suit, and we both got out of bed. I wasn't exactly shocked that Lydia had breakfast all laid out for me—cereal, fresh fruit, and a note saying to make myself at home and that she'd see me after work. An envelope marked "spare key" was under the note.

I ate and then called my office.

"Good morning, Malloy and Marlowe," came the sugar-coated greeting.

"Can you say that three times fast, Clarissa?"

"Oh—hello, Irene. Where are you? Kevin said if you called in, to tell you that you could have a few days off if you'd like."

"What?"

"Kevin told me about what happened to your friend—he showed me the article in the paper. Kevin said that he had really loved the guy who got killed and that you were almost like the guy's daughter or something, so he didn't expect you in for a few days. I'm real sorry it happened, Irene."

All morning I had wondered what I'd tell Kevin, who seldom takes no for an answer; but I had failed to keep in mind just how much

Kevin and O'Connor had meant to each other. The two of them had been friends for many years.

Clarissa was babbling on. "Hey—somebody called for you. A man. Asked if you were in this morning, but wouldn't leave a name. Said he'd call back later to see if you had come in."

The hairs on my neck stood on end.

"Did you recognize the voice?"

"Nope, not one of our regular clients, that much I know. You got a new boyfriend or something?"

"Huh? Oh, no. No, I don't know who it could have been. Look, Clarissa, if he calls back and won't leave his name, don't tell him I called, okay? Just tell him you don't know when I'll be in, all right?"

That was fine with Clarissa, who was quite used to telling callers something other than the truth when they asked about the whereabouts of Malloy & Marlowe employees.

I dreaded the next call. I knew I'd have to talk to my sister, but I was worried about flying off the handle with her, betraying my knowledge of Kenny's being at her house yesterday before she was ready to tell me herself. I took a lot of deep breaths, took long strides around the den while swinging my arms up over my head to throw off some of the tension.

Cody, perched on the back of Lydia's couch, looked at me like I was a lunatic.

I made the call.

"Hello?" she answered.

"Hello, Barbara. It's Irene."

"Oh, Irene. Do you know where Kenny's car is?"

"Your father-in-law, my best friend, is dead—no, make that murdered— and the first thing you ask me about is Kenny's fucking car?!?"

There was silence on the other end of the line. I'd blown it already.

"Barbara, I'm sorry. I'm a mess. A real mess." Deep breath.

Still no response. I waited.

"No need to be foul-mouthed, Irene. Mama would be so ashamed to hear you talk like that."

"I'm sorry." Damn that bitch for trying to invoke our dead mother to stop me from swearing. Frank was asking too much. But I couldn't think of anyone else besides Kenny who could tell me what might be behind all of this. And Barbara was the only way I could find Kenny.

"Kenny's car was towed by the police after my window was shot out," I said. "We don't know if they shot my window out because of the car or not, but since Kenny hadn't been truth——since Kenny wasn't where the police thought he'd be, they thought it'd be better to keep the car out from in front of other people's houses; the last two houses it was parked in front of didn't fare too well."

"So that's what happened to your window?"

"That's what happened to my window. And my armchair. And nearly to me and someone who happened to be in my living room."

"Not Granddad's armchair?"

"The very one," I said, clenching my teeth at her priorities. "Barbara, if you know where Kenny is, you'd better call the police and ask for Detective Frank Harriman in Homicide. I'm not kidding around about this."

Silence.

I decided to try another approach.

"Barbara, Kenny's life is in danger. And, for that matter, until he talks to the police, so is mine." I refrained from mentioning how much of our grandparents' furniture might also be at risk.

"So you think he's in danger, too?"

"What do you mean, 'too'?"

She hesitated. Apparently she was figuring out that by asking me about the car, she had as much as admitted that she'd seen him yesterday.

"You really hate him, don't you?"

"No, I don't," I lied, "I just felt protective of you after the divorce. I didn't like how he treated you, or all the hurtful things he said to you then. I feel protective of you now, Barbara. I don't want you to get hurt again."

She mulled this over.

"Kenny wasn't himself then, Irene. He was having a crisis."

Right, I thought. Temporary insanity. Unfortunately, Barbara took this silence as meaning she needed to keep selling me on him.

"I know he said some awful things, but he's taken them all back. He's begged my forgiveness."

I'll bet he has, I thought. Out loud I said, "So you've seen him?"

More hesitation. "He was here yesterday. Irene, the poor man is scared out of his wits. He's upset about his dad, but he's sure someone's after him, too."

"He thinks someone wanted to kill both of them?"

"Yes. Yes, exactly."

"Did he say *why* he thought someone would want to kill him?" Impatience was creeping back into my tone.

"You don't believe him?"

"Yes, I believe him. Not a doubt in my mind that's true." ·

This appeased her. "Well, then you can see why I couldn't refuse to help him in his hour of need."

His hour of need? Kenny had a lifetime of need.

"But did he tell you why they are trying to kill him?" I pressed.

"No, Irene, he didn't want to put me in danger. He told me that he had already lost his father and he couldn't stand to lose me. That's why he didn't want to leave the car in front of my house. He said everyone knew that deep down he still loved me, and that this is the first place they'd look for him."

"But it was okay to park the car next door to *my* house?"

"Kenny said it would be safe there."

Well, he was right. The car was safe. It was Frank and I who almost got in line right behind O'Connor at the Pearly Gates.

"Irene?"

"Yeah, Barbara?" I was suddenly feeling weary and depressed.

"I'm really sorry putting the car there caused you trouble."

"You had no way of knowing. Don't worry about it. Where's Kenny now?"

"I promised not to tell."

"Barbara, it's literally a matter of life and death. Please tell me."

"I'm his wife. You can't make me testify against him."

"You're his ex-wife, and we aren't in a courtroom. If you're happy he's come back, more power to you. I mean that. Be happy. But for God's sakes, Barbara, someone is trying to kill me, so tell me where he is."

"They weren't trying to kill you, Irene. They were after Kenny."

I wasn't getting anywhere. I decided to pick up a rather cruel cue stick and play dirty pool.

"Barbara, what would our mother say to do?"

I knew this would get to her. I prayed my mother would forgive me. After all, as Barbara and I used to say when we were children, she started it.

"I'll think about it. What was that policeman's name?"

"Detective Frank Harriman."

"I'll tell you what. If I see Kenny, I'll tell him what happened to your window, and that you think they're trying to kill you. I'll ask him if it's okay to tell you where he is."

This idea did not seem likely to bear fruit. But it was obvious that if Mom couldn't make her do it, I couldn't begin to budge her out of this position.

"Okay, but please think about blood being thicker than water and all that. I need you, too, Barbara."

That really confused her. "Where are you anyway? I just tried calling you at work and they said you wouldn't be in today. Are you at home?"

"No, but you can leave a message on my machine or get in touch with me through Detective Harriman. I'm—I'm going to be moving around a lot. I'll keep checking in with you, okay?"

"Okay," she said uncertainly.

"I have to handle it this way, Barbara."

"I know . . . Irene?"

"Yeah."

"Is there going to be a funeral for O'Connor?"

I thought of the men with forceps and plastic bags, but shook it off.

"I guess that will be up to Kenny. But he's probably too upset to deal with that right now."

"I'd like to have—I don't know—a wake or something for him."

"He'd like that, I'm sure. We may have to wait awhile, though, because of the investigation."

"Yeah, well, anyway, I don't know how to give a wake, do you?"

Ah, the plight of second generation Irish-Americans—proud of the culture but not knowing near enough about it. Granddad would have known. Dad may have. We had never been to a wake.

"No, Barbara, but call Great Aunt Mary. She can tell you how."

"Well, I'm sure there's more to it than Chieftains' records and a bunch of booze."

"I'm sure you're right."

"I'm going to miss him."

"Me too."

"Oh, of course."

Of course, I thought.

"Take care of yourself, Barbara."

"You too, Irene."

What an ungodly mess, I thought, as I hung up the phone.

I took the spare key from the envelope and watched the street from a window at the front of the house. No dark blue Lincolns or shiny red Corvettes. Still, I felt scared going out of the house.

I climbed into the Karmann Ghia and headed for the Thai section of town, feeling a craving for satay and pad Thai. But as I drove, I decided I should let Frank know what Barbara had said, and stopped at a phone booth to invite him to join me. I called his work number.

"Homicide," said a deep male voice.

"Frank Harriman, please."

I found myself watching the street while I waited for Frank to pick up the phone.

"Harriman."

"Frank?"

His tone was abrupt. "Where are you calling from?"

"A pay phone in Little Thailand."

He relaxed. "I was going to call you in a minute anyway. Are you getting antsy?"

"A little. Frank, are you having Barbara followed?"

A pause. "Yes."

"Good. I don't think Kenny's with her now, but I'm almost certain she'll be in touch with him later today."

"You've talked to her?"

"Yes. Can you meet me for lunch at the Thai Royal over on Broadway and Pacific?"

"Give me about twenty minutes."

I was fairly sure I wasn't followed to the restaurant. It was about eleven-thirty, and Sam, the owner, was just setting up in preparation for the noon crowd.

"Miss Kelly!" he greeted me. Then his face fell. "We were very sorry to hear about Mr. O'Connor. We liked him very much. I know you have lost a good companion."

"Thanks, Sam. Can you get me one of your private booths? And when a tall gentleman with scratch marks on the right side of his face comes in, will you please show him to my table?"

Sam beamed at the thought of my meeting a gentleman, scratches or no, and happily showed me to a booth behind a curtain made of wooden beads. He and Roselynn, his wife, had been concerned about my single status for years.

We talked for a while, then he brought me a Tsingtao beer. As I drank it, I watched the restaurant start to fill up.

Frank was late.

7

The place was packed and humming with the tension of people who only have forty-five minutes left for lunch. I was just getting fidgety again when Sam walked back, and told me I had a phone call.

We hurried our way through the tables into the hot and steamy kitchen, where Roselynn waved to me from a counter where she was cutting fresh vegetables. Sam handed the receiver to me.

"Frank?"

"Irene? They found Kenny. Somebody's worked him over pretty good. I'm at St. Anne's Hospital. Can you meet me here? If not, I'll meet you later at Lydia's."

I told Frank I would meet him in the ER waiting room and hung up. When I turned around, Sam was holding a white grocery-store bag with two Styrofoam containers in it.

"You've got to have lunch. Lucky for me, you always order the same thing every time."

I couldn't turn him down, and when he adamantly refused payment, I promised to bring Frank in to meet him someday soon.

St. Anne's is in downtown Las Piernas, not far from the old Wrigley Building, the gargoyle roost that houses the *Express*. It's run by the Sisters of Mercy. Like the Wrigley Building, one part of St. Anne's was built in the late 1920s, but some Las Piernas millionaire that no one had ever heard of before died and left a large part of his fortune to the place, so they had added new wings. They were not only very up-to-date in facilities and equipment, but they were known as one of the best trauma centers in the area. That and the nun factor gave it a high reputation. It also made its emergency room one of the busiest for miles around.

Despite traffic and my tendency to check the rearview mirror a lot, I got to St. Anne's fairly quickly. Frank was standing outside the ER entrance, waiting for me.

"Hi," he said, when I got nearer. "They're working on him, not much we can learn right now. Your sister's in there, too. She found him. My partner, Pete Baird, was two steps behind her and was able to radio for help or I don't think Kenny would have made it. Still not sure he will. Whoever it was really beat the living hell out of him."

"How's Barbara?" I asked, anxious to find her.

"Your sister has seen something that would be pretty disturbing to anybody. It's even worse when somebody you care about gets messed up like this. The doctor gave her a sedative; she was . . . well, she was really upset. Had a little difficulty getting her to leave the ER so they could work on Kenny." He paused and asked, "What's in the bag?"

"Lunch," I said, feeling more than a little bit foolish. "I didn't want to leave it in the car. It's a gift of the restaurant owner, who was a great fan of O'Connor's. He insisted."

"Sorry about keeping you waiting there. You know how it is. Why don't you try to coax your sister into coming outside? I'd like to ask her some questions, and I think it would be easier if we were away from all the other people in the waiting room."

I handed him the bag and went into the waiting room. There wasn't the crowd that would be there on a Friday or Saturday night, but every chair was taken. Barbara was leaning against a wall near a doorway, twisting a Kleenex to shreds. She looked up at me and I could see she had been crying hard. Fresh tears started as I approached. I put my arms around her. She leaned on my shoulder and I felt her heaving with quiet sobs. I heard myself softly comforting her with the same singsong—"shh, shh, shh"—sound our mother used to make as she held us when we cried as children. I reached into my purse and brought out a fresh packet of Kleenex. She nodded her thanks and straightened up and blew her nose.

"Let's go outside for a minute, Barbara. There's someone who needs to talk to you out there."

"I . . . can't . . . leave . . . him," she said, sharp breaths between each word.

I put my arm around her and walked her over to an elderly nun who was at the admitting counter.

"Excuse me, Sister?"

"Yes?" She had gentle, knowing eyes that took in the situation in a glance.

"This is Mrs. Kenneth O'Connor, whose husband was just admitted a little while ago. I'm her sister and I'd like to take her out to the courtyard for a while. Would it be possible to have someone let her know when her husband comes out of the emergency room?"

"Of course," she said, smiling gently at Barbara. "I promise to come out there myself just as soon as there's word on his condition. I'm Sister Theresa. Just ask for me if you need anything."

The Sisters of Mercy had lived up to their name.

Barbara allowed me to lead her out into the courtyard, but as we got to the double glass doors, she stopped me.

"You shouldn't have lied to that nun."

"I didn't lie to that nun."

"Yes, you did. You told her I was Mrs. Kenneth O'Connor."

"In the eyes of the Church, you still are."

It made me feel good that she'd hassle me over anything; it was a sign she was capable of being distracted, however momentarily, from the problems at hand. And here I was, leading her out to talk with a cop who would make her rehash it all. I could feel her tense up when she saw Frank. She stared down at the ground the rest of the way over to the concrete table and bench where he sat waiting for us. As we approached, he stood up and said, "Mrs. O'Connor, we haven't really been introduced. I'm Frank Harriman."

Barbara nodded her head without making any eye contact.

"I know. You're Irene's detective."

I made a sign to Frank not to pursue it for a moment.

"Why don't we sit down for a while?" he said. "Are you hungry? Your sister has brought some lunch."

She looked up and glared at me. "You went out and bought lunch before coming here?"

"No, Barbara," I said, wondering when the sedative was going to kick in. "I was at a restaurant when Detective Harriman—Frank— was kind enough to call and let me know you needed me." Not the exact truth, but she didn't seem to question it—or how Frank would know I was at a particular restaurant. In any case, this story of Frank's searching for her sister for her at least got her to look up at his face.

"That was very kind of you," she said to Frank.

"No problem."

No one was going to make a move toward the food. Frank was the only possible candidate for an appetite at that moment, and he wasn't diving in.

The courtyard was private and serene. It was bordered by carefully tended beds of bright-colored flowers and tall trees. A hedge with an opening into a walkway to the front entrance shielded the yard from the parking lot. We sat there listening to birds and smelling the now chilled satay and pad Thai.

Barbara seemed to be growing calmer. Frank asked me if he had ever told me the story of the time he was called out to rescue a lady who was stuck in a dog door. I said no.

"It was out in Bakersfield, oh, about midnight one night. The owner of the house was this lady's former boyfriend. He had tried to break up with her for two weeks. She refused to let go, as they say, and on four other occasions within these two weeks she had shown up drunk on his doorstep. He'd open the door and she'd try to shove her way in, calling him every name in the book, then crying on his shoulder and telling him she couldn't live without him. At first he felt so guilty about hurting her that he put up with it. But this particular night he just got tired of it, so he didn't open the door. She went around back."

"And tried to get in through the dog door?"

"Right. And, well, let's just say she was a little more fully developed than the dog. The guy only had a beagle. Anyway, she was stuck between her hips and bra-line."

He looked over to see if this was offensive to Barbara, but to my amazement she was sitting there with a little grin on her face.

"How'd you get her out?" I asked.

"Well, by the time I got there, she'd sobered up quite a bit, and felt more than a little embarrassed. I asked the guy if he had any mineral oil or petroleum jelly and a sheet. He brought in a bottle of baby oil and a sheet. I told her I'd need her to take off her blouse, and we'd put the sheet over her for the sake of modesty. She said she was past worrying about modesty, her back and knees were killing her and would we please hurry up and get her the hell out of the dog door.

"So we stripped her from the waist up, and lubricated her skin and as much of the door liner as we could. I went out and around through the backyard gate so that I could pull from the other side. I'm sure it didn't feel great, but eventually she slid right out. She thanked me, took her blouse and bra and told the guy she never wanted to see him again."

"I'll never feel like the most desperate woman in the world again," Barbara said.

"Frank and I knew each other when I worked in Bakersfield," I said.

"Oh," said Barbara, "I didn't know you were such old friends."

"We haven't been in touch in a long time."

Barbara looked between us. "Oh."

"I know you've really had a shock today, Mrs. O'Connor," Frank said gently.

She nodded. Tears welled up in her eyes and she looked back over toward the glass doors, but she stayed put.

"Did Mr. O'Connor call you today?"

She turned back to Frank. "You mean Kenny? Yes, he called. He said he needed me to give him a ride to a new hiding place. Someone was trying to kill him."

Frank waited.

"He said he couldn't tell me more over the phone because the cops—I mean, the police—might have the phone tapped."

"Why was he afraid of the police?"

"I don't know. I think he was afraid of everybody. He was just so scared. Anyway, he asked me to come and give him a ride, since he didn't have his car—" She looked at me and reddened. She turned back to Frank. "I guess you already know that."

"Did he mention the names of anyone who might be causing him trouble?"

She hesitated. "I've been thinking about that. He said he couldn't tell me what his problems were or who was after him, just that they were very powerful people who could get away with anything. But when we dropped the Corvette off at your house, Irene, he said something like, 'All because of Hannah.' I thought that might have been the young girl he was trying to impress when he bought the Corvette. Do you think she could be behind this?"

Frank and I looked at one another.

"Well, maybe that's crazy," she added quickly. "I don't know. But who is Hannah?"

" 'Who Is Hannah' . . . " I repeated slowly. "O'Connor's column."

"Oh, for pity's sakes, Irene, that Hannah died almost forty years ago. And there's more than one Hannah in the world. She probably wasn't even a Hannah. Who knows what her name really was."

"That's what I want to know, Barbara. Who is it that might know her real name?"

Frank shot me a look that clearly said he wished I would shut my big mouth. Barbara saw it and went into a pout. "No one tells me anything!"

"I'm sorry," Frank said. "I just think your sister is doing a lot of speculating on slim evidence and I don't want her to worry you."

"Worry me! After today?" She turned to me. "Do you know what happened to me today?"

The shrill edge in her tone made me realize Barbara was a powder keg and I was playing with matches. I shook my head "no" and looked at Frank, who was now looking down at his hands. He was rubbing his right thumb over the knuckles of his left hand.

"That's right," she went on, "you don't. When Kenny called he said he'd be ready to go in an hour. Just one hour. I was ready to go get him then, but he wanted me to come down in an hour. He was down at the beach house. The front door was open. Just wide open."

"Barbara . . ."

She was white as a sheet. Her voice scared me—it had become mechanical, as if she were describing a scene in a movie. "There was blood everywhere. Everywhere. I walked in and I called out, 'Kenny!' But I already knew he wouldn't answer. There was so much blood. It was sprayed on the walls. And there was a trail of it on the carpet leading to the back door. I got some of it on my shoes."

She stopped and looked down at her shoes, and then back up at me. She started to cry.

"Barbara—" I reached out and she recoiled from me. I looked to Frank for help.

He said, very quietly, "Let her tell it."

She started to speak again, tears rolling down her face.

"When I looked out into the backyard, I saw this red baseball bat stuck in the sand. I wondered why it was sticking up there in the sand, right where this trail of blood stopped. And then there was Kenny's hand, just barely showing. He was moving his fingers. He was trying to dig himself out. They had buried him alive."

"Oh, Jesus Christ, Barbara . . ."

"That's when I started screaming. I just screamed and I screamed. I was screaming the whole time I was digging him out. At first I couldn't find his nose. I wanted to make it so he could breathe, you see. I guess I got his mouth free, because he made these gulping and wheezing and then coughing noises. Then there was Detective Baird. I don't know when he got there, but he helped me dig Kenny out. He pulled me away from Kenny and made me sit in the sand. He called some help somehow, and he tried to help Kenny breathe, but it was hard because . . . well, they had smashed his face. His teeth were all broken on one side and I could see . . . bone. And his nose was broken. His eyes were swollen shut and he had sand in all his cuts. The blood made everything stick. Detective Baird got some of the bleeding to stop. And then there were lots of people and Detective Baird drove me here, right behind the ambulance. Detective Baird had Kenny's blood all over him."

She looked at Frank, and took his hands. "You sent Detective Baird to look after me, didn't you?"

"You might put it that way," he said.

"I want to thank you for that." She started sobbing again, but she wouldn't let go of Frank's hands. He didn't try to take them away.

I thought of how often I misjudged her, thought of all she had been through just this morning. I stood up and took the bag of Thai food over to the trash can. A shame to waste it, but I didn't expect to be hungry again for about five years.

As I turned to go back to the table, I noticed Sister Theresa walking toward us. I prayed a prayer I never thought I'd pray—I prayed to God that Kenny was still alive.

8

Sister Theresa and I reached the bench at the same time.

"Mrs. O'Connor?" she said to Barbara, "Come along now, the doctor is ready to talk to you about your husband."

"Is he . . . ?"

"Yes, he's alive. Now, more than that, you'll have to learn from the doctor."

I murmured a prayer of thanks to a God who would listen to hypocrites.

Barbara and Sister Theresa started back. I was about to follow when Barbara turned and asked me if I'd wait outside with Frank. I felt hurt, but I stayed where I was. Frank looked over at me.

"Hey, don't take it so hard. Later on she's probably not even going to remember being upset with you."

"I've never been—what did you call it the other day?—'sympathetic' enough with her. I'm always wanting her to be a little tougher, less vulnerable."

Frank was good enough just to let me kick myself in silence for a while.

"I don't suppose there are any leads on this?" I asked.

"Nothing solid. We've got a forensics team combing every inch of that beach house."

"I wonder if Kenny was the intended target all along."

"It's possible. But then there's this Hannah business and a couple of other things that bother me. For example, why shoot out *your* window? If they thought he was at your place, and were planning to kill him, why not wait for a clear shot? For that matter, why not just shoot him today? If they wanted to kill him, why not just do it outright?"

"O'Connor must have figured out who Hannah was," I said, "or at least worried someone into thinking he was getting too close to figuring it out. But why be so vicious with Kenny?"

"I don't know. We're talking to people with whom Kenny has been in recent contact, trying to find out if anyone knows anything that might help us figure out how he comes into it."

"I talked to Lydia. I think things look pretty good for my getting my job back at the paper."

To my surprise, he didn't seem very happy about this. "Irene, what happened to Kenny changes everything. I don't think it's a good idea for you to stay in Las Piernas. At least not until we figure out what's going on."

"And what if you never figure it out?"

"We will."

"Who are you trying to kid? Maybe some people expect you guys to be supermen, but I don't. I'll bet even the Canadian Mounties don't always get their man anymore. I've worked the crime beat, remember?"

"Look—doesn't my experience count for anything with you?"

"Doesn't mine count for anything with you?"

"Goddamn it, Irene, this guy's a freak. Burying Kenny in the sand—that's not the work of some hood on an errand."

"I appreciate your concern; but think about it, Frank. I'm in danger until we figure out who's behind all of this. That will be easier to discover if I pick up the threads of O'Connor's investigations. I know how O'Connor's mind worked, the way he attacked a problem. You've probably already gone into the newsroom and gathered whatever Wrigley could hand over, and I know enough about O'Connor's note-taking to know you probably haven't been able to make heads or tails of it. I'm not trying to be a hero here, Frank. I just don't see any quicker or better way to get my own life back in order."

I waited. He was rubbing his knuckles again.

"I'm not going to be able to talk you out of this, am I?"

"In a word, no."

"Well, hell."

"This isn't something I take lightly. I'm about to compromise the hell out of my journalistic ethics. I don't like Wrigley, but that doesn't make me feel any less like a double agent, working with you on this. The only way I'm going to be able to face myself in the mirror is by telling myself that this is beyond reporters versus cops. That, and I trust you."

"Thanks, but I also happen to know you see yourself as O'Connor's Avenging Angel."

"I've never been any kind of angel, Frank."

"Hmph." He shoved his hands into his pockets. "Look, I'd better get going. All hell will be breaking loose at headquarters. I'll call you at Lydia's tonight."

I watched as he walked off, then went back to the ER waiting room. I walked over to the counter, where Sister Theresa was concentrating on something on her desk. I looked down and noticed she was doodling—a fairly good caricature of one of the nurses I had seen going in and out of the ER. She had captured the nurse's semi-military bearing and grim facial features rather well.

"Remarkable resemblance," I said.

She gave a start and then two bright red spots appeared on her cheeks.

"Not very Christian of me, I suppose," she said.

"I won't tell."

She smiled. "You want to find your sister."

"No, I don't think she really wants to see me, at least not now. I just want to know if she's okay and where she'll be later on—I know she'll want to stay with her husband as much as possible."

"Yes, I'm afraid your sister is the kind of person who will exhaust herself with dedication. And you're wise to let her have some time to, well, to get used to things. It's very hard to adjust to extensive, critical injuries to those we love. She may not be herself for a while."

"I understand."

She looked at me with those gentle eyes. I grew up thinking nuns had X-ray vision where your guilty conscience was concerned, so I never really enjoyed getting the old eyeball from them; but I didn't feel uncomfortable with Sister Theresa.

"Don't worry," she said, "you're a good sister to her."

Damn. X-ray vision after all.

9

Before I left, I learned from Sister Theresa that Kenny was in a coma, had multiple fractures and facial injuries. Both collarbones and several ribs had received bone-breaking whacks from the bat. Brain damage might or might not be permanent. She explained that most of the beating had been on his face, which gave him a better chance of recovery than he would have had if the blows had landed on other parts of his head. Most of the blood probably had come from his face—especially the mouth and nose. He was also lucky that the broken ribs hadn't punctured his lungs. His condition was listed as critical.

It was late afternoon when I got back to Lydia's place. Cody was starved for attention and gave me a grand welcome, prancing and yowling and purring loudly. The phone rang.

I let the machine get it, but listened in, then picked up the receiver when I recognized Lydia's voice.

"What's up, Lydia?"

"I've been worried sick about you! Do you know what's happened to O'Connor's son?"

It dawned on me that as assistant city editor, she would have heard the police and paramedics calls on the scanner and sent some general assignment person out to check out the beach-house story.

"Yeah, I know. That's where I've been, down at St. Anne's."

"Is he going to make it?"

"Don't know. He's a mess, but he's hanging in there so far. Can't get nuns to quote odds. How are things going with Wrigley?"

"He wants to take us both out to dinner tonight."

"Are you game?"

"For an evening with Wrigley? Now we're talking sacrifice. But I wouldn't send my worst enemy out alone with that wolf."

"I take it he's not in the newsroom."

"You'll make a fine newspaperwoman someday."

"Gee, thanks. So he took the bait?"

"Hook, line, and sinker."

"So where's dinner?" I asked.

"Café La Fleur, eight o'clock."

"How trendy."

"That's our Wrigley."

"Are you coming back home first?"

"Of course; I need to change."

This struck a note of panic in me. "Lydia, I haven't got anything fancy with me."

"Fancy? My dear, the look at La Fleur is studied dishabille. Got anything left over from the hippie days with you?"

"No, gone to Goodwill. But I get the picture."

"Anyway, I've got stuff you can borrow."

Lydia got home about half an hour later and invited me to go for a run. Paranoia about being out in the open almost made me beg off, but I decided I could use the stress relief. It was the perfect time of day to go running—still light and yet cooling off. We took a couple of turns and ended up in a nearby park. There were lots of other joggers and skaters and bike riders, and somehow we avoided being bumped into by all this fitness traffic. Lydia and I took off over the grass to avoid some of the crowd on the pathways.

We reached that point where all you hear is your own breathing, the air going past your ears, and the rhythm of your feet on the ground. I started feeling all the tension leave me; I was bathed in sweat and happy as a clam. We made a wide turn in the park and headed home. We slowed to a walk without anyone saying a word, just smiling and breathing hard.

We each showered, and I put on a simple blouse and long cotton skirt, a dark-blue number that showed off my eye color. Barbara has the green-eyed, redhead Irish looks of my mother, while I have the dark brown hair and blue eyes of my father. Unless you saw us with our parents, you wouldn't know we were related.

Lydia had a sort of romper on, with a plain blouse underneath and all the buttons but one—the bottom one—open on the romper.

"You were serious about the dishabille. Shall I tuck my skirt into my panty hose?"

"Come on, now," she laughed, "I got this look straight out of the *L.A. Times Magazine*. Don't tell Wrigley I said so. You know how he is about the T-word."

Good Italian that she is, Lydia drove and talked with her hands at the same time, and I was fearing for my life again. I thought that it would be too ironic to die in a traffic accident after everything else that had happened. To my great relief we made it safely to the restaurant.

I'd never been to Café La Fleur, even though it's not far from my house. It's on Allen Street, which was "rediscovered" about five years ago. From dilapidated storefronts, thrift shops, and laundromats, some real estate genius had fashioned a local hot spot, now filled with art galleries, restaurants, and boutiques. Everything is in salmon pink or pistachio ice-cream green, or else it looks like *Casablanca* could be filmed there. La Fleur is in the pistachio mode. Glass bricks line its street-side exterior, 1930s-style.

We stepped inside. The interior of the restaurant was brightly lit, with large ceiling fans turning lazily above. Everything else was white or salmon pink. I guess they saved the green for outdoors. There were little planters with bromeliads in them between the booths. The tables were tall and circular, with backless white metal stools pulled up to them. This encouraged table-sitters to lean their elbows on the tables, and gave them all the look of being in intimate conversation.

A blackboard arrayed in colored chalk announced specials of crab soufflé and squid with asparagus pasta. A young anorexic who looked like she was wearing her father's pajamas greeted us and asked for our names. We told her we were with Mr. Wrigley. She told us her name was Crystal and offered to show us to where he was seated in the bar.

The lighting in the bar was only slightly more subdued, but the clientele was slightly less so. As we were being seated, I thanked Crystal. "Do you eat here?" I asked.

"All the time," she said, "I love this place."

Wrigley was in fine fettle. He must have sworn himself to his best behavior, as he didn't try to hug or kiss us on arrival. He bought us a round of drinks; it looked as if he had a good head start.

"Irene, dear," he cooed as the waitress left the table, "we are all very saddened by this whole sad, sad business."

When he's been drinking, Wrigley tends to have redundancy problems.

"Yes," I replied, "I know you'll miss O'Connor." This was pure horseshit. O'Connor had always been highly regarded by both the board of directors and the staff of the paper, and nothing Wrigley did could demean O'Connor. Wrigley had always felt threatened by him. Worse, O'Connor had annoyed Wrigley by simply ignoring him.

"Miss him!" Wrigley replied. "The man was an absolute gem. He was a jewel in the crown of the *Express*. And such a horrible fate! Horrible!"

I didn't say anything. I was relieved to see the waitress coming back with our drinks.

Crystal came padding over to us just as the drinks were delivered and told us our table was ready. I fervently hoped I would not have to lean forward into Wrigley's martini breath on one of those metal seats.

Fortunately, she took us to a booth. I sat down and Lydia immediately fielded the position next to me, forcing Wrigley to sit alone on the other side. He grabbed Crystal's hand as she started to leave. That was more like the Wrigley I knew.

"Crystal, darling," he hissed, "tell us what's good tonight."

She repeated the blackboard choices and said, "Avoid the Cajun-style red snapper." She pulled her hand away from Wrigley and shuffled back to the door.

Wrigley stared after her departing form, then seemed to remember we were at the table. "So," he said, "let's pick out what we want and then we can talk. Hate to be unprepared when the waitress comes by."

We looked over the menus. Almost everything sounded like a combination of things I would not like to find on my plate at the same time. I turned to Lydia. "What's pancetta?"

"Bacon," she said with a grin.

I shrugged. "At least I knew arugula."

Wrigley was lost in space. He came to with a start when he discovered the restaurant, in its infinite wisdom, had sent us a waiter— not a waitress. Not just any waiter. This was obviously Super-Waiter. He was a hunk. He had jet black hair and blue eyes and a bod as solid as a brick shithouse. A gorgeous man. He smiled. Lydia and I smiled. Wrigley looked forlorn.

Lydia ordered the pasta carbonara, my question about pancetta apparently whetting her appetite for it. The waiter, who had introduced himself as Michael, gave a great deal of attention to Lydia's order—salad dressing, wine choices, and bread—and gave her another big smile, as if he were proud to be of service. I ordered the Sante Fe chicken, and while he was very polite, I could tell who was going to be spoiled rotten all night. And it wasn't Wrigley or me. In fact, when Wrigley ordered his squid and asparagus pasta, he got a "Very good, sir," and that was that.

"This place has really gone downhill," groused Wrigley.

Michael had our salads and wine out to us in record time. He fussed endlessly over Lydia, who gloried in the attention. This also seemed to have the effect of inhibiting Wrigley's desire to make passes. I wondered if Michael had any interest in journalism.

"Well," Wrigley said in a peeved tone, "now that we have a few moments to ourselves"— he shot a meaningful look at Lydia—"now that we can talk without being overheard by every Tom, Dick, and Harry with an apron on, I just wanted to ask you if certain rumors I hear are true, Irene."

"Rumors?" I repeated with perfectly feigned innocence.

"It's been said that you might be looking to get back into the newspaper game."

Reflecting that for Wrigley, who had inherited a large share of stock in the paper and made himself executive editor, it was indeed nothing more than a game, I told him that rumor was true.

"Well, how exciting! How thrilling! And of course you will come back to work for us then! It couldn't be any other way, Irene. We're your family. Why, we practically raised you. You came to us as a mere child, and we would welcome you back. It's only right."

This was going to be easier than I thought. Lydia must have really done a job on the old boy if she had him this eager. Still, I had to make sure of my position.

"Actually, I had thought of going to work at another paper."

"The *Bee*? Oh, yes, I know all about it. I can't let that happen. Why, O'Connor would come back to haunt me. He would be rolling in his grave if I let you go to work anywhere but the *Express*."

The spinning and haunting O'Connor already invoked, I thought I might as well go for broke.

"Well," I said slowly, as if thinking it all over for the first time, "O'Connor and I were close friends. It would be nice to be back in the old newsroom, near his desk. I'd feel closer to him somehow."

"Yes, yes!"

"In fact, he always told me all about the stories he was working on—in confidence, of course, seeing how I was really one of the *Express* family, as you say. Some of his most recent stuff will really turn some heads. Make those snobs at the *Times* take you seriously."

"Yes, yes, I can see it will!"

Time to set the hook. "Who did you give his stuff to?"

"Oh, the police have most of it, you know, murder investigation."

"I mean, who have you assigned the stories to?"

"Why, Irene, that's what I've been trying to say! It's what I've been trying so hard to tell you! You! You're the one I want for his stories. Couldn't be anybody else."

"You're willing to overlook our last . . . discussion?"

He waved his hand in a gesture of dismissal, dipping his sleeve in blue cheese dressing. "Forgive and forget, I always say. Let bygones be bygones, that's my motto. Isn't it, Lydia?"

"Yes, sir," she said, smiling as she lied.

Just then Michael brought our main courses. I noticed Lydia's portion seemed substantially larger than Wrigley's or mine. It fact, mine left me no doubt that Crystal did indeed eat here. A piece of reddish-orange chicken, about the size of the sole of a baby's shoe, graced one side of a white plate, with two halves of a potato too small to have left its mother on the other; they were fenced off from each other by what looked like something that had been weeded from between the bromeliads.

Wrigley's pasta looked so weird, I was glad there wasn't too much of it to look at.

Queen Lydia continued to reign as Michael asked her if everything was satisfactory and left right after she told him it was great. I didn't begrudge her all her fun—she deserved it, and I owed her big time for working Wrigley into such a fervor for me.

As he ate, Wrigley continually dropped bits and pieces of his food on his clothing. In the space of about five minutes, you could have figured out what he ordered by looking at his lapels. Early on he captured a peppercorn between his front teeth, making it very hard not to look at his teeth while he talked.

And talk he did. On and on about how he had visions for the *Express* and how I was a part of those visions. How the newsroom just wasn't the same without me.

I told him I'd need a fairly free reign to follow up on O'Connor's stories.

No problem.

I told him I'd like access to whatever the police hadn't hauled off from O'Connor's desk.

No problem.

I told him I wanted more pay.

Problem. These difficult times, the need to stay competitive, and so on.

Michael came by again, insisting that Lydia order dessert. She went for the chocolate-mousse pie. I ordered creme brûlée and Wrigley ordered profiteroles. When they came, I realized how this place stayed in business—from now on, people would have to invite me out for dessert if they wanted to meet me here.

Wrigley finally agreed to a very slight increase in my former pay, and I felt that after hoodwinking him into buying us dinner and begging me to do everything I wanted to do, I should be satisfied. We shook on it. I had to wipe sauce off my hand afterward.

Lydia excused herself for a moment and I got a little panicked that with her gone, Wrigley would wax romantic to seal the deal.

"Excuse me," I said, "I didn't want to say anything in front of Lydia, but you have a peppercorn stuck in your front teeth."

"Why, thanks for letting me know," he said, "that's so embarrassing."

He then took out a slim silver object which I first took to be a cigarette case. He opened it and took out a length of dental floss, and using the polished lid as a mirror, proceeded to floss his teeth at the table.

"Nothing beats good dental hygiene, I always say," he said between teeth.

Let bygones be bygones, I thought to myself, trying not to watch.

Lydia finally got back. She had missed the demonstration of Wrigley's table manners completely. Michael brought our check and told Lydia he hoped she had enjoyed her evening and would return soon, and left the check. I was sure Wrigley would stiff him his tip.

As we crossed the parking lot, I could see that Lydia was dying to tell me something. As soon as we were in the car, she revealed that Michael had asked for her phone number.

"He said he'd call when he got off work tonight, about eleven."
She frowned for a moment. "I suppose I shouldn't get my hopes up.
He's quite a bit younger than I am. He might not call."

"Don't talk yourself into or out of anything yet, kiddo. Enjoy it."

"You're right. I'm not going to spoil it."

I thanked her for paving the way for my getting everything I could
hope for out of Wrigley, and she laughed so hard at my description
of Wrigley's flossing that I didn't even think about her driving.

10

When we got home, there was a message for me from Frank on the answering machine, asking me to call him. He sounded weary on the tape. He wasn't in at headquarters, but they said he was expecting my call, so they would contact him out in the field.

About fifteen minutes went by, and the phone rang. It was Michael. He was still at the restaurant, but was calling Lydia to ask if she'd like to go out Thursday night. He worked Fridays and weekends, so that was his next night off. She said yes, hung up and was bouncing off the walls in excitement for the next half hour. Cody, whose affections for Lydia had been won with lasagna, got in the act and started tearing through the house as if he were being chased by a pack of wild dogs.

Sometime around twelve o'clock Lydia and Cody finally wound down. We were sitting together on the couch, scratching Cody's ears and catching up on newsroom gossip, when Frank called. Lydia handed the phone to me.

"Hi, Frank."

"Hello, Irene. Do you have a few minutes?" That weary tone again.

"Lately I haven't been booked at midnight. What's up? You sound kind of down."

"Do I? I'm okay, just tired. Can't keep the hours I did when I was twenty-three. Anyway, I need your help with something. We've got copies of O'Connor's handwritten notes and you were right—they're in some kind of code. Do you know how to read it, or am I going to have to hire a cryptographer?"

"I can usually make out most of it."

"Great."

"Can you get copies of what you have to me?"

"Yeah. You going to be up for a little while?"

"Yeah, probably. Lydia's catching me up on the latest rumors at the *Express*. Did you want to drop them by on your way home?"

"If you don't mind . . ."

"See you soon."

We hung up and I let Lydia know what was up.

It took Frank about thirty minutes to get over to the house. Lydia had fallen asleep on the couch by then, but woke with a start when he knocked on the door. After making sure who it was, she let him in. I introduced them to each other, and watched them quickly appraise one another.

"I'll leave you two sleuths to do your work," she said, adding, "Are you going to give Kevin any notice, Irene? I thought we could ride in together tomorrow, if you'd like."

The thought of another car ride with Lydia, and my uncertainty over how things would go with Kevin when I told him my plans, led me to decline politely. She said goodnight and went off to bed. To my dismay, my two-timing cat followed her into her room.

"So, you've got your job back already?" Frank asked casually.

"Yes. I've got to let my boss at the PR firm know what's up, though. I'm probably going to take a leave—this doesn't seem like a good time to make decisions about my career—I'm too emotional."

"All things considered, you're doing great."

We went into the kitchen, where we would be least likely to keep Lydia awake with the noise of our conversation. We sat on stools at the counter. He was carrying a bulky clasp envelope, from which he pulled out a five-inch-thick sheaf of photocopied pages from one of O'Connor's notebooks.

"Your pal O'Connor must have never thrown a piece of paper away in his life. The guys who went through his desk told me every drawer was stuffed with notebooks, scraps of paper, you name it."

"He was something of a pack rat, I'll admit," I said.

"Well, these copies are from the notebooks. I've had someone trying to put them in order all day today. These seem to be the most recent; at least, they are if these dates aren't in some kind of code, too."

"No, no secret date system." I thumbed through the notes, pleased at how quickly O'Connor's shorthand system came back to me. "I've been reading this code since I was a GA—general assignment reporter—and he started working it out so that I'd always get assigned to his stories." I laughed, remembering. "Boy, talk about your rumor mill—the paper was buzzing then. Most of them thought he had the red hots for me.

"Anyway, unlike some of the older staff, he didn't have any trouble using the computer terminals, but he didn't trust them entirely— didn't believe they were very secure. He suspected some newsroom hacker might call up his work somehow, even though there are passwords and all of that. So he used a system of abbreviations, nicknames, and good old-fashioned shorthand notation."

As I glanced through them, I saw that most of the notes were pretty routine. Over the last fifteen years, O'Connor had had fairly free rein to pick his stories. Lately, a lot of his work had been on political stories. For every hot item there were a hundred deadly dull ones. He had notes from press conferences, campaign interviews, and so on.

"What's this?" Frank asked, leaning over my shoulder to point to a page where O'Connor had scrawled the letters "RCC."

"Rubber-chicken circuit," I explained. "Political fund-raising banquets. Refers to the delicious fare at those gatherings." I looked at the notes below this one, on the same page. O'Connor had placed a dot with several lines angling off it.

"See this?" I asked, pointing to them. "It's a rat's nose and whiskers. O'Connor used those to mean, 'I smell a rat.'" I smiled, thinking of him making the rat-nose notation, a hound on the trail of some faint scent. "I once asked him why all his political notes weren't covered with these rat noses. He told me I should watch out, that working for newspapers had made me a real cynic and that was just another way of losing objectivity. Then he laughed and said, 'Besides, this means a real rat, not every little mouse that thinks he's a rat.'"

Frank laughed, and his laugh made me feel good. The O'Connor in these notes was alive; his wit and sense of humor, his curiosity, his ability to puzzle it all out. I went back to reading them, feeling as if they were letters from home.

"You miss him, don't you?" asked Frank, watching me.

"Oh, yeah, sure I do," I said. "I keep asking myself, 'How would O'Connor handle this? How would he pursue it?' So many times I saw him stop and examine some minor point the rest of us had just sailed right by. It would turn out to be the key to everything."

"He must have been quite a character. I've known some cops who were the same way—just doggedly pursued something until it gave out. I think I'm just now getting to be old enough to really appreciate that kind of patience and persistence."

We sat quietly, going back over the notes more slowly. I stopped when I came to a page I had missed the first time through. The heading was "JD55," O'Connor's way of writing, "Jane Doe 1955."

"Here! Look at this, it's about Hannah! 'JD55' was his code for her. He's got all these arrows—he doodled arrows when he thought something seemed like it was an important break in a story. Let's see. It's shorthand for 'Mac teeth,' and then here's the letter *F*, circled."

"Great, when can I make an arrest?"

I looked up at him. "Remember what O'Connor said about being a cynic, smart-ass. It goes double for cops."

"Why not? Everything else does."

Frank stood up and stretched, and walked into the living room, which was off the kitchen, and started pacing around. Out of what I took to be some kind of innate detective nosiness, he was reading the titles on the spines of Lydia's books and looking at her family pictures.

I tried to make out another section on the page about Hannah.

"Hey, Frank—do you know someone in the coroner's office by the name of Hernandez?"

"Yeah," he said, walking back over, "Dr. Carlos Hernandez. He's the new coroner. He took over about a year ago, when old Woolsey retired. Why?"

"He's in the notes. Something about Hannah's teeth. Has he talked to you about seeing O'Connor?"

"No, but he hasn't been around the last few days. He had to fly back to Colorado to testify in a murder trial. That's his previous jurisdiction." He leaned over my shoulder again. "What do the notes say about Hernandez?"

"It says, 'Old Sheep Dip wrong about teeth'—Sheep Dip is Woolsey. O'Connor had a rather strained relationship with him." I felt a little embarrassed to mention this nickname for Dr. Emmet Woolsey, coroner of Las Piernas for over forty years, but when I glanced at Frank, I could see he was amused by it.

"Woolsey felt like O'Connor was pointing out some failing of his when he talked about Hannah in the paper every year," I explained. "He was bitter over it. On the other hand, as I've said, the same column sometimes helped to identify a John or Jane Doe left in the morgue, so Woolsey had to grudgingly acknowledge O'Connor's help."

"Woolsey could be a real pain in the ass. I've never thought much of him. Always preferred to deal with just about anybody else in that office. Hernandez, on the other hand, is sharp. He came on board just before that double homicide down at the beach last year—his work on that really helped me out."

"Any way to reach him?"

"Shouldn't be too hard. I can at least get word to him, ask him to get in touch."

Frank pulled out his notebook and wrote a memo to make the call. He folded it up and put it back in his pocket. He had a grin on his face. "Old Sheep Dip, huh? Are all these nicknames so colorful?" He sat back down next to me. "I wonder if Hernandez will know what 'Mac teeth' means. Are you sure that's what it says?"

"I think so," I said, and tried to puzzle it out again. "Yeah, I'm pretty sure it says 'Mac teeth.' Look, I'll get into his computer files tomorrow. You have copies of those?"

"Yes, but other than stories he was actually in the process of writing or ones he had already filed, it's this same gobbledygook. Without the help of arrows or whiskers." He sat leaning on the counter with his face in his hands, rubbing his eyes. He suddenly looked tired again. I watched him for a moment.

"You'd better get some sleep," I said, standing up.

I straightened out the papers and put them back in the envelope, trying to keep my idle hands from temptation. "Can I keep these?"

"Yeah, sure," he said. "If you can manage to keep going over them, I think we're bound to get a better handle on this."

"When I get into his computer files tomorrow I'll have more to work with."

"I guess you were right about working at the paper," he said, looking down. "Sorry if I got a little hot under the collar this afternoon, I just . . ." He didn't finish the sentence. Instead, he shrugged and said, "Well, be careful anyway, okay, Irene? For my sake?" Quickly he added, "I'd hate for you to get killed before I learned what the hell 'Mac teeth' means."

"Gee, thanks."

He laughed and said goodnight.

That night I dreamed again and again that I was buried under sand, suffocating. I couldn't move my hands or mouth, but somehow

I was crying out. The sand muffled the cries. Frank was walking right over the place I was buried, and I couldn't get him to hear my screams. Sometimes O'Connor would be there, and he'd tell Frank, "She's here," and Frank would dig me free. Other times O'Connor wasn't in the dream, and Frank kept walking on down the beach. I'd wake up drenched in sweat either way, afraid to fall back to sleep.

I had a hell of a time making the bed the next morning.

11

Two nights without much sleep threatened to make me a cranky baby, so I had to talk myself into getting going the next morning. I was excited about digging into O'Connor's files, but first I had to face Kevin.

Kevin was the Malloy of Malloy & Marlowe, the public-relations firm I had been working for since I quit the *Express*. He had worked at the paper at one time as well, but left just after old man Wrigley died. Kevin had the foresight to see what was coming with Son of Wrigley. He had left amicably, hooked up with Don Marlowe, who was another former reporter, and formed a very successful firm. Always able to smooth-talk if need be, Kevin had also been a real go-getter, and the energy had paid off. He wasn't the writer Don was, but the combination of the copy Don turned out and Kevin's ability to work with people made for lots of happy clients.

Kevin had been a great friend of O'Connor's. They often went drinking together, and O'Connor used to say that Kevin made him feel like a true Irishman. They would tell stories all night, and Kevin was one of the few who were a match for O'Connor's silver tongue. As one of the members of the circle that revolved around O'Connor, Kevin embraced me as a friend, but I've no doubt it was his love of the old man which led to his hiring me after the great brouhaha at the paper.

I had gone into the newsroom pissed as hell one day after learning that Wrigley was not going to take any disciplinary action against an assistant city editor who had all but raped one of the women working as a night-shift GA. It was part of a whole atmosphere that had festered under Wrigley's inability to keep his hands to himself. He never touched me, but he made sexually provocative comments to me and other women staff members on a nauseatingly recurrent basis.

I made a lot of unflattering references to his ancestors and his own person, told him I was through working for an ass-pinching sleazeball and stomped off. I got a loud cheer and some hoots from my longtime companions in the newsroom. Lydia told me later that as the applause died down, O'Connor stood up and told Wrigley that he wasn't going to have much of a staff left if he didn't take better care of people who depended on him to see the right thing was done. Word got out to the Publisher's Board, which could still outvote Wrigley, and was starting to do so more and more frequently. Some pressure was brought to bear, and Wrigley fired the assistant city editor.

I, of course, for all the personal satisfaction that had given me, was out of a job, finding myself in the position of many a person who has told the boss to shove it. The bills came anyway.

O'Connor tried to get me to swallow my pride and come back, but I couldn't make myself do it. Kevin Malloy heard what was no doubt a richly embellished version of this story one night when he was down at one of the local newshounds' watering holes; he called me up the next day and gave me a job. Although he was a demanding boss, he had been nothing but good to me since. Trouble was, my heart wasn't in the work.

So when I went into Malloy & Marlowe that Tuesday morning, it was with the lousy taste you get in your mouth from biting the hand that feeds you. Kevin was talking to Clarissa, his back to me. Clarissa's eyes widened in surprise and she called out, "Irene, you aren't supposed to be in for another week!"

Kevin turned around. I asked if I could talk to him for a minute. He stood there looking as if he were making his mind up about something, and then invited me back.

I sat in one of the four chairs surrounding what we jokingly referred to as the "Aircraft Carrier Malloy," Kevin's gigantic marble-topped, dark cherry-wood desk. Kevin opted for a chair close to my own instead of the one behind the desk.

He was a sandy-haired man with boyish but not foolish looks, and a smile that could melt the world's hardest heart. "We've both lost a very good friend," he said, and halted, a sadness so sudden and complete coming over his face that when I saw it I felt a tightening in my chest. Tears began welling up in his eyes, and in no time flat we were both crying quietly, neither of us able to speak. Eventually, we both went digging for our handkerchiefs.

"God, I loved that man," he said, unbashedly weeping now. "He was one of the best. I can't believe it. I can't."

"He thought a lot of you, Kevin. You were one of his favorites. He didn't have many real favorites."

He just wept.

After a while he sat up straight and said, "I'm sorry," giving me that strange apology we Americans make for our grief. Between the two of us, there was a lot of nose-blowing for a few minutes. We both sighed and tried to pull ourselves together.

"How are things going here?" I asked.

"Hectic as usual. We miss having you around, even though you've only been gone for a day. The Kensington project and the various campaign work going on is keeping me from sitting around using up boxes of Kleenex. It's a busy time of year."

I was feeling more and more like a heel. "Kevin," I said, "I have a very difficult request to make of you. I need an extended leave of absence."

"Oh."

I thought he was going to say more, but he waited for me to go on.

"The police think O'Connor was probably killed because of some story he was working on or had written in the past. And yesterday someone tried to murder his son."

"I heard about it at Calhoun's," he said, referring to a bar that's the current hot spot for the staff of the *Express*. That saved me a lot of explaining, because that meant he already had heard any news in more detail than was printed in the late edition. Doubtless in more detail than would ever be printed. Most people don't like to read that stuff over breakfast.

"Did you ever meet a guy in Homicide named Frank Harriman?" I asked.

Kevin thought a moment. "Yes, in fact, Mark Baker introduced us down at Calhoun's a few months ago, when he was working on that double homicide at the Legs."

"The Legs," or, in Spanish, "Las Piernas," were two tall, rounded cliffs above the beach. From out on the ocean, they did indeed look like two long legs, and were so named from the time the Spaniards first sailed past them.

"Well, he's on the O'Connor case now. The only way he's going to get anywhere is if somebody who knew O'Connor, knew his notation system, knew how he worked—if somebody like that gets back on the paper and digs up whatever dirt is making this bastard kill people."

"And you think it should be you."

Long silence.

He studied me again. "I'll be honest with you, Irene. I knew the minute I heard about O'Connor that you would go after this guy. I've known you too long. I've also known that you haven't been happy here . . ."

I started to object, but he cut me off.

"Hear me out. It's true. You've done everything I've asked of you and more, and I've asked a lot. O'Connor used to take me out to Banyon's or Calhoun's and tell me how I was never going to take the black ink out of your veins. He'd kid me about how I was trying to harness a racehorse to the plow, and while a racehorse might pull steady, it would always be looking over the fence at the track, longing for a good run for the money. 'One day, she'll bolt the harness,' he'd say.

"Well, he was right and I knew it. I hope you don't mind my extending the analogy, but I told him you at least were making hay, more hay than the *Express* offered. But, to my advantage, this day took longer to get here than even O'Connor imagined."

"Kevin, I know I'm leaving you in the lurch now, but it's not because I'm not grateful to you. I always will be. I could be slinging hash if it weren't for you."

"You underrate yourself. And don't feel guilty. There never would be a good time to leave, and we both know it."

"You're being very understanding."

"I can't keep you here if you want to go. Your work would suffer, you'd resent me, and I'd probably end up resenting you. Not worth it. O'Connor would haunt me to no end."

"I owe you, Kevin."

"Well, leave that sort of thing to people who keep such accounts. Anyway, before you go, there's something else you should know. Someone has been very curious as to when you'll be coming back to work here. I was just talking to Clarissa about it. I don't like it at all. The caller won't leave a name or number, but he called several times yesterday and he's already called twice today. What would you like me to have her tell him?"

"Tell him I've gone back to work for the paper."

"You in a hurry to have someone harm you?"

"Look, they're going to find out the first time I have a byline, the first time they call the paper, or the first time they bend an ear to conversations at Banyon's or Calhoun's. The *Express* staff loves to talk about nothing so much as the *Express* staff. This won't be a secret for long."

"Okay, Irene. But keep in mind that you're worried after. It's okay to help, but let the professionals go after the criminals."

"Don't worry, I'm cooperating with the police on this. I'm not as crazy as I sometimes seem."

"One other thing—speaking of crazy people—how the hell did you ever get Wrigley to ask you back?"

"Kevin, if she ever gets tired of the newsroom, hire a woman named Lydia Ames. I've never seen so great a PR job done on anybody."

"She's your school chum, isn't she? Well, I'll keep that in mind. And don't forget, there's always room for you here if you want to come back."

We shook hands warmly. On my way out, I said good-bye to Clarissa and Don, and then left for the grand old offices of the *Express*. As I drove along, I had a feeling that O'Connor was watching over me. He might not be the only one, but together he and I had the luck of the Irish.

12

Coming within sight of the newspaper meant coming within sight of the hospital, and I wondered how Kenny and Barbara were doing. I decided I would stop by there after I had done some work at the paper.

As I walked up to the double glass doors and went into the marble-and-brass entry of the *Express*, a great sense of anticipation filled me. I hadn't been inside those doors since I marched out two years before.

I couldn't take in enough of the place. In the center of the room sat Geoff, the reedy gentleman who served as our security man. Geoff was so old and had been with the paper so long, we used to say he was put into the foyer by the architect and greeted the original Wrigley when he first came through the door. A big smile lit his face.

"Welcome back, Miss Kelly! You're a sight for sore eyes!"

"And you are, too, Geoff. It feels good to be back. Are they running now?"

Geoff laughed his wheezy laugh and said, "I told myself this morning, when Mr. Wrigley said to send you right upstairs when you came in, I said to myself, 'Miss Kelly is going to want to go downstairs before she goes upstairs.' " He wheezed and shook in glee. "And I was right, wasn't I? Yes, ma'am, they are most certainly running. Special sections right now, I believe. So you go right on down, and if anybody asks, I ain't seen hide nor hair of you yet."

"Thanks, Geoff."

I went down the stairwell and through a maze of doorless hallways. The building was laid out by someone whose previous work was in rabbit warrens. But through the ancient walls I could already hear the rumble of running presses. A sound I loved almost as much as the smell that permeated this basement area—ink and newsprint.

Overhead the open ceiling was crisscrossed with wires and rollers which would later carry finished papers to the machines that would bundle them for distribution. I turned a corner and stepped into the main press room. I grabbed a pair of "visitor's" ear protectors and listened through them to the magnificent roar of rolling paper and press. Coburn and Parker, two of the operators, saw me and waved, grinning from ear to ear.

Straight ahead was the tall black housing of the Motters, our newest presses, which had color-printing capabilities. The older, green Goss presses surrounded the two Motters. Newsprint rolled into them and streamed from them in a blur of speeding print. Eight pages at a time, cut, rolled, turned, folded, and moving, moving, moving in a web of fantastic design. I stood and watched for a while.

Coburn walked over and shouted, "Good to see you back!" It was a greeting I would hear again and again as I made my way upstairs.

Wrigley was smoking a cigar in his glass-paneled office. We called this his "God office," which was one of two he had in the building. The God office was the one he sat in when he wanted to watch what was going on in the newsroom, or hold conferences with the editors. He had another one upstairs that he spent most of his time in; that one commanded the much more attractive view of the skyline and was more impressive to visitors.

I knew that he had watched as I made my way over to the office, stopped every few feet by an old, familiar face, or to be introduced to someone new. When I stepped in to his God office, it was as if we were in a glass cage—I realized that every face was watching from the other side. I also realized that Wrigley had orchestrated our first reunion as employee and employer in this manner to make a point to the staff. Bygones were going to be bygones.

"Irene, dear!" he beamed and stretched out a hand. "Come in, come in."

What the hell, I thought, and shook it. He glanced out the windows behind me and the staff went back to work. He didn't say anything for a while, just sat there grinning like a fool. It was a scary sight.

Finally, he said, "Well! I guess you'll want to get going. Your ah, old desk—" He floundered, circling the cigar in the air as if it would help him speak. "Your old desk is in use. But I want you to take O'Connor's desk. I think it's—it's appropriate. It's just the way he left it—well, except for what the police took."

I had wanted to work with whatever O'Connor had left here, but I guess I hadn't considered the possibility of being given his desk as my work station. It was crazy, of course, to think that no one would be using my desk over a two-year absence—after all, I had quit and refused to come back. But so much at the paper had seemed to stand still in time, I suppose I had figured that would too; now I saw the nonsense of it.

Wrigley handed me a small brass desk key and shook my hand again, and once more all eyes seemed to be on me as I stood up and walked toward O'Connor's desk. Except for the crackle of the scanners, the room was as quiet as I ever remembered it being.

As close as O'Connor and I were, as I approached his desk I felt like an intruder. And as curious as I was about what secrets I might learn there, I couldn't make myself sit down in his chair. So many, many times I had seen him there. I walked around the outside of the desk, running my fingers along it. I could feel my co-workers staring at my back. Suddenly I heard a booming voice say, "Haven't you rubberneckers got some work to do?"

It was John Walters, the news editor. John was a great old gruff bear of a man, about seventy pounds overweight and all of it cantankerous. The room was startled back into motion at his command, as if a stern teacher had walked back into a schoolroom. We got along famously. In John's book, I was "a feisty broad."

"Welcome back, Irene," he said to me in his low, growling voice. "Have a seat. He's not going to put an Irish curse on you for sitting in his chair."

Reluctantly, I sat.

John laughed. "You'll get used to it. That chair was lonely until just this minute." He winked, an incredible gesture on his stern face, and strolled off to harass somebody.

For a few moments, I simply sat there, thinking of O'Connor. Finally, I reached over and turned on the monitor at his computer terminal. It glowed to life, the bright cursor pulsing on and off below the words "Sign-off completed."

Not yet, I thought. Not yet.

13

I needed a password to get into O'Connor's files. Unlocking the desk and looking through its drawers, I realized that the detectives who had searched it had been thorough. No loose papers, no calendar, no notebooks. I was going to have to spend some time down at police headquarters if I wanted to go through anything handwritten.

Just as I was about to give up, Lydia stopped by the desk and handed me a small piece of paper with what looked like a license plate number on it. "It's a new password," she said. "You'll need it to access O'Connor's computer files. They had to override the old one so that the cops could copy the files onto a disk."

"Thanks."

I entered the password into the terminal. There was the usual delay while the computer looked for the files. Just as O'Connor's notes were coming up on the screen, the phone rang.

"Kelly," I said, picking it up.

"Oh, I'm sorry. I was trying to reach Mr. O'Connor. Is he in?"

Now what should I do? I couldn't bring myself to say, "Mr. O'Connor is dead," or "He won't be in today," or "Not at the moment." I settled on "May I ask who is calling?"

"This is Dr. MacPherson at the Los Angeles College of Dentistry."

"Mac teeth," I said half-aloud. It had to be the man referred to in O'Connor's notes.

"I beg your pardon?"

"Oh, excuse me. This is Irene Kelly. May I help you with something?"

"Well, I'm not sure that he would want me to talk about this with anyone else, so maybe you could have him give me a call when he gets in."

"Dr. MacPherson, I'm sorry to say that Mr. O'Connor was killed this past Sunday."

"Killed!"

"Yes, someone delivered a package bomb to his home."

"A bomb!"

The conversation wasn't going at all like I wanted it to. I tried to get it back under control. "Dr. MacPherson, I think you can be of help. I'm a friend of Mr. O'Connor's, and I've worked with him on many of his stories. I think I saw a reference to your name in his notes."

"This is all so shocking! I just talked to the man last week." He paused. "If he's been murdered, I suppose I should talk to the police."

I could tell he was going to be a tough nut, and that he was scared out of his pants by what I had blabbed to him so far. I could try to badger him into talking to me, but I doubted it would do any good. I thought it might be better if I could see him face to face. "I'll be happy to have someone contact you. Where can you be reached?"

"I have classes to teach this morning, but I'll be in my office this afternoon."

"I'll contact the Las Piernas Police and let them know you may have some information. If I can arrange to have someone from the police with me, could I talk to you at your office this afternoon? Say, about one o'clock?"

"Well, if someone from the police is with you, I suppose it would be all right." He gave me directions to the campus in San Pedro.

I called Frank. He was as curious as I about what the good doctor might have to say, and we decided to meet for lunch before going over to the college. He told me he would pick me up at the paper at about eleven-thirty.

I spent about half an hour on the computer, but found I had no patience for it right at that moment. I kept wondering what Mac-Pherson would be able to tell us. I thought about O'Connor's obsession with Hannah. It was one of those aspects of his life that he kept to himself. He wrote the article every year, but for the most part it was usually more about missing persons and John Does in general than about Hannah herself. He would open with the story of the body being found, and note how many years had gone by without identification, but nothing more than that. And yet he was always trying to learn more about her.

The Hannah articles were among his most moving. Perhaps because of his family's own loss, he had a way of writing about the victims in these cases—both living and dead—with a dignified empathy. He could portray the anguish of the families without being maudlin.

In these stories, he never actually wrote anything about his own sister.

I remember the night he told me about her. O'Connor drank, and on occasion got drunk, but he was seldom absolutely plastered. On this particular night, he was three sheets to the wind. By the time I got him home, he was sobering up a little, but was still pretty sloshed. I don't remember now what brought it on, but he got on the subject of his sister.

With bitterness in every word, he told me about the night she disappeared. He was full of self-loathing and misplaced blame. He talked about the misery of the years she was missing, of his frustration that the murderer had never been discovered, of the injustice of it all. It was a difficult story to hear; it was painful to watch him tell it. He was not one to cry on others' shoulders.

The next day, I had wondered if he would remember telling me about her. He did, and said, "I know you heard my sad tale with a kind heart, Irene, so I won't regret the telling of it. But I have no right to use my sister's memory in such a way. I would be grateful if we did not speak of it again."

But of course he did, if not directly. He would muse aloud about how hard it must be for Hannah's family not to know what had become of her. He would say that someday her murderer would be caught, and so on.

I knew he sought his retribution this way; he meant to be the one to do the catching.

Mid-morning, I decided to see how Kenny and Barbara were doing. I told Lydia where I was going and then stopped by Geoff's desk on the way out and asked him to tell Detective Harriman I was over at St. Anne's and would be back soon.

I walked the two short blocks to the hospital and went into the main entrance. Behind the information counter, a thin woman with a pinched face peered at me over her glasses and refused to direct me to Kenny's room.

"He's in ICU. You can't see him," she sniffed.

"I'm a family member."

"Oh, really?"

"Really."

"Well, they still won't let you see him."

"A very pleasant day to you, too," I said, and went back out the doors and around the corner to the emergency room entrance. I went into the waiting room and up to the counter, and sure enough, there was Sister Theresa.

"I need your help, Sister," I said.

"Yes?" she asked with a smile.

"The lady at the main entrance won't let me near my brother-in-law's room. I know he's not in any shape for visitors, but I'm sure my sister could use a little diversion by now."

"I think you're right," she said. "Come along, I'll take you to her."

We went out a set of doors down a wide white hallway and took a set of turns that got us to the ICU. Sister Theresa nodded to the nurse at the unit's central desk and guided me to Kenny's room. I hate everything outside of the maternity wards in hospitals, and I could feel my heart beat faster and my palms grow clammy as we walked into the room.

Kenny was almost hidden by the array of tubes and monitors surrounding his bed. He was on a respirator and his heart was being monitored. He was being given intravenous medication. His head looked oversized and was swathed in bandages, with openings where his eyes, nose and mouth should be. His respirator tube went into his throat; he had evidently needed a tracheotomy to get the tube in. Most of his upper body was bandaged as well. He looked like a mummy whose head had been filled with helium. I fought the sensation of my stomach plummeting.

Barbara was holding on to his hand through the bedrail, staring at him. She turned when she heard us, and Sister Theresa said, "Your sister is here to see how you and your husband are doing. Why don't I sit with Mr. O'Connor while you two take a little stroll?"

If I hadn't had a nun with me, I doubt she would have left his side, so the lady at the front desk had done me a favor. Barbara got up slowly and walked out of the room with me.

"How is he?" I asked her in the hallway.

She shrugged. "He's what they call semi-comatose. Every hour they come in and give him neurological tests—see if his pupils respond to light and if he reacts to mild pain—like having his skin pricked, things like that. So far, he has. They tell me that's good," she said woodenly.

"And what about you?"

"I'm okay. I try to talk to him and read to him. The nurses told me Kenny might be able to hear me."

We walked in silence for a moment. We passed a couple who sat in a waiting area, tension etched into their faces. Who could help wondering about the stories behind the people in hospital hallways and waiting rooms?

"Barbara, if you need to get some sleep or do some errands or something, maybe I could come down and give you a break. I would be grateful if you'd let me help you out a little."

"I'm okay," she said again. After a moment she said, "But thanks."

She was anxious to get back to the room, so we turned around and headed back. Sister Theresa walked me out the main entrance, right under the receptionist's surprised nose.

"Patience, Irene," she said to me as I left.

"Not my strong suit, Sister, but I'll try."

On the walk back to the paper I thought about Barbara's devotion to Kenny. Had she stayed secretly attached to him through the years of being divorced? Or was she just so lonely now that she was happy to be needed by someone, even someone who could make no response? I wondered if my own anger with Kenny made it impossible for her to tell me that she would, in fact, jump at the chance to be back with him. She did complain about him to me, but maybe it was that brand of complaining that turns about-face if you agree with the complainer.

I had never thought Kenny treated her well, and though I couldn't help being softened in my attitude toward him by his current condition, I wondered what would come of it—for Barbara's sake. Could I have been wrong about him? Like any other couple, they had a life of their own together, a private one that I could not learn of from family gatherings and the like.

Truth be told, somewhere inside me a voice that would like to be mistaken for my conscience said, "You wished this on him." All those times Barbara had cried to me on the phone about him, all those times I'd said, "Don't worry, Barbara, someday Kenny will get his. It's only a matter of time before he crosses someone who'll teach him some manners."

Of course, I hadn't expected Amy Vanderbilt to be carrying a baseball bat, but I hadn't exactly wished him well, either. So now he lay half-dead, while my sister spun a web of fragile hope around him.

14

This kind of thinking is not good for one's optimistic outlook in life, so I was a little down when I reached the door of the Wrigley Building. As I opened it, I saw Frank politely signing in for Geoff, who took no one at his word. As he pushed the clipboard back across the counter, I realized how happy I was to see him. He gave me a smile. Just what the doctor ordered. "Sign him back out, Geoff, I'm making him take me to lunch."

Geoff, another member of the "Coalition of Those Who Are Terribly Concerned About Irene Still Being Single," gave me a knowing look.

Frank walked me out to his car, a battered, old gray Volvo. "Is this thing going to make it to L.A.?" I asked, trying not to laugh out loud. "What'd you do, steal it from Columbo?"

"Well, excuse me, Princess Di. Here I am, being a nice guy and offering to take you to lunch, and you give me grief about my car. I'm not a glutton for freeway driving—I'll let you take us in your car, if you prefer, your highness."

"I love to hear men talk that way. No, you can drive, and I promise to try not to make jokes about your car."

"I just drive this thing to make the taxpayers feel good, anyway."

Despite its external appearance, the car was very comfortable and clean on the inside.

"So where are we going for lunch?" I asked, as we pulled out of the parking lot.

"You'll see," he said. "By the way, I got in touch with Hernandez."

"And?"

"He talked to O'Connor twice last month, once in person, once on the phone. O'Connor had come down to the morgue about the middle of May, to start gathering information for his Hannah article. The anniversary of the day they found her is next weekend—June seventeenth—and I guess that's the day he does the write-up on the John Does. Hernandez told me it was the first time he'd met O'Connor, and he took a real liking to him. He wasn't too happy when I told him what had happened."

"So what happened in May?"

"Not much, I guess, except that Hernandez had never heard the Hannah story, so O'Connor told him all about it and about the annual articles. Hernandez talked to him about a couple of stiffs they haven't been able to identify, and they shook hands like pals and said so long."

Frank broke off long enough to negotiate getting on the 405 Freeway going north. Traffic was, as usual, ridiculously heavy. Where could all of these people be going at noon? We hunkered down for some "slow and go," and Frank took up the conversation again.

"I guess O'Connor managed to spark his interest. He just took a real liking to the guy. Talked to each other for a couple of hours. They're starved for the company of folks that can still breathe down there in the coroner's office anyway—not too many people just go down there for a chat—and he said O'Connor was quite a talker."

"That he was."

"So after O'Connor left, Hernandez figured he'd go check out this Hannah story. He dug out the case file, and saw a reference to an evidence number. He was especially interested in the dental section of the report."

Frank stopped talking, and seemed to be watching something in his rearview mirror for a moment. I turned around and looked behind us. A dark car changed lanes, and began to pass us on the left.

"Don't do that," Frank said. "It's not the Lincoln."

"Don't do what?"

"Don't turn around and stare at somebody if you think I'm looking at them in the rearview mirror. If they're following us, I'd like to know for sure before you spook them off."

"Sorry."

"It's okay. I'm pretty sure they're just in a hurry to get past us."

This seemed to be the case, as the car continued to weave in and out of traffic, moving on ahead of us.

"So what happened with Hernandez?"

"He got curious and put one of the assistants on the task of finding the evidence file. I guess the assistant wasn't too happy with the job, since it was down in the morgue's basement somewhere.

"Hernandez starts reading through the remarks about Hannah's teeth. The autopsy report says that although her front teeth were broken, they found all the fragments and were able to reconstruct the jaw. No sign of decay, or of any dentistry work. Now, in 1955, Hernandez thinks, this isn't too common, but it's not unheard of.

"So he reads on. There were some tobacco stains, according to Woolsey. Hernandez looks back through the rest of the autopsy report and notices that there was no sign of nicotine in her blood work and that her lungs were clear and undiseased. He sets it aside and goes to work on something a little more recent."

"And that's it?"

"No, there's more. Over an hour goes by, and the assistant comes back, mad as hell because he's had to really dig around to find this evidence file. He's carrying a box labeled 'Jane Doe 6-17-55' with the matching evidence number on it. Hernandez opens the box, and guess what he finds?"

"Her teeth?"

"Her skull."

"Good Lord," I said. The thought of Hannah buried without her skull disturbed me. I didn't know why it should; it all happened so long ago, and she was dead. But it just seemed you ought to have your head with you when you're in your grave. Of course, you ought to have your feet and hands, too.

Frank negotiated an exit onto the Harbor Freeway. We headed south, toward San Pedro. The campus was down near the L.A. Harbor. I figured he had picked out a place near the harbor for lunch.

"So what else was in the box?" I asked, getting impatient for him to pick up the story again.

"What? Oh, sorry. No, nothing else in the box. But there's more to the story. Hernandez is convinced that the teeth are not tobacco stained, but that the stain is something different. He said he's pretty sure it's a condition called fluorosis. It's usually caused by drinking water that has too much fluoride in it, especially before the age of ten, when teeth are coming in."

"I thought fluoride was good for teeth."

"It is, at the right level. Too little, and you're more prone to cavities. Too much, and your teeth can be mottled or stained. He told me that in some parts of the country fluoride occurs naturally in relatively high levels, and people from around these areas will get this staining on their teeth."

"How does a coroner know so much about tooth stains?"

"Colorado is one of the places that has pockets of high-fluoride water supplies, and Hernandez had seen this staining on the teeth of some of the older people who were brought into the morgue there."

I caught myself running my tongue over the surfaces of my teeth.

"He called O'Connor the next day," Frank went on, "and told him to get in touch with this Dr. MacPherson, who's an expert on forensic dentistry. He lectures all over the country. Hernandez sent the skull to MacPherson for some kind of special analysis on the teeth. He said they could tell more if they had the rest of her bones, but he had thought it could give them a start. They could always do an exhumation later."

We got off the freeway and went down Gaffey. We wound our way around to the cliffs of Palos Verdes. The scenery was soon distracting me from my morbid thoughts of Hannah. He turned down a small road and pulled off to the side. We were high above the ocean, the harbor off to our left.

Frank turned and said, "This is it."

I knew there weren't any restaurants or other buildings out on these cliffs. Watching my face, he laughed, and got out of the car. He went around to the trunk and opened it. I got out and walked back to see him taking out a blanket and a large white paper sack. "Ever eat at the Galley?" he asked. "It's a great deli down on Hermosa Avenue. I picked up a couple of ham on ryes. That okay?"

"Fine," I said, still caught off guard. "You're full of surprises, aren't you?"

"All pleasant ones. Just thought you might need a little change of scenery."

We walked about halfway out to the edge of one of the zigzagging cliffs and spread the blanket. Good thing I wear sensible shoes. He gave me a sandwich and then handed me a small carton of milk. "Hope it didn't get too warm," he said.

The milk was very warm. "Perfect," I said. After all, who cared?

The Pacific spread out below us, whitecaps tossing in the wind.

Sailboats glided effortlessly behind and beyond the breakwater, while huge ships made their way more cautiously. Who cared about anything but feeling the sun and the wind?

We sat there and ate a leisurely lunch. We didn't say a word to one another, but enjoyed one of those rare companionships that are comfortable in silence.

15

We arrived at the campus at a little before one, and wound our way to the visitors' parking lot. A student at the parking kiosk pointed us in the right direction, and we walked across a common to a tall brick building. As we walked, I was struck by how young the students looked to me. I stopped to calculate the number of years it had been since I got my bachelor's, and realized why. To these people, the Beatles were what the Andrews Sisters had been to me—something your parents had danced to.

We found MacPherson's office, but he wasn't in. It was on the second floor of a building filled with labs and lecture rooms, with an occasional faculty office here or there. Between the rooms, the hallways were lined with lighted display cases. They were the old wooden-style cases, and they were all full of human jawbones and skulls. We started browsing among the displays while we waited.

There were little tags next to each set of bones and teeth, telling about conditions that could be found in them, as well as the gender and approximate age of the former owners. There were also some historical collections of dentures and an array of rather intimidating antique dental instruments. It made me glad I was born after Novocain was invented.

A tall, gray-haired gentleman in a tan corduroy sports jacket came walking past us, and put a key in the office door. He looked up at us as he let himself in.

"Miss Kelly?"

"Dr. MacPherson?"

We both nodded yes, and shook hands. He had a nice firm grip. I introduced him to Frank, and we went into the small cubicle of an office. He sat at his desk, the windows backlighting his hair, which was done up exactly like Albert Einstein's. He looked like God had sent him.

"So, if you will excuse an old man for being particular, could I please see some identification, Detective Harriman?"

Frank obliged. Dr. MacPherson didn't just glance at it; he could have written a dissertation on the subject if he had studied it much longer. He handed it back, saying, "Well, everything seems to be in order."

"Dr. MacPherson," Frank began, "I spoke with Dr. Carlos Hernandez of the Las Piernas Coroner's Office earlier today."

"Then you know how I came to be involved?"

"Yes. Dr. Hernandez told me that last month, he sent you the skull of a Jane Doe who has been unidentified since 1955. He said you might be able to learn if there was a condition called fluorosis in the teeth, and possibly to give his office information that would help to identify the woman."

MacPherson slammed his open palm on the desktop, making us jump. "Exactly!" he said, as if we were students. He stood up and went over to a file cabinet. From the top of it, he gathered up a box and some loose papers. He sat down and leaned back in his chair, pulling on his left earlobe. He swiveled in the chair and looked out the window. Frank and I looked at one another and shrugged.

Suddenly he swiveled back toward us and slammed his hand on the desk again. You'd think we would have wised up, but he got us to jump the second time too. He was going to have to quit that.

"We begin with some background. According to the copy of the coroner's report—by a Dr. Woolsey—" He spoke the coroner's name with a disparaging tone. "Well, let's just say you are quite fortunate to have Dr. Hernandez now." He found this immensely funny, and we waited for him to get himself settled down again.

"Oh, forgive me. I just haven't seen work this bad in years. To continue—according to the report, this is a pregnant female who was approximately twenty to twenty-five years of age. Now, the body was found—or, I should say, most of the body was found—in June 1955. That means this woman was most likely to have been born between 1930 and 1935. Most unfortunate. If she had been born just a few years later, her teeth might not have carried these stains."

Here he pulled out the contents of the box, and there, grinning at us with brown teeth, was Hannah.

Although I had known what was in that box, it was still an unsettling sight. Her eye sockets staring out, areas around her nose and teeth obviously made up of fragments glued in place.

After the first shock of seeing her passed, I felt ashamed to be looking at her. Although I had just looked at cases full of skulls, I didn't know anything at all about those people, while I had known at least one part of Hannah's story. It dawned on me that nothing was private for a victim like her. Everything that could be, would be examined, studied, displayed, and written up by people she had never known.

"Just about the time she was born," MacPherson went on, "a group of American dental researchers had figured out that high levels of fluoride in the water supplies caused this stain, but nothing was scientifically proven until about 1931, and it was sometime after that that the U.S. Public Health Service surveyed fluoride levels.

"As anyone who has waited for the tooth fairy knows, teeth are developed in childhood. The staining appears to occur partly from surface contact, but mainly from fluoride in the bloodstream. During the years of dental development—that is to say, in children under ten—those who ingest too much fluoride are likely to develop fluorosis. So your Jane Doe—I believe Mr. O'Connor called her Hannah—Hannah was most likely to have received these stains from the water she drank as a child."

He stood up and paced the two or three steps he could pace in the area behind his desk. He gestured as he spoke, a natural showman.

"Fluoride occurs naturally in a great many substances. It occurs in varying levels in water supplies, generally low in most areas, especially in the Great Lakes region. There are primarily three regions of the country where the levels would be high enough to produce fluorosis."

"So we might narrow down the areas she could come from by knowing she had this condition?" I asked.

"Precisely!" *Bang!* went the hand again. I won't say we didn't jump, but we were starting to brace ourselves whenever we saw him raise his hand near the desk.

"As I told Mr. O'Connor, your most likely candidates are three regions." He counted them off on his hand. "They are: one, that part of the Midwest comprised of Indiana, Ohio, and Illinois; two, the Rocky Mountain area, especially South Dakota and Colorado; and three, the Southwest—Texas, New Mexico, Arizona."

I didn't think this did much narrowing, although I supposed it was better than nothing. Dr. MacPherson must have noticed my disappointment.

"You give up too easily, my dear. Your friend Mr. O'Connor was not so easily dismayed. Now, within these regions, there are only so many places with fluoride levels that could produce fluorosis this severe. But setting that aside for the moment, I must tell you that your previous coroner really did not follow up on a great many clues to her identity."

"Such as?" Frank asked.

"According to the autopsy report, her skin was fairly tanned. This makes the Southwest the most likely candidate of the three regions, although she could have been from a farm or worked outdoors in the others. But we have other evidence that she was from the Southwest.

"The autopsy report also indicates that the time of death was about seven P.M. the evening she was found. Her stomach contents showed she had been killed shortly after she ate her dinner. Guess what she had eaten?"

Frank and I shrugged.

"Tacos!" he shouted, slamming his hand on the desk again. It must be harder than hell to doze off in this guy's classes.

"This blond woman ate tacos for dinner in southern California in 1955! Now, there were Mexican restaurants then, of course, but Mexican food was not available through big chain restaurants all over the country.

"This is just a hypothesis, of course, but I believe that this woman may have spent at least some of her childhood years in a sunny border state, somewhere with a considerable Hispanic population. It had to be an area where high fluoride content in the water stained the local children's teeth. I would say that narrows the field to Arizona, New Mexico, and Texas."

"Can we be certain that she didn't get the stains from fluoride added to the water supply or by fluoride tablets from a dentist?" Frank asked.

"Certain? No, nothing is certain. Reasonably sure? Yes. Fluoride wasn't added to water in the United States until the mid-1940s, and Hannah here probably would have been too old to receive these stains then. But the most compelling reason to doubt it is that fluoride additions to water supplies are done very carefully, and at low levels. I believe stains like hers would be from a source three to four times higher in fluoride than the highest fluoride addition."

"Is there any kind of listing of communities that might fit that level of natural fluoridation?" Frank asked.

"Of course. I've had copies of a fluoridation survey of the Southwest prepared for you."

He thumbed through the papers and handed over a few pages. "I gave a copy of this same report to Mr. O'Connor. I've highlighted the communities which are the most likely candidates for this degree of fluorosis."

"Thank you, Dr. MacPherson," said Frank, glancing at the report. I tried to read over his shoulder.

"Of course," MacPherson said as we read, "you'll also want her picture."

"What!" we shouted in unison, both startled into looking up at the old man.

MacPherson couldn't have been more pleased with himself.

"The picture is what took so long. Amazing what these computers can do. I sent copies of the photos from the autopsy and measurements of the skull to a fellow who is quite good at visual reconstructions."

From his papers, he pulled out a computer-generated drawing that, across the desk, did not look unlike a photo.

"Ladies and gentlemen," he said, "allow me to introduce Hannah."

16

Looking back at us from the photo was an attractive young woman with medium-length, curled blond hair and a tan complexion. She had high cheekbones and dark, arching brows over dark eyes. The computer artist had given her make-up and a hairstyle circa 1955, and, with an understanding of human frailties, a closed-mouth smile.

The professor had several other views, a couple with smiles showing the stained teeth; there were even some with slightly different noses.

"The nose suffered the most damage in the violence done to her face," MacPherson explained. "Interestingly, the eyes weren't touched. As I said, this case was, in my opinion, badly mishandled. Had the head been severed and removed from the scene with the hands and feet, then I could understand the lack of progress. But this type of battering is not impossible to reconstruct—indeed, someone did take the time to remove the flesh from the skull, to painstakingly glue her face and skull back together, but then, it seems, did not proceed from there. The photos from the autopsy wouldn't be a pretty sight for the lay person, but to someone who works in a field which constantly exposes him to the very worst sorts of damage human beings can suffer, it would not be so bad."

At this point, he pulled out one of the autopsy photos. I guess I'm still a lay person; to me it looked awful. Frank didn't flinch, though, so I suppose the professor was right.

"I'll let you take all of this," MacPherson said, carefully replacing the skull in the box and gathering up the papers. "I will be happy to answer any questions which arise after you've had a chance to read the material. Would you please make sure that Hannah's skull is safely returned to Dr. Hernandez?"

"Certainly," Frank answered, taking the box. I was glad he had handed the box to Frank. I'm not especially squeamish, but the idea of riding back in the car with a skull in a box was enough to give me the willies.

"Dr. MacPherson," I said, "I know this would have meant a great deal to Mr. O'Connor. You've undertaken a lot of work here on his behalf. We do appreciate it."

"Not at all, not at all. Your friend had a way of piquing one's curiosity. I am the luckiest of men. I find this type of thing fascinating, and I'm paid to do it. Please let me know what you learn."

We all shook hands and Frank left his card, in case Dr. MacPherson had questions of his own later on. We started to leave, when Frank hesitated, then said, "One other thing, Dr. MacPherson. We have to advise anyone even remotely connected with Mr. O'Connor on this case to be very careful. Mr. O'Connor's son has been critically injured. Shots have been taken at Miss Kelly's home. We're dealing with a very violent person here."

"Detective Harriman, when you have testified against as many psychopaths as I have, you become cautious by habit. But how interesting! I would have thought the odds of the killer still being alive and in the area slim, but this is obviously not the case. When Miss Kelly told me Mr. O'Connor was killed, I considered it, but complications from such an old murder case seemed unlikely. It raises a number of questions."

"We're not sure it is in connection with this case, sir, but we are following up on any possibilities."

"In that case, it is I who should advise you to be careful. Anyone desperate enough to kill a journalist won't think twice about harming an officer of the law."

We said good-bye again and walked out to the car. Frank tucked the box under one arm and fished in his pockets for his keys.

"For God's sakes, Frank, don't drop her."

"That was quite an experience, wasn't it?"

"Not at all what I expected."

Frank started to put Hannah's head in the trunk, then thought better of it. "She might roll around back there and get damaged. Let's put her on the floor of the backseat."

I was relieved not to have to hold her on my lap.

As we drove off, I looked at my watch. "We might get back in time for me to make deadline."

"You think they're going to want to print the pictures of her? It's not as if this is really fresh news."

"The murder itself is old news, but the pictures and the progress in identifying her are another story. Our readers have been seeing articles on this woman at least once a year for the past thirty-five years. I think they'll be curious."

"Something tells me your boss will want to save this up for one of those anniversary stories."

"No, I'm going to write it up as a possible link to O'Connor's murder. Maybe Wrigley will go for it. It won't work as the kind of 'help us find her' story; too many years have gone by, and I doubt she was in Las Piernas for very long before she was killed. Otherwise, someone would have noticed she was missing."

"Maybe you're right." For a moment he seemed distracted, glancing at the side and rearview mirrors.

"Somebody following us?" I asked, willing myself not to turn around.

He was quiet, concentrating on getting onto the Harbor Freeway, and subtly checking the mirrors again. "No, I guess not," he said at last.

He looked over at me. "Hey, you okay?"

"Yeah, just jittery, I guess."

"Sorry."

We rode in silence while I tried to find my gumption. We reached the 405, and Frank did the routine with mirrors again, and there went any nerve I was building.

I was beginning to wonder if two years in PR work had ruined me for being a reporter. Where was all that spunk I had shown in other crime cases? Okay, so I had never been a target, but you had to have a certain amount of grit if you were going to succeed in the business.

"It's okay to be scared, you know. It keeps you from being foolish," he said, looking over at me. I was going to have to give up poker if I kept showing everything I was feeling.

"I was just wondering if I am going to be able to cut it as a reporter. Maybe I'm getting too old for this stuff."

"Well, Granny, hold off on the retirement party. Benefits are lousy when you've only put in one day and quit before you're forty. Stop being so tough on yourself all the time."

"How many pep talks a day are you geared up for?"

"Whatever it takes."

After a while I settled down and started thinking about Hannah again. I kept coming back to one of MacPherson's comments.

"Frank?"

"Mmm?"

"If the person we're after is Hannah's killer, why do you think he stuck around?"

"I've been asking myself the same question. Assuming it is a 'he'— and this would not be the kind of action you'd expect from a woman, true, but we should keep that option open—anyway, I guess there could be any number of reasons and they'd apply to either sex. First and foremost, he or she got away with it, and is still a long way from being discovered, let alone convicted of anything. That in itself might keep him in the area. Second, he may have some job or position that requires him to be in Las Piernas—or maybe he's dependent on someone here. Third, leaving might have attracted more attention than staying."

"Something else," I said. "If Hannah came from another city or part of the country, and it has always looked like she did, then her killer went to a lot of trouble to make sure no one could trace her back to her home. Maybe he can be connected to the same place."

"Maybe. Woolsey's behavior in all of this is damned odd as well."

"All those years of O'Connor pestering him, and he was still holding back."

Frank took the off-ramp at Shoreline, the street that runs along the cliffs by the ocean in Las Piernas.

"Taking the scenic route?" I asked.

"You might say that," he said, looking in the mirrors again.

After three or four minutes, he said quietly, "Make sure your seat belt's snug."

I did, glancing at my side mirror long enough to see a big blue Lincoln two cars behind us.

17

"**Now what?**" I asked.

"Let's see what they have in mind. Keep your eyes open for a black-and-white—we may want to attract some attention."

He accelerated slightly, and began to work his way in and out of traffic. The Lincoln stayed with us.

"If I get a chance, I'll try to get you out of the car. But I don't want to make you a target if he's got his gun with him."

"Forget it, Frank. I'm not getting out of this car."

"Goddamn it, Irene, you'll do as you're told."

"That line only worked for my father, and he wore it out in less than fifteen years."

He sat there clenching the wheel, seething and muttering under his breath. But soon he was concentrating on the Lincoln again, which was making a move to close the distance between us. I realized that traffic had fallen off—we were entering an industrial area near the harbor. Quonset huts and old brick warehouses lined the streets.

"Hang on."

He floored the accelerator and pulled the car into a hard left. The wheels squealed in protest and the car fishtailed onto a short street that ran alongside the warehouses and away from the water. He made a sharp right onto an alleyway so narrow it didn't seem we would fit. We didn't—the car scraped along between two corrugated tin buildings on either side, metal screeching against metal, throwing sparks. Both side mirrors went flying off in the first few seconds. The doors grew hot, but the car kept moving. Frank looked up in the only remaining mirror.

The Lincoln had reached the alley, but was too wide to follow us.

It roared off. Frank reached the end of the narrow passage and made a series of turns and came out on McKinley Road, which leads back into downtown. We were still going full speed. For a moment I thought we had lost them, but soon I heard the squeal of tires behind us—I turned around and saw that the Lincoln had found us again. There still wasn't much traffic, but we were going faster than anything else on the road, and were weaving around cars that seemed to be standing still.

The street became less and less industrial as we swerved along it. We reached a flat stretch near some old houses, and the Lincoln began closing the distance between us. Within seconds, it seemed, it was right behind us. Frank took a turn up a curving hillside residential street. The Volvo cornered well, but the Lincoln had more power. It began to pull alongside us. Frank jerked the wheel hard to the left, bashing its back end into the Lincoln's front bumper. Both cars swerved wildly, the Volvo recovering a little more quickly as we pulled ahead again. But within seconds the Lincoln had regained the lost ground.

Once again it pulled alongside us, this time the barrel of a gun clearly visible on the passenger side. Frank grabbed me by the neck with one hand, forcing my head down. I could see nothing, but felt the car veer from side to side. Suddenly a blast of shattered glass fell all around me as the gunman fired through the back windshield.

Frank took the wheel with both hands again, and I started to sit up, ignoring him when he shouted, "Stay down!" We reached the crest of the hill and began rocketing our way down the other side. That was when we saw the garbage truck.

Coming up the hill from the opposite direction, almost as if in slow motion, the lumbering white giant filled the road. There was no time to stop. Both cars were plummeting downhill side by side, heading straight for the truck. Frank gave a hard pull to the right, driving up onto the sidewalk. The car jolted as we went over the curb and mowed down a picket fence. We heard a sound like a bomb going off, the loud boom of the Lincoln hitting the truck. We kept going, Frank trying to regain control of the Volvo as it bounced wildly through front yard after front yard. The front windshield shattered as we came to rest with a bone-jarring halt in a large hedge. Beads of glass and sticks and leaves came flying at us, with Frank's side of the car taking the brunt of the impact.

There was that eerie peacefulness that follows collisions. For a moment, it seemed all was still. I was a little dazed, but came around quickly. I became aware that my forehead was cut in several places and bleeding, but not too badly. I may have hit the dash. I was shaken up, but nothing seemed to hurt much.

Then I heard Frank moan softly.

He was slumped over the wheel.

"Frank?"

Another small moaning sound. Afraid to move him, I called his name again, without response. He was breathing through his mouth, as if he were sleeping. There was a streak of blood down the front of his shirt, but it all seemed to be from his nose and some facial cuts.

People from the neighborhood were starting to come toward the car. An elderly man reached us first. He spoke to me though the open windshield. "You okay, honey?"

"Yes, but please call an ambulance. And the police."

"Already called 'em. They're on the way. Is your friend all right?"

"I don't know. He's breathing and there's some blood. He's unconscious. I can't tell how badly he's hurt. I'm afraid to move him."

"That's all right, now. Shouldn't move him. Can you open your door here? It's pretty smashed in on this side."

I tried, but it was no use. The trip through the alley had sealed us in.

Frank moaned again. I felt utterly useless to him.

"Don't let that worry you, honey, he's just trying real hard to come around. My name's Charlie. What's yours?"

"Irene," I said. "This is Frank. Detective Frank Harriman," I added, not really knowing why.

"Oh, a policeman? Well, it looks like you two had quite a chase. You came out better than the folks in that blue car. Those boys didn't have a prayer." I looked around, still in something of a fog. The garbage truck and what was left of the Lincoln seemed far, far away.

If it hadn't been for that old man, I would have gone crazy. I couldn't tell how badly Frank was hurt, I couldn't get out of the damned car. But Charlie would see my face grow worried, and console me. "He's going to be okay, Irene," he would say, "I know you wish there was something you could do, but you can't, you've just got to hang on for a little while. He's gonna make it, it looks worse than it is. You listen to this old man; I know."

I was calmed by his constant stream of conversation. His gravelly voice went on and on, telling me his life story, trying to distract me. Before I knew it, I heard the wail of sirens coming up the hill.

"There, now, you see?" Charlie said. "That didn't take too long. They'll have you out of here in no time. And they'll get your friend fixed up, too. He'll be all right. He just needs a little time to come around is all."

As if he heard Charlie, Frank moved himself to a sitting position for a moment, eyes closed; he moaned, then slumped over the steering wheel again. His nose had been bloodied, his upper lip was swelling; much more I couldn't see before he fell forward.

The paramedics arrived. They got a crowbar and went to work on the car doors, Frank's side first. They got the door open and tried talking to him, checking him over and cleaning him up a little without moving him. He didn't come to, so they gently strapped his back and neck to a support board. I watched as they carefully managed removing him from the car, taking no chances with his injuries. By this time, one of the other men had helped me out of the other side. I felt shaky and tired, but was okay. They cleaned my cuts out and bandaged my forehead, and made sure I could answer questions like "How many fingers am I holding up?"

Someone had called in a report of an injured officer, and more sirens soon howled their way to the scene. I was watching Frank get loaded into an ambulance, feeling afraid to see him taken away, when I heard someone say, "Miss Kelly?"

I looked over to see a short, dark-haired man in a suit. He introduced himself as Pete Baird, and told me he was Frank's partner. He offered to take me over to the hospital, but would I mind answering a few questions on the way? Before we left, I walked over to Charlie and said, "Thank you isn't enough, Charlie. I won't forget your kindness."

He looked genuinely bashful as I shook his hand.

As I passed by the remains of the Volvo, I suddenly remembered Hannah. To Pete Baird's surprise, I got back in the car and crawled halfway over the seat. I picked up the box with Hannah's skull in it and retrieved the papers from under broken glass. I opened the top flap of the box, and there was Hannah, grinning at me, unscathed by it all.

"What have you got there?"

"This," I said, gently closing the box, "is the beginning of a long story."

18

Pete led me over to a black-and-white where two uniformed officers stood waiting. As Frank's partner, Pete already knew about O'Connor's notes and Frank's conversation with Hernandez. As we drove to the hospital, I told him about the visit with Dr. MacPherson. I asked him if they could please have someone check on the professor. I thought of MacPherson's last cautioning words to Frank—he was right, harming a cop was no big deal to whoever had come after us.

"Do you know who was in the Lincoln?" I asked.

"No, not yet. I don't know if anyone told you—they're both dead."

"Somehow that doesn't make me feel any better."

"Do you think this was the car that fired the shots into your house?"

"Yes, pretty sure. But I'm not positive."

"That's okay. If it is, ballistics will probably be able to match the gun to the bullets from your wall. These guys followed you from San Pedro?"

I told him about the drive back, and the chase. It seemed as if it had all happened to someone else, except that I was holding a skull in my lap. It was funny in a way. I didn't want to have it near me earlier. Now it was my link to believing we still had an edge over whoever wanted Hannah's identity to remain a secret.

"Here," I said, reluctantly handing the box to Pete. "It's her skull. And here are the computer drawings. If you don't mind, I'd like to take one set in to the paper. And this is a list of places she was most likely to have lived before coming here, or at least, where she lived as a child."

"Thanks, we'll get the pictures out to all these places and make some phone contacts with the local PDs. If somebody hadn't made all this noise, I probably couldn't get anyone to take a look at it, you know? But now we've got a homicide, two attempteds, and a long list of other charges to excite people about."

We pulled up to the ER entrance of St. Anne's. It was getting to be familiar territory. I got out of the car and rushed into the waiting room. The nurse at the counter told me that Frank was still in the ER; they would let me know when I could see him.

I sat down on one of the plastic chairs. Pete checked in with the desk as well, showing his ID and telling the nurse he would be waiting with me.

"Hey, how's your sister's husband?" he asked as he sat down next to me.

"Still critical. Thanks for helping him and taking care of Barbara."

"Your sister's okay. It was rough for her, you know? But all things considered, she did okay."

"Yes, she did."

"You hanging in there? Most people would want to go home and crawl under the covers after what happened to you today."

I shrugged, and felt the stiffness that was starting to set in on my back and neck. I stood up and stretched.

"Starting to get sore?"

"Yeah, a little."

The nurse came over to Pete and me, told us Frank was being taken to a room, and that the doctor would talk to us now. We went through the door to the hallway outside the waiting room and were met by a young man in scrubs. He introduced himself as Dr. Baldwin.

When I told him my name, he said, "Detective Harriman has been asking about you." Then, talking mainly to Pete, but giving me polite eye contact now and again, he told us that Frank had suffered a concussion and a broken nose, two cracked ribs, and various minor facial injuries. Luckily, the ribs hadn't punctured his lungs. Frank was conscious now but we should keep our visit brief.

Frank was lying in the bed, his head and shoulders slightly elevated. His face was chalk-white. His eyes, nose, and upper lip were puffy; he lay very still. Even knowing that he was probably going to be okay, it scared me to see him like this. As we approached the bed, he opened his eyes and tried to focus on our faces. "Hi," he managed to say.

"Hello. Good to see you're awake," I said.

"You're hurt," he said, seeing the bandage.

"Look who's talking."

He swallowed, and made a motion for the water glass. I held the straw up to his lips and he took a long drink.

"Thanks." He closed his eyes for a moment. When he opened them again, he said, "Hi, Pete."

"Hey, Frank. Doctor tells us you're gonna be fine, but that it will hurt like hell for a while."

"It already does," he said. I wondered if we should leave, but it was hard to make myself do it.

He managed an odd, lopsided grin. "Glad you're okay. I was worried."

I took his hand, held it between mine. "You worried me, too. Get some sleep. I'll be back to see you in the morning."

"Okay," he said, and squeezed my hand as I let go. As I turned to leave, he said, "Irene?"

I turned back. "Yes?"

"Miss your deadline?"

"There will be another one tomorrow, and another one the day after that. Don't worry about it. Get better."

I moved to the foot of the bed, and Pete moved up toward him. "She's right, Frank, just get better. And don't you worry about Irene. I'll watch out for her."

"Thanks, Pete," he whispered.

He closed his eyes again, falling asleep this time; Pete and I, like tiptoeing children, stepped quietly away from his bed.

On our way down the hallway, we met Captain Bredloe, Frank's boss in Homicide. He was a tall, strapping man with a deep voice. I stood to one side while Pete told him Frank was asleep and not able to talk much right now, but that he should be okay. The captain hesitated, looked down the hallway toward the room, then turned and walked out with us.

Pete went over the list of Frank's injuries. The captain asked a few questions, then looked over at me as Pete gave a brief summary of what I had told him about the day's activities.

"You're a reporter?" Bredloe asked.

"Yes, sir, I am."

"You worked with O'Connor, didn't you?"

"Yes." That seemed like something as long lost as childhood right now.

"I liked O'Connor," he said. "You be careful." He paused, then said, "Can we give you a ride somewhere?"

"My car's just over at the paper. Frank met me there before we went to San Pedro." I thought of the picnic on the cliffs.

"So your car has been there all day?"

"Pretty much. Since about nine this morning."

"Hmm. Pete, have it checked out before she gets in it."

A simple phrase, but it made me feel queasy.

He noticed. "I'll tell you what, you look like you could use some rest. Why don't I take you home and let Pete deal with your car?"

It sounded like a good idea. I told them I could get a ride in with Lydia tomorrow. I gave Pete my car keys and left with the captain.

On the way to Lydia's, he talked to me about O'Connor, told stories of his own first days on the force, when O'Connor was already a journeyman reporter. Apparently they had lifted a few glasses together at Banyon's back when Bredloe was a single man. "O'Connor always gave us a fair shake," he said. "He wasn't as sympathetic as some would have liked him to be, but he was always fair." We pulled up in front of Lydia's house. "A pleasure to meet you, Miss Kelly. I'll just watch you to the door."

I thanked him and said goodnight, feeling the stiffness again as I got out of the car. I waved to the captain as I let myself in.

Lydia exclaimed over me, mothered me, fussed over me once again. My weary, lifeless retelling of the day's events brought further sympathy and care. "Take another hot bath tonight or you'll be supersore tomorrow," she advised. I agreed, and went down the hall to run the bath. She came in with a coffee-colored drink.

"What is it?" I asked.

"A B-52—Kahlúa, Grand Marnier, and Irish Cream."

"Jesus, Lydia, what are you trying to do, embalm me?"

"Trust me."

My resistance was low. I climbed into the bath and sipped the sweet drink that went down my throat like liquid fire. The bathroom door opened, and in strolled Cody. He climbed up on the edge of the tub and started meowing at me. I scratched his ears and chin with my dry hand, and he rubbed against it and almost fell in. He settled down on the bath mat and watched me. I could hear him purring. It's nice to be loved.

When the water got cold and my face felt numb from the drink, I crawled out and dried off. Cody pranced ahead of me and jumped up onto the bed. I definitely had a buzz on. I fell asleep quickly, saying a little prayer of gratitude. I don't know if it was the prayer, exhaustion, the booze, or Cody's purring, but that night I didn't have any nightmares.

19

I woke up at about six the next morning, acutely aware of every muscle in my back and neck. I forced myself out of bed and hobbled into the bathroom. I took a hot shower to help get limbered up a little. I stood there, aiming the water on my neck and then between my shoulder blades, wondering how Frank was feeling, thinking of him lying there in the hospital. I wondered how Barbara and Kenny were doing. Thought about the fact that O'Connor had been killed three days ago. By the time I got out of the shower, I was depressed.

As the steam cleared off the bathroom mirror, I was a little startled to notice my forehead had started to bruise. I looked pretty weird with that and the cuts. For some reason it struck me as comical. I could hardly brush my teeth, I wanted to laugh at my odd appearance so much. "Well, Miss Mood Swing," I said to myself in the mirror, "get a grip."

I rode to work with Lydia. She was nice enough to walk at my pace as we made our way into the building. Geoff gave me a look of great concern. I felt self-conscious now that I was exposing the public to this purple band above my eyebrows. "Not as bad as it looks," I said to him.

"Glad it isn't. Miss Kelly, the night man left me a message to give you. It says the police checked your car and it's okay. Here are your keys."

I thanked him and we took the elevator up the one flight. I knew if I kept moving I would feel better, but stairs were not yet on the program.

One of Wrigley's assistants stopped me on my way back to O'Connor's desk. Staring at my forehead, she said, "Mr. Wrigley asked me to give you all of Mr. O'Connor's mail. I put a couple of letters that arrived yesterday afternoon on his old desk for you."

"Thanks."

"John Walters wants to talk to you."

She was right. I had just picked up the two envelopes that constituted O'Connor's mail and was about to sit down, when John yelled across the room, "Kelly, get over here." "Here" was Lydia's desk; he had apparently cornered her the moment she walked in.

I stuffed the envelopes in my purse and made my way slowly over to Lydia and John. He was leaning his ample behind on Lydia's desk, watching me. As I got closer, he glanced at my forehead, and said, "You'll be better off if you don't sit down for a while. Try to keep moving around a little." Lydia looked at him in surprise—Walters as caretaker was a rare sighting.

I asked what I could do for him.

"We did a short piece on the car chase yesterday, but I could use more information than I'm getting from the cops."

So someone at the paper had picked up the calls going out to the accident, I just hadn't seen any reporter before we left for the hospital. That story was pretty late-breaking, and must have just made the final edition.

"You want me to write it?" I asked.

"Sure, why not? But first tell me about it, so Lydia can get some people on any other angles we might need to cover."

"It's a complex story. I've got something here that ties in." I handed him the computer drawings of Hannah.

"Who is it?"

"That's Hannah."

"Hannah who?"

"Handless Hannah, the woman O'Connor wrote about every year; the Jane Doe they found under the pier in 1955."

"What does this have to do with an attempt on the lives of a cop and a reporter?"

"I think it has something to do with the murder of O'Connor as well."

I told him about Hernandez, the skull, and MacPherson. As I spoke, I could tell I had started to pique John's interest, but he didn't have that look that said I had sold something for page one. Nothing to do but finish telling him the story. "I've been thinking about it,

John. For some reason Woolsey didn't follow up. Why not? He may have intentionally misled O'Connor for years. I think someone should talk to Woolsey."

It was the first time I had mentioned Woolsey's role, and John and Lydia exchanged a wide-eyed look.

"What's wrong?"

Lydia reached across her desk and pulled a large sheet over—copy for today's run. She handed it to me.

"Dr. Emmet Woolsey," I read aloud, "former Coroner for the City of Las Piernas, died of self-inflicted gunshot wounds early Tuesday evening . . ."

I stood there, re-reading it, trying to let the words sink in. John was telling Lydia that we needed to have someone go back over the Woolsey story. He looked at me.

"Go on with your story, Irene."

I told him about MacPherson getting the computer images made, about taking the skull and being followed, and the chase.

"Any ID on the guys in the Lincoln?"

"Not that I know of, but I'll put a call in to Pete Baird—he's one of the cops working on this with Frank Harriman."

"What about this Harriman? Is he gonna make it?"

I then told him about Frank's injuries, trying to sound clinical and shoving away the memories of the wait for the ambulance.

"Hmm. So you want me to run the pictures on A-one in hopes that someone comes forward and says, 'Oh yeah, this girl stopped in and bought a taco from me in 1955. I remember it well.'"

"You have a lovely way of putting things, John. No, I want you to run the pictures on A-one because it's tied into everything that happened to us yesterday, and probably everything that's happened for the last few days to several other people, including Woolsey. I think it will make someone nervous, and nervous people tend to make mistakes."

"Nervous people can also be dangerous—and if you haven't figured that out by now, you've got a thicker skull than old Hannah there."

"It's a break in a case that everyone who ever read O'Connor's column knows about."

He made a motion as if waving off a pesky fly. "I'll think about it. Go back to work."

• • •

I turned on the computer at O'Connor's desk, thinking that it might still hold clues about Hannah. I also owed Wrigley some work on that mayor's story. I signed on and was getting ready to do the write-up on the chase, when the phone rang.

"Kelly."

"Hi, Irene. Pete Baird. Just wanted to let you know I saw Frank this morning and he's doing a lot better."

"Thanks for letting me know."

"I also wanted to let you know what we learned about the guys in the Lincoln. Couple of local hoods, Bob Cully and Jimmy Blake. I don't suppose you knew them?"

"Never heard of them."

"They've got records. Ballistics made a match between the Desert Eagle .357 we found in their car and the bullets lodged in your wall."

"You've made a lot of progress then."

"It gets better. When we went to check out their home sweet homes, it turns out Cully had a little factory set up in his garage with the makings for an explosive device—the bomb squad is still checking that out, but it seems pretty likely that these guys are the ones who set up your friend. Cully had priors on explosives and Blake was a gunman. Up to now they mainly stuck to holding up jewelry stores and blowing safes, but I guess they were looking for career advancement."

I knew Pete was waiting for me to say something, but I was choking with rage. A simple hundred-miles-per-hour head-on collision with a garbage truck was an easy way out for the people who had killed O'Connor. It was too easy, and way too quick.

"Irene, you okay?"

"Sorry, Pete. Any chance they were acting alone?"

"I don't believe it for a minute. Do you?"

"Not for half a minute."

"So those names don't give you any ideas, huh?"

"No, I'm sure I've never met or heard of them. I'll look through O'Connor's computer notes, but I doubt he mentioned them."

"Probably not. Just hired hands."

"You know about Woolsey?"

Pete sighed. "Yeah. Strange. I had some questions for that guy."

"You're not the only one. Any ideas on why he shot himself? Are you sure it's a suicide?"

"It looks like it, though it takes a while to really check that out.

Hernandez got back in today, so he'll do the work on it. As for why—no note or anything. His wife died about a year ago; he lived alone. Neighbor was out in the backyard, just a few feet from his window, and heard the shot."

"This whole thing just gets harder and harder to grab on to."

"I know what you mean, but I think you're right about Hannah. It's got to be connected. We'll send the drawings out today, along with a letter explaining why we're just now tracking her down."

"Great. Is MacPherson okay?"

"LAPD found him safe and sound."

"Were Cully and Blake the guys who went after Kenny?"

"No, I guess they had a good alibi for that one—not that it does them any good now. They had appointments with their parole officer."

"Same parole officer?"

"Yeah. We think that's how they met—waiting around before their appointments to see this parole officer. We really rehabilitate them, don't we?"

"Well, Pete, I'd better get some of this into a story, or I'll be out of a job again. Thanks for calling. And thanks for letting me know about Frank."

I hung up and got to work on the story. It felt good to be writing like this again. Something came alive in me, a part of myself I had not used in a long time. The uncertainty left me after about the fourth sentence. It was going to be a good story.

I finished, let John know, and he called it up on his screen. I watched his face as he read it. I don't know why; as usual, he was like granite while reading a story. You never knew if he loved it or hated it.

He got to the end and looked up from the screen. "Nice to have you back, Irene. But why are you standing around kibitzing? You need another assignment?"

"Nice to be back, John—I've missed you so much."

At O'Connor's desk, I started looking through the computer files. His code wasn't so hard to decipher on the computer—no drawings or shorthand. But he did use nicknames and even had a way of making a rat nose: =o=.

On one of the more recent entries, I found another reference to campaign fund-raising banquets:

RCC—DA + MYR =o=. LDY? $ VS $ BLP AM W/C.

Rubber-chicken circuit, district attorney and mayor. Rat nose. I wasn't sure about the rest of it. Something about money and then a note that someone "will call." I studied it for a while, but couldn't make out any more. I went back a few pages, to an entry marked with arrows:

>>>MYR PD FR DA RCC $? CK W/AM @ BLP.

Mayor paid from DA's fund-raiser money? Check with AM at BLP.

Who was AM at BLP? Someone who was going to call O'Connor about the BLP or about the district attorney and mayor's races? Did AM know O'Connor had died? Or would I get another call at some point, like the one from MacPherson?

I leaned back in the chair and tried to stretch a little. Time to do some moving around or I'd be walking like Frankenstein by the end of the day.

O'Connor was pursuing the possibility of something dirty going on in the mayor's and DA's races. After lunch, I'd go down to City Hall, and then maybe over to the California Fair Political Practices Commission office in the City of Industry; campaign-funding reports were on file there.

I also wanted to go over to the hospital and visit all my friends and relatives—the walk would be good for me. I turned off the computer monitor and slowly stood up. I started to push the chair in and swore under my breath—my purse was on the floor. I bent over—a big mistake—and couldn't make myself straighten up again. Blood started rushing to my head as I stared at my purse and the floor.

I made a grab for the shoulder strap of the purse, and managed to dump its entire contents all over the floor. My head was throbbing and I could tell my face was red. The swearing was getting out from under my breath now. I turned my head a few degrees to see if anyone was nearby. John Walters was. I looked back down in mortification.

It was then that I noticed the two envelopes that had been O'Connor's mail. The return address on one of them was "The Global Guru," O'Connor's nutty travel agent. Had O'Connor been planning to go somewhere?

20

I picked up the envelopes just as John, still chuckling, came over to help. "It's not funny, damn it," I said, but proceeded to disprove that by laughing myself. I managed to creep back up into a standing position with his support.

He was good enough to gather up my pens, notebooks, hairbrush, wallet, and other assorted items that had spread across the floor.

"What?" he said with mock surprise. "Where the hell could that lipstick have gone to? And where did that mascara go?"

"I only wear makeup on Holy Days of Obligation and you know it."

"Your religion must not have had a feast day since the Flood."

"Since before the Flood."

"You okay now?"

"Yes, thanks, John."

He walked off, still snickering. I opened the letter from the Global Guru. The familiar letterhead proclaimed, "Peace, Love and Understanding Through Travel." The Global Guru was Fred Barnes to those of us who knew him in high school. Poor old Fred just never got over the sixties. I could picture him in his bell-bottoms and beads, burning incense in the travel agency.

The strange part was that, for all the trappings, he was a real wheeler-dealer. He could find low fares going anywhere, anytime. He knew his stuff—so I guess he was a sort of a guru. He actually had a pretty-decent-sized client list. O'Connor said he liked going to Fred because Fred had flair. In that way, he was much like all the people O'Connor went to for services, a little oddball but highly capable.

The envelope contained a single round-trip ticket for a flight to

Phoenix, Arizona, on Thursday—tomorrow morning. The letter explained that a rental car would be waiting there for O'Connor, and that if he changed his mind and decided to stay overnight, he should give Fred a call to arrange lodging.

A trip to a sunny border state, with an Hispanic population. And some high fluoride levels. I reached for the phone and dialed Fred.

"Global Guru, Shalom."

"Specials on Israel this month, Fred?"

"Irene? Oh, Irene. I'm so sorry about O'Connor. He was a true human being. I know he's around here, watching all of us and having a laugh, but I will miss him. I wonder what he'll come back as? Something inquisitive. Did you know I just mailed some tickets to him?"

"Yes, I've got them. That's why I called."

"Oh?"

"Did he tell you why he was going to Phoenix?"

"He wasn't going to Phoenix," he said. "I mean, he wasn't staying there. That was just the closest spot with an airport."

"Where was he going from Phoenix?"

"I was afraid you'd ask that. Well, let's see. It's a funny name, something to do with lizards, I think . . ."

"He was going somewhere to do a story about lizards?" My hopes momentarily sank.

"No, no, no! Oh, I see what you mean! Oh, no. Not about lizards, I mean the name of the town has something to do with lizards. Iguana? No, no iguanas. Oh, now I remember—Gila monsters!"

"Gila monsters?"

"No, the name of the town is Gila Bend. Gila Bend, Arizona. Near the Gila River. Yes, that's it."

I thought about the list MacPherson had given us. I was almost positive Gila Bend was on it. "Did he tell you anything more?"

"No, just that he had to see someone in Gila Bend. He wanted a flight in and out of Phoenix for the same day, no overnight stay."

"You're sure about Gila Bend?"

"Yes. No doubt about it."

"Thanks, Fred."

"Irene? Are you going to be using the tickets? Or should I refund them?"

I thought about this. "I'm not sure. Can I let you know by this evening?"

"Sure, that's cool. Just let me know, okay?" He gave me his home number and told me that he could make changes in the tickets from his home computer.

"I appreciate this. Take care, Fred."

"Peace."

Poor Fred, flair or no flair, he had missed all the interesting parts of the last couple of decades. I was trying to remember what these were when my stomach growled and reminded me to go to lunch.

Before leaving, I made a quick call to Pete Baird to tell him about the tickets and have him check MacPherson's list. Yes, Gila Bend was on it. Yes, it was one of the highlighted places on the list. Pete told me he would call the sheriff in Gila Bend after lunch—maybe someone was expecting O'Connor. I hung up the phone and stared at it for a moment, wondering about Gila Bend and what O'Connor might have been up to there.

"What have you found out?" It was Lydia. She had walked up without my noticing. I guess I was still jumpy, because I gave a start and felt it everywhere. "Sorry," she went on, "didn't mean to scare you. It's just that when you pull a little on your lower lip like that, I know you've just learned something—something's up."

I put my hand down from my face, caught in the act. "Didn't realize I do that. Guess that's another liability of staying single—no one to point out all your little idiosyncrasies."

"I don't know that I'd call that a liability."

I filled her in on what I had learned. "I'm headed over to the hospital. See you later?"

"You know where I'll be," she said, looking over at the City Desk, where a general-assignment reporter was waiting to see her.

Walking over to St. Anne's was a lot slower process than the day before, but moving around did make me feel better.

As I walked down the hallway, I tried to decide whether to see Frank or Barbara and Kenny first. I realized I was starting to think of Barbara and Kenny as one unit in the critical-care ward. She seemed so much a part of his being a patient here, that I couldn't think of it as "seeing how Kenny is doing." Since I had no reason to believe that Barbara would welcome my visit, I decided to stop by Kenny's room first and get that over with.

As soon as I walked in, I noticed that more of Kenny's face was showing, although he still had a great deal of swelling and bruising.

Barbara sat next to him in exactly the same position I had left her in the day before. She turned to me and on her weary face I could see exhaustion taking its toll.

"Irene!" She stood up and came over and hugged me. I was so shocked that it took me a minute to hug back.

"Irene, I'm so sorry I was rude to you yesterday. Pete Baird came by—he's been so good to me—and he told me about you and Frank. I felt so bad. I could have lost you—and the last time I might have ever talked to you, I was mean. I saw Frank. He looks awful. And look at your poor forehead!" She was crying.

I don't know why, but these reconciliations with Barbara are so welcomed and yet so awkward that I always feel a little inner sting when they occur. It passes, and while I know that we will inevitably go back to driving each other crazy, for a few moments we both know how really important we are to each other.

"I'm okay, Barbara, but I'm really worried about you. Have you had any sleep at all?"

"A little."

I could see how little. "How's Kenny?"

"He's actually doing a little better. He's been conscious a couple of times—well, sort of—he didn't know where he was or what was going on, but he opened his eyes. Today he looked at me and said, 'Barbara? What are you doing here?' It's the most he's talked. He recognized me; they tell me that's a good sign."

"Could you sleep here in his room?"

"I've tried, but it's hard. People are constantly in here checking on him. I know I should go home and go to bed, but I just can't make myself do it. What if he wakes up and he's frightened or disoriented? He might need me."

I put my arm around her shoulders.

"Well, well," came a lilting voice from the doorway. "How nice to see you two girls together." Sister Theresa walked in, smiling until she saw my forehead. "Irene, I heard you just couldn't bear to stay away from us. Look at those bruises."

"It was a real letdown when I realized that you don't just hover around in here all night like a guardian angel, Sister."

"Sorry to disappoint you, dear. But I understand you left someone special for us to look after. Detective Harriman has had many visitors from the police force, all very concerned about him." She paused, then added, "But I dare say he will be especially happy to see you."

There was an impish grin on her face. Great. A nun matchmaker.

"Well, I guess I'll go over and see him then," I said.

"Good. Now, Barbara, I think you need to trust an old nun to watch your husband's bedside for a while. Go tell the nurse at the station out in the hall that I sent you. Our census is just low enough that we can spare a quiet place for you to sleep for a few hours. I won't take no for an answer. You need to sleep. Go on now, go."

I felt like I was back in Catholic school. An irresistible force, Sister Theresa. We thanked her and headed out the door. Barbara gave me one last hug and headed over to the nurses' station. I went in the other direction, to Frank's room.

I was surprised, then relieved, to see a uniformed officer outside Frank's door. I told him my name and he checked a list. He took a look at my ID and said, "Sorry to have to check this, Miss Kelly. You understand." I told him I did, and that I was glad he was there.

As I opened the door, I saw the room was full of flowers and cards from well-wishers. Frank was sleeping. In some ways, he looked worse than the night before. His bruises were quite dramatic, even on his sleeping face. He had two terrific shiners from the broken nose, which was still very swollen. His forehead was swollen, too, and much more discolored than my own. The swelling on his lip had gone down a little. I noticed he wasn't so pale today.

He opened his eyes and took a while to wake up completely. His face suddenly went ashen, reflecting a wave of pain that was hard to watch. I found myself remembering visits to my father during his last illness, and how he had told me that he always hurt the most when he first woke up. I wondered if it was the same for Frank. He saw me and smiled a little. "Hi," he said. He tried to bring himself around.

"Hi yourself. How's the head?" I asked. Damn silly question.

He didn't answer right away. "Truth?"

"Truth."

"Hurts. A lot."

He was talking slowly, with difficulty.

"Do you want me to come back later?"

"No, stay a while. Okay?"

"Sure. But you don't have to talk."

"I know," he said. He reached for my hand and held it. His was a rough hand, with calluses here and there, but it felt good to hold it. A little scary, but good. He closed his eyes and soon fell back to sleep.

I sat there with him like that for about an hour. Throughout that time, I fought down the panic welling up within me, a rising desire to leave. During the eternity spent sitting in that wreck the day before, waiting for the ambulance to arrive, I had tried not to focus on my fears about the seriousness of his injuries. Now I had to admit to myself that even knowing that they were not life-threatening, I was still uneasy. Too much experience with hospitals as places where people were lost to you forever. Too many good-byes to people dressed just as Frank was now, in rooms like this, with rolling trays and curtains and bedrails.

I argued with myself that Frank was not critically injured, did not have cancer like my father had, would only be here for a few days. I didn't let go of his hand.

As I sat and listened to the steady rhythm of his breathing, I realized that I had naively expected to be able to come in and chatter away with him, as if a good night's sleep would get him over the concussion. I also realized that I missed having him to talk to about the case. I would have to do what I could on my own until he was up and around.

As if he could hear my thoughts, he woke up again. He seemed a little more alert this time. "You okay?" he asked.

"Yes, it's just that . . . well, I just feel bad that you got hurt like this."

"Don't be scared."

"It's not a matter of being scared."

He grinned that half-grin. "I'll be okay soon."

He didn't look as if he'd be okay soon, but I smiled back anyway.

He started to move his head, then seemed to get dizzy for a minute. He blanched and drew in a breath, closing his eyes. He never increased the pressure on my hand, but I saw him clench the sheets in his other hand.

I waited for it to pass, then said, "I'm going to go now. You need to rest. I'll try to come back later today, after work."

"Irene, wait," he said, just above a whisper.

I waited.

"Talk to Pete about everything. No secrets, okay? You can trust him."

I gave his hand a parting squeeze and said, "Get better, Frank. I'll come back to see you tonight."

He held on. "Promise—no secrets from Pete."

"If Wrigley has this room wiretapped, I'm a dead woman. I'm in here holding hands with a cop, for Christ's sakes." I looked at his battered face, then added, "But being as you have saved my life twice in about as many days, okay, I promise."

He relaxed and let go of my hand. "Thanks. Come back, okay?"

He was asleep again before I was out of the room.

21

On my way out, I decided I would stop by a burger stand I had passed on the way to the hospital. As I exited the double doors of St. Anne's, I glanced up at the tall monolith of dark mirrored glass across the street and froze on the sidewalk. At the top of the building were the initials BLP.

BLP. Bank of Las Piernas. The fact that I had failed to think of this when reading a reference to money in O'Connor's notes made me feel like I was losing my edge. I tried to remember the computer phrases. Something about AM. I crossed the street and went into the bank.

The Bank of Las Piernas's downtown branch was done up in a modern style. Contemporary-art sculptures with intriguing but unidentifiable shapes bedecked the interior courtyard entrance. Inside the building itself, the tellers and other branch officers worked in a room that was cavernous and marbled, so that those who applied for loans felt akin to Dorothy stepping up to meet the Great Oz. It was fairly busy for a Wednesday afternoon.

I walked past the dozen or so people corralled in the stanchions and ropes waiting for tellers, and started reading their name badges. This behavior was frowned on by the customers in line, who thought I was trying to butt in front of them, and by the tellers, who were wary of the strange bruised woman wandering outside the cattle chute.

Soon a pencil of a woman came striding toward me, purpose in every step. She was tall and thin; there was absolutely no shape on her that couldn't be drawn with a ruler. She had a gold-plated name tag that said her name was Miss Ramona Ralston. "Can I help you?" she asked, but help didn't seem to be what she had in mind.

"No, thanks," I said, stepping around her and continuing my walk past the teller windows. She seemed not to know what to do about it for a minute, but only a minute.

"Excuse me, miss?"

I turned around and looked at her as if she were interrupting a Nobel Prize-winning effort, and said, "Yes?"

"What you need to do is talk to the branch manager."

"How can you possibly know what I need when you don't even know why I'm here?"

"Well, if you want to see a teller you need to go over where it says, 'Please Enter Line Here.' But if you aren't willing to abide by the rules of common courtesy, then you need to see the branch manager."

"Look, Miss Ralston, I am not trying to cut in front of everyone in line. I won't stop at a teller's window. I don't need to talk to you or to the branch manager. You may go back to whatever you were doing before I came in."

She decided to shadow me, following a few paces behind me. I passed about ten windows, reading the name plates on the desks in the operations area behind the tellers. I stopped abruptly when I saw "Ann Marchenko" on one of them. Miss Ralston plowed into my back, hard enough so that it ended up being a tackle. Before I knew it, I was sprawled on the floor, with Miss Ralston right on top of me.

Unfortunately, my stiff muscles made getting to my feet a slow process. While I listened to a constant stream of flustered apologies from Miss Ralston, I tried to force myself back up to my feet. Soon a small crowd had formed around us, and a tall man with an athletic build came striding over to us.

"Give her some room, everybody," he commanded. "Give her some room." He put a burly hand down and I grabbed on, and he lifted me up effortlessly. "Are you all right, miss?"

"Yes, I think so," I said. He was a handsome man, with dark hair graying at the temples and almost jet-black eyes. He spoke with a slight French accent. There was something familiar about him, but I couldn't for the life of me figure out what it was.

"Miss Ralston, what is the meaning of this?" he asked.

"Why, Mr. St. Germain, I—I—" Miss Ralston was stuck in neutral, but the name had helped me place him.

"Guy St. Germain?" I asked, giving it the best French-Canadian pronunciation I could muster. "Didn't you play defense for the Buffalo Sabres?"

He beamed. "Yes, ma'am, I did. How did you know that? Not too many hockey fans around here, and most of them are only interested in Gretsky and company."

"You'll have to forgive me, Mr. St. Germain, the Sabres are my second-favorite team. You've met another Kings fan. But I do remember seeing you play."

"You're too young for that, I'm afraid."

"Nonsense."

I introduced myself and we spent a few minutes discussing the recent Stanley Cup play-offs, taking advantage of that rare—in southern California—pleasure of talking serious hockey in the off season. Miss Ralston was dumbstruck, totally unable to comprehend our conversation.

She sidled off and Guy St. Germain led me over to his large desk. He had a vice-president's title on his name plate and a fancy pen set. The visitors' chairs were plush. Eventually we wore down on hockey and he asked me if Miss Ralston had hurt me when she gave me that hard check.

"No, I got a few bumps and bruises in a car accident yesterday, and so I'm a little stiff and sore today. She didn't mean to run into me; I just stopped suddenly when she was right behind me."

"I'm glad you're not hurt, and it is kind of you to be so understanding. Is there some way in which I may be of help to you?"

"I'm trying to get in touch with one of the employees here," I said, praying to God that Ann Marchenko was the AM of O'Connor's computer notes.

"Really? Which one?"

"Ann Marchenko."

"Our branch specialist? You have a problem with a safe deposit box here or something of this nature?"

"Oh, no, she doesn't even know me. She helped a friend of mine who died recently and I wanted to thank her. He mentioned her in some notes he left."

"I see. Well, Mrs. Marchenko is off today, but she'll be in tomorrow. Shall I have her contact you?"

"I'm not sure I'll be in town tomorrow; I'll stop by again. Is Wednesday her regular day off?"

"No, her daughter was ill today and she couldn't arrange child care in time. She's usually here Monday through Friday."

"Well," I said, standing up and extending a hand, "I'll call if I'm out of town, or come by if I'm still in Las Piernas. Thank you for your help, Mr. St. Germain."

"Please call me Guy," he said, returning the handshake with a firm grasp. "And please stop by my desk and say hello if you do come in. You have provided a very pleasant change of pace today, even though our acquaintance had such an unfortunate beginning."

"Don't worry about it. And I will definitely stop by if I come in, if you promise to call me Irene." We shook on it and I left him.

As I walked out, Miss Ralston spotted me and started following me again, her long strides catching up to me quickly. She had found her voice again and was chattering away at me. "I'm so sorry, ma'am, I don't know what got into me. I didn't realize you knew Mr. St. Germain. I don't mean knew him—but knew of him, or whatever . . . " She kept this up, following me all the way out onto the sidewalk. I stopped and turned around, ready to ask her to please forget all about it, when I heard the roar of an engine and noticed something very much out of place: A car was barreling down the sidewalk, headed right for us.

22

I took two long running steps and wedged myself between two parked cars, as the car on the sidewalk, an old brown Camaro, sent newspaper stands outside the bank flying as it steered toward me. Next I heard a sickening *thunk*—similar to the sound a football makes when it's kicked—and watched Miss Ralston hurtling through the air. She had frozen in place, and now was knocked halfway down the block by the impact. The car never slowed down. There were no plates on it. It jumped back over the curb and onto the street and went squealing out of sight before any of us on the sidewalk had moved again.

A woman who had just missed getting hit as she walked out of the bank started screaming at the top of her lungs. I was shaking, unable to make myself come out from my haven. It took a moment to grasp what had actually happened, and once I did I felt sickened by it.

Eventually I made myself go down the sidewalk to the place where she'd landed. I didn't have much hope for what I'd find there. It was just as well. She was absolutely motionless, lying face-up with her eyes open, and would have seemed unscathed if it weren't for the fact that her head was in one of those unnatural positions that can only be achieved with a broken neck, and that her skull was completely cracked open where she had landed on it, spilling its contents out onto the sidewalk. I stumbled over to the gutter and retched.

In moments, I saw emergency-room people coming from the hospital across the street, and Guy St. Germain was running down the sidewalk from the bank. I turned and caught another glimpse of Miss Ralston, and almost passed out.

Next thing I knew, Guy had taken hold of my shoulders and was shaking me gently, shouting, "What happened to her? What happened to her?"

I started crying. "A car—oh, God, have mercy on me, it's my fault. Sweet Jesus, it's all my fault—it was me they wanted to kill. It was me. They wanted to kill me." I was losing it rapidly.

He was taken aback, then put his arms around me and held me, saying, "No, no, *chére*—hush." I felt dizzy and sick; once again, I almost passed out, but fought it off. As if it were happening miles away from me, I felt my own crying become sobs. Guy turned me away from where Miss Ralston lay and held me to his shoulder while they found something to cover her. I concentrated on the weave of the fabric in Guy's suit and calmed down.

Someone came out of a nearby café and gave me a glass of water. It was one of those little kindnesses that make a person feel human again. I washed the taste of being sick out of my mouth, pulled out a Kleenex and blew my nose. I was getting there.

In no time at all, police pulled up, sirens howling. One of the officers gently took me from Guy and sat me down in a patrol car. I asked him to contact Pete Baird. He turned his head to one side and took a longer look at me. "You the lady who was with Frank Harriman yesterday?"

I nodded through a stream of tears.

"Sister, you better think about getting out of town for a few days."

I had thought about it. I thought about Gila Bend. I thought about running away to some place not even connected to all of this, just long enough to feel sane again. But how could I feel in control of my own life if all I did was run? I had to face this head on; even if I got scared or cried or whatever—I had to deal with it.

I thought about Miss Ralston, and how sarcastic and mean all my thoughts of her had been, when she was just a busybody who was in the wrong place at the wrong time. If she hadn't knocked me down, she wouldn't be dead. If I hadn't been walking around in a suspicious manner, she wouldn't have come over to talk to me. If only I hadn't looked up and seen the BLP on the building—if, if, if, if.

I thought of something O'Connor once told me. He had read an article somewhere that made an impression on him, and as was his wont, he repeated its salient points for my benefit.

"Irene," he said, "do you know what the two saddest words in the English language are?"

"Boo and hoo?" I had guessed.

"No, wise-ass. The two saddest words in the English language are 'if only.' "

I used to hate it when he'd get into going on and on with all of his quotes and proverbs and old saws, but somehow they always came back to me in times of trouble. And so I left off with the ifs.

By the time Pete got there, I was much calmer; still a little shaky, but calmer.

He sighed. "Hell. I was hoping these jokers would need a little while to regroup. You know, give you a day off." He turned to one of the uniformed men and asked them to go over and double check on the guard for Frank's room, and to ask the hospital about tightening security around Kenny as well.

"Have you heard back from the sheriff in Gila Bend yet?" I asked.

"Yeah. They said they had been trying to dig up something for O'Connor since early last week. They think they might have something."

"I'm thinking of going there."

"By yourself?"

"My traveling companions aren't faring too well these days."

"Don't start thinking like that, Irene. It'll make you crazy."

"That's what I was just telling myself."

"Let me run this by Bredloe. Maybe I can work it out so that I can go along. I don't like the idea of you going somewhere connected with Mr. O'Connor on your own."

"What time is it?" I asked.

"About three o'clock."

"Criminy. They're going to think I quit again. I've got to get back to the paper."

"Let one of these guys make sure you get to work okay," he said, motioning to one of the patrolmen.

The officer walked over and introduced himself as Mike Sorenson. It seemed silly to get in a car for a two-block ride, but I didn't feel like walking over near the sidewalk where Miss Ralston's body was still lying.

"You're Frank Harriman's friend, aren't you?" he asked.

"Yes," I said. "You know him?"

"Oh, sure. Great guy, Frank. I saw him earlier—he didn't look so hot, but they said he'll be one hundred percent before too long. I don't know, seeing him there just made me boil—really got to me. We all want to nail these bastards. Frank's a good cop. And he says you're okay. No offense, but I don't usually get along so hot with reporters. But if Frank says you're okay, then you're okay."

"Thanks. I wondered if—if people might blame me for what happened to him."

"Naw, are you crazy? We know who's who in this mess. Hell, lady, you're damned lucky to be alive, and you know it."

"You're right."

We pulled up at the newspaper and he got out and walked me in. I could hear the presses rolling. Snap out of it, I told myself, you're lucky to be alive. I thanked Officer Sorenson, waved hello to Geoff, then made my way upstairs.

I talked to Lydia—she had been worried. Someone was already covering the hit-and-run.

I went over my progress on the funding story with John Walters and then I asked if we could go into his office. He looked up at me with a raised eyebrow, then motioned me inside the little glass cubicle he called home and shut the door on the nosiest people in the world.

I told him that I wanted to go to Gila Bend, and that I'd probably be taking a cop along with me, both for protection and for entrée to any business I might need to do with the Gila Bend cops. I told him that there really wasn't any way for me to do this story on the sly from the cops, and if that bothered him, he ought to can me or get somebody else to cover it.

He started laughing. Not the reaction I expected.

"You are so damned ethical, Irene. I love it. You haven't been here forty-eight hours and you've got the news editor in his office, giving him ultimatums so you can work with a clean conscience. Brother."

I waited.

"God save me from girls who went to Catholic school. Guilt just eats them alive."

I still waited.

"Irene, you know what the dangers are of getting too chummy with the people you may have to write some story about later. You're a professional. I'm not going to give you advanced absolution for any sins you are about to commit against the paper, I'll just trust you to use your best judgment. Just between the two of us, I'm happy as hell that you're not going out there alone."

"I know, John, I know. Don't think I'm not frightened. You should have seen me fall apart out there today. I even puked on the street."

"What the hell do you expect? You see someone you were talking to five minutes earlier get their head cracked open and die. Are you supposed to just stand there and say, 'Gee, that reminds me, I didn't have lunch today'?"

"I didn't."

"Didn't what?"

"I didn't have lunch today."

This broke him up again.

"Hell, John, I don't ever remember making you laugh like this before. Either I ought to go on stage or you're becoming a raving lunatic."

"The latter, I assure you, my dear, the latter. Now call it a day. Go home and make travel arrangements."

On the way home, I bought a couple of steaks. By the time Lydia came in, I had a small feast waiting; Cody serenaded us with loud noises of anticipation for the leftovers.

Pete called to say Bredloe had okayed the trip, and I told him I'd take care of the reservations. I called Fred back and cancelled O'Connor's arrangements. Fred worked it out so that Pete and I could get on a flight to Phoenix the next morning and reserved a rental car. He needed to ask Pete some questions about seating preferences and so on, so I gave him Pete's number and said goodnight.

At about seven-thirty, over Lydia's protests, I headed back to the hospital. I hated the drive there, hated the walk in. But when I got to Frank's room, all of that changed. He was awake and seemed fairly alert, and I realized I was damned glad to see him.

"You did come back," he said.

"Sure. You remember my visit this afternoon?"

"Yeah, of course."

"You look better tonight."

"Thanks."

I sat down and reached for his hand. We were quiet for a while. I was debating whether or not to tell him what had happened that afternoon. I decided not to. It would probably just worry him; besides, I reminded myself, I was there to comfort *him*.

"Something wrong?" he asked.

"Hospitals scare me, I guess." It wasn't a complete lie.

"Hmm. That all?"

"No, that's only part of it. I'm not going to be able to see you tomorrow. I'm going to Phoenix for the day with Pete. We're going to check something out there."

"Glad Pete's going, too. I'll be okay."

I stayed a little longer, and he seemed to be wearing down again. He tried to stay awake, but I could tell he was feeling drowsy. I didn't want to push it. I started to leave and he roused himself enough to say, "Take care."

"You too," I said.

When I got back to Lydia's I took a hot bath for my sore muscles' sake and climbed into bed. Cody wasn't ready to turn in and so he hung out with Lydia. I'd given the little bastard steak and he still snubbed me.

23

I **woke up** before sunup, about 4 A.M., and couldn't get back to sleep. I dressed as quietly as I could, so as not to wake Lydia. I was a lot less sore than the day before. I felt restless, and I still had a few hours before the flight to Phoenix, so I decided to take a drive down to the beach. I grabbed a sweatshirt and eased the front door open, holding the knob to keep the latch quiet. Outside, the streetlights reflected softly in the cloudy June sky, and the air was damp and cool. Crickets sang. The car was covered with dew.

I started the car, and in the quiet of the neighborhood the sound seemed incredibly loud. As quickly as I could, I put it into gear and headed down to the water.

I reached the shore just as the pre-dawn light was filtering above the horizon. I parked and walked out to the end of the pier, passing only a few avid fishermen silently standing along its sides. Without the traffic and beach crowd to distract from it, the Pacific roared in an endless, uneven rhythm of waves.

"Peaceful," her name meant, and though I had seen her storms and wrath, I always felt restored when I saw her. She stretched to the horizon, a reminder of the power of nature at the doorstep of southern California's posturing artifice. All my worries seemed so small before her.

I watched a terrific sunrise, one full of gentle color and changing hues in water and sky. The gulls were beginning their day noisily, their *cree, cree* echoing off the cliffs. I went down the stairs to the beach, took my shoes off and chilled the bottoms of my feet in the soft, cold sand. They soon felt numb. I plodded along, letting the wind pull my hair across my face, taking deep breaths of salt-sea air.

I walked until I reached the Las Piernas cliffs. Above them the sun was glinting off the windows of the upper sundeck of the enormous Sheffield Estate. Here, for as many generations as Las Piernas had been a city, the Sheffield family had reigned. The earliest Sheffields had started a general store, then a bank, then a pharmacy, and so on and on; they bought and sold real estate in and around Las Piernas to amass the original fortune, and added to it when one of the Sheffield grandchildren developed a knack for making ice cream. Sheffield Ice Cream stores were everywhere, and always seemed to be one step ahead of the latest ice cream craze. The last of the Sheffields was Elinor Sheffield Hollingsworth, who had married a handsome young Harvard law graduate who was now the district attorney of Las Piernas.

The Hollingsworths spent most of their time in one of the other family mansions, one up in the hills above the city, where they could socialize more easily with the other members of the upper crust. And so it was that today, like most other days, the cliffside estate looked vacant and lonely. Completely isolated, no other houses for two miles on either side, it stood sheltered on three sides by deep stands of trees that stretched from shore to road.

I turned and walked away from the twin cliffs and headed back to the pier. I watched a fisherman reel in and toss back a small perch. I thought about how strange an experience that must be for the fish, imagined the act of eating breakfast leading to a yank up into outer space and then a sudden fall back to earth.

I padded barefoot back to the car, the asphalt of the parking lot much warmer than the sand. I brushed the sand off my feet and pant cuffs. I put my shoes back on, then sat looking out at the water a little while longer. On this side of the pier, surfers had been riding waves since just before daybreak. I checked my rearview mirror and looked around. No one watching, as far as I could tell. I started up the car. No bomb under the hood. Whoever was trying to kill me had missed a golden opportunity. Not even that kind of thinking could disturb me much as I drove back to Lydia's.

24

Pete came by to pick me up just after Lydia had left for work. It was only about a fifteen-minute drive from Lydia's place to the Las Piernas Airport. The airport was built in the late 1930s and it has a certain appeal because of it. The architecture has the curving chrome, brass, and green-glass look of the time. It's small, just six gates. Only three major carriers use the Las Piernas Airport, but between them and the smaller airlines we get pretty good service and a hell of a lot less hassle than LAX. I don't even think I've ever seen a Hare Krishna recruiter there.

Our flight was on American Southwest Airlines. We pulled out our plastic and paid for our tickets. Pete checked his gun in with security; they put it in a special box for the flight. We walked about forty feet to the gate and had a seat. Pete offered me a piece of gum.

"No, thanks," I said.

"I gotta have gum before a flight. I quit smoking fifteen years ago, but every time I get near an airplane I want to light up so bad, I can't stand it."

"Gum's easier on your lungs."

"Yeah, no kidding. You ever been a smoker?"

"Never really was a smoker. As a kid I tried it a couple of times— never really learned how to inhale. Thought I looked pretty cool just carrying one around, but the charm of that wore off fairly quickly."

"Yeah, well, you're lucky. Took longer for the charm to wear off for me. Now I've got what they call the zeal of the convert—I hate being around it, you know? But not when I'm in an airport—then it's all I can do not to go into the bar and buy a pack of cigarettes. It's crazy."

"You afraid of flying?"

His cheeks colored. "Naw, I wouldn't say that." But after a moment he added, "I don't know. Maybe. Yeah, I guess it does make me nervous."

"I won't tell a soul, Pete," I said.

"Thanks."

By the time they called our flight he had gone through half a large pack of Big Red Chewing Gum. He smelled like a cinnamon stick. I still preferred it to the smell of smoke. I stood up and started for the gate. He grabbed my arm.

"Not yet," he said.

"You're not going to completely balk at getting on the plane, are you?"

"We're in no rush. I'd just prefer we let everybody else get to their seats. We don't have any luggage or anything to put in an overhead compartment."

I sat down again. I wondered if Pete was nervous about flying with one of Las Piernas's leading targets.

Although they were supposedly boarding by sections, it seemed like most people just got on as soon as they could. Phoenix is a hub for American Southwest, so the flight was almost full. They got to the final boarding call. Pete looked around in the waiting area and didn't seem to find anything out of the ordinary. We walked down the ramp and on to the plane.

People were still standing up in the aisle, trying to shove impossible amounts of carry-on baggage into the overhead compartments. Eventually we made our way back to our seats. Pete asked me to take the window seat, and he sat in between me and a kid who looked to be about sixteen.

The kid was dressed for effect. Except for his Day-Glo green shoelaces and a bleeding-skull-and-crossbones necklace that looked as if it came out of a gumball machine, he wore a basic black outfit, complete with knee-length jacket. He was listening to a radio whose earphones were smaller than his earrings. He had one of those haircuts that was what we used to call a 'butch' on one side of his head, but from his crown forward was straight and about chin length. I wondered if a person could wear that haircut and feel in balance at all times. I admonished myself for this kind of thinking, remembering the guy I dated in high school whose hair was twice as long as my own, and how loudly I protested over my parents narrow-minded reaction to him.

The kid caught me looking at him. I smiled and said, "Hi." Apparently reading my lips, he flashed me a peace sign. I think it's still a peace sign.

Pete looked at me and rolled his eyes.

One more passenger came on board, a tall, thin man with hollow cheeks. He had hard, piercing eyes that roamed over the faces of the passengers as he walked down the aisle. He moved just past our row and sat down right behind Pete. I could think of no specific reason to feel uneasy about this man, but we had failed to be the last ones on board and I couldn't help but wonder about the way the man had looked over the passengers.

I felt my palms break out in a sweat. There were only a few open seats left on the plane. Had he just been looking for an empty seat? No, he was looking at people, not just scanning the rows for an available place. Then I noticed that he had passed up one of the ones closer to the door.

Why sit right behind us? Was that his assigned seat, or did he just choose that seat on his own?

"Got any more of that gum?" I asked Pete.

"Sure," he said, offering me a stick, and then holding one out to the kid.

"Thank you, sir, that's very kind of you," the kid said politely.

I know we both looked slack-jawed. I don't know why. The hippie I dated in high school was the most well-mannered of any of the handful of guys I went out with.

We started down the runway and I saw Pete's knuckles go white. I thought about how odd it was—here was a guy who could handle resuscitating a bloody man who was buried alive in sand, but he was scared silly by an airplane's take off. For my part, few sensations were better than the rush of being airborne.

It was a short flight. They barely had enough time to hand out peanuts and drinks before we landed. Pete seemed to be bothered even more by landing. We were going to have to buy more gum before the day was over.

Once we were on the ground, Pete gradually relaxed. But as we pulled into the gate, he motioned to me to stay seated. "Wait," he said.

We watched all the other passengers leave. The man whom I had started to think of as "Hawkeyes" was one of the first ones off the plane. Maybe I was imagining things after all.

Not having any baggage makes flying a totally different experience. Except for my windbreaker and purse, I had nothing to keep track of. We retrieved Pete's gun from Phoenix Airport security, then went down to the car-rental counter to pick up the compact Fred had reserved for us. As I gave the information for the rental contract, Pete leaned with his back against the counter, watching the people around us.

Outside, the morning was already turning warm. Only 9:00 A.M. and it must have been about eighty degrees out. I asked Pete if he would mind if I did the driving. He didn't, and after accidentally turning the windshield wipers on while trying to adjust the steering wheel, we were on our way to Gila Bend.

Traffic in Phoenix was a bitch, so it took us a while to get clear of the city and its immediate neighbors on U.S. 10. The road became less and less crowded as we moved west. We passed the dark-green swath of farmlands along the Gila River, crossing over the river itself near Buckeye. We made the turnoff on Highway 85, and the landscape changed as we went south through clusters of dry Arizona mountains.

For miles we saw few signs of human inhabitants. Scattered here and there were vacant farm houses along the road. Broken windows gave them a forlorn look, as if they were ashamed of their shabbiness. Already scrub brush and cacti were reclaiming the abandoned fields.

Pete yammered away throughout the trip.

"I grew up in upstate New York," he told me. "Like a friend of mine says, 'Only penguins should live there.' You ever been to upstate New York? No? Well, I suppose for some people it's got attractions. But every time I even start to miss it, you know what I do? I go out to my garage. I got a snow shovel out there. Honest to God. I'm probably the only guy in southern California with a snow shovel in his garage. Yeah, I just look at that snow shovel and think about what it feels like when there's a good windchill factor and a driveway full of snow, and I say, 'Just sit there, you bastard, I'm never picking you up again in my lifetime.' No kidding. That's what I do."

Outside the car, it was probably nearing a hundred degrees, and I was listening to stories about snow shovels.

"How long you known Frank?" he asked.

"We met years ago in Bakersfield, but I haven't seen much of him until—well, until this week," I said, thinking of that morning on O'Connor's front lawn. Was that only a few days ago?

"No foolin'? You knew him back in Bakersfield? I've just known him since he's been in Las Piernas—what, about five years now? Smart guy. Really smart guy. You know, I'm not saying he's Poindexter or anything, just sharp—you know what I mean? I mean, he never makes anybody else feel dumb. He's good that way. You know, a lot of guys want to be homicide detectives, so when somebody gets promoted quickly, there might be resentment. But Frank, he's the kind of guy that made it easy on everybody. They just like him. Works hard, don't put anybody down, doesn't go around with his nose stuck up in the sky—he's a good cop. He doesn't make the guys in uniform feel like lackeys.

"Yeah, I worked with him on his first case here. It was tough on him then, getting used to Las Piernas, new guys to work with. Plus, he broke up with his girlfriend. I guess he transferred down here partly because of some broad he knew in Bakersfield. She gets a job in Las Piernas, begs him to move; he no sooner gets transferred and she quits and goes back to Bakersfield. God knows why. She was with the Highway Patrol. He shoulda known right there. You know her? No? I don't know what he saw in her. I told him, 'Good riddance—a woman like that will make you crazy.' But he hasn't really been with anybody special since. You know, dated here and there, but nobody special."

He gave me a meaningful look, and I casually tried to steer the conversation in another direction. "I didn't know you and Frank had worked together so long."

"Aw, five years is all. I've been tracking down corpse-makers for ten years—before that I spent another seven in uniform—all of it in Las Piernas. Place grows on you, you know what I mean?"

"Yes. I've lived in Las Piernas most of my life. There are only a handful of places in southern California where people really settle down, and Las Piernas is one of them. Lots of third generation locals. I suppose that's no big deal compared to some parts of the country, but in the L.A. area . . ."

"You're right. People are born and die in Las Piernas, and you look around and most people in neighboring towns are moving every few years. I love the place."

We reached the outskirts of a town that looked like it hadn't changed much in fifty years. A pockmarked sign announced that this was "Gila Bend—Home of 1700 Friendly People and Five Old Crabs." The highway joined up with Interstate 8 at Gila Bend, and in turn became Pima Avenue. It looked as if Gila Bend was struggling through some tough times. Every third or fourth building stood abandoned. There were four or five motels designed on varying themes, and about as many fast-food places and gas stations. A couple of convenience stores rounded out the picture. I had just about reached the end of the town when I spotted the City Hall, which was attached to the Gila Bend Museum and Arizona Tourist Information Center.

"You passed the sheriff's station several blocks ago," Pete said, as I started to pull in to ask directions.

"If you knew that, why didn't you speak up?"

"I wanted to see the rest of the town."

Exasperated, I turned the car around and headed back up the street.

Soon we came to a fairly new one-story building of brown brick with Spanish tiles on the roof. The Maricopa County Sheriff's Office. I pulled into a parking space.

"Okay," I said, "let's find out what they have on Hannah."

"Don't get your hopes up," Pete warned.

We opened the car doors and were met with a blast of dry heat. We made our way into the building and felt the chill of air conditioning inside. "Out of the frying pan, into the freezer," mumbled Pete.

It was a small station that also served as a part of the court system and as a detention center. We went up to a window and pressed an intercom button. A woman detention officer came to the window. Pete showed his ID and asked her if she would please let a deputy sheriff know we were there. A few minutes later, a door to our left was opened, and a tall man in a tan uniform came out to greet us. There was a warm smile on his rugged features. "You must be the folks from California. I'm Enrique Ramos," he said. He was a big man, but he moved with ease and grace. I guessed him to be about fifty.

Pete extended a hand. "Pete Baird. I think I talked to you on the phone. This is the friend of Mr. O'Connor's I told you about, Irene Kelly."

Ramos gave me a firm handshake. "Sorry to hear about Mr. O'Connor. I got a kick out of talking to him on the phone. I was looking forward to meeting him in person. Come on back."

He motioned us to follow him through the door to a small back office.

"You know, as slow as it is around here sometimes, I don't think anybody but your friend could have talked me into going through our old missing-persons files from the 1950s. But he kind of got my interest going with all his talk about teeth and so on. Besides, I figured him to be the kind of person who would bug the hell out of me if I didn't respond to his request."

"You figured right," I said. "He always tried the friendly approach first, but he could make a royal pain out of himself if need be."

Ramos smiled. "I thought so." He gestured to a couple of straight-back wooden chairs and we sat. He pulled a folder out of a filing cabinet and sat behind his desk.

"Had to go into the old archives to find stuff like this—all on microfiche now. Well, anyway, when you've only got a few hundred people in town, you don't have many go missing in a year. In 1955, we weren't the great metropolis we are now. I know it's hard for people from a big city to imagine this place being any smaller than it is now, but it was." He opened the folder and looked over some notes.

"In 1955, we had three missing persons. One was an old woman who probably had what we now call Alzheimer's, and she wandered off along the fence of the damned gunnery range—it's just across the road—the MPs found her, but it was winter and she never really recovered from her time outdoors.

"You might say we also found a young boy who ran off from home, but really he came back on his own; according to the notes here, no worse for the adventure.

"There was one more we didn't find: a young woman, about twenty, who worked in the feed store. She was still living with her folks at the time. Her mother reported her missing on June 16, 1955, but there was evidence that she left on her own; she had purchased a bus ticket to San Diego the previous evening. Couldn't trace her from there. Guy at the Greyhound depot here said she gave him just about every last cent she had to go to California, and San Diego was as far as it would take her. So we figured she might have just got tired of life in Gila Bend. We checked around and a girl she worked with said she had talked a lot about how she was going to marry a rich kid from Phoenix. Well, we couldn't figure out why she'd go to California if the rich kid was in Phoenix, but maybe he was going to meet her there."

"Had she ever mentioned this kid to her parents?" I asked.

"No, but it was pretty clear she hadn't been abducted, and she was over eighteen, so there wasn't much we could do about it. Her folks never made much out of it once we told them about the bus ticket.

"Now along comes your friend Mr. O'Connor, thirty-five years later, with his story. I did a little more digging around and found this. A picture from her high school graduation, in 1953." He pushed a small black and white photo across the desk, and Pete and I both rose from our chairs to look at it.

"Well, I'll be goddamned," said Pete.

Except for small differences in her looks, a little something about her nose and lips, there was no mistaking the resemblance to MacPherson's computer composites.

"It's Hannah," I said.

"Who?" asked Ramos.

I handed the computer drawing over to Ramos. "Hannah's sort of a nickname we've used for her over the years." I didn't want to tell him why. "What was her real name?" I asked.

"Assuming this is the same woman—and I agree, it looks a lot like her—her real name was Jennifer. Jennifer Owens."

"Jennifer Owens," I said aloud, then repeated it in my mind. Suddenly, I felt tears well up in my eyes. O'Connor should have been the first one to hear her name. She had been his obsession for thirty-five years. It was his work that had led us this far. He had come so very close to learning who she was. God, how proud he would have been. It might have eased a little of that pain he carried around for his sister.

Ramos was looking at me. "You okay, Miss Kelly?"

"Yes, I'm sorry. Just thinking of how pleased O'Connor would have been. He was . . . especially concerned about Hannah—Jennifer. Had been from the start. It's hard to explain."

"He told me about his sister," Ramos said.

I was surprised, and didn't hide it. Ramos met my look with an understanding smile. "I think he was afraid I wouldn't take this seriously."

Pete was looking between us, but neither of us offered him an explanation. "So," he asked Ramos, "are her parents still around?"

"Yeah, her mother is still living," Ramos said. "Old man's been dead some years now. But her mother lives out in a trailer off Highway 85. You probably passed it on the way here. She doesn't have a phone. I'll take you out there if you want to go."

Pete stood up. "Yeah, if you don't mind." He sighed and ran his hand through his hair. "If I live to be a hundred, I'll never get used to this part of the job."

We climbed into the front seat of a large green-and-white Jeep Cherokee that had the sheriff's logo on its doors. About five miles back on Highway 85, we turned off onto a dirt road that ran through some fenced acreage with cattle here and there. It was easy to see why a four-wheel drive vehicle was necessary. We jolted our way down a road that had so many potholes, NASA could have tested lunar-landing vehicles on it. Finally we came to a stop outside an opening in the barbed-wire fence; from the opening, a gravel drive led back to a trailer. Ramos honked and waited awhile. Soon the trailer door swung open and a thin gray-haired lady stared out and then waved to us. Ramos slowly pulled into the drive, trying not to raise dust.

"Hello, Enrique!" she barked out in a raspy voice. "Who you brought with you?"

"A couple of folks from California, Mrs. Owens."

"California! Well, come on in out of the sun. It's hotter than hell out. A couple of old devils like Enrique and I can take it, but you folks are probably just about baked."

The trailer was an old silver one, with light wood paneling. By the time the four of us had squeezed in, it felt as if we had quite a crowd in there.

After introductions, she motioned us to sit down on a couch behind a Formica table. On a shelf below a window were several framed photos of Jennifer. Baby pictures, family pictures. Jennifer with another young girl. Jennifer standing outside the trailer. A larger version of the graduation photo. She had been a beautiful blonde with a shy, closed-mouth smile.

Mrs. Owens went over to the refrigerator and came back with a big pitcher of lemonade. She brought out four ornate glasses on a tray covered with an old lace doily.

I felt like shit. I glanced at Pete, and knew he felt the same.

"So what brings a police officer all the way out from California to see a seventy-year old desert rat?" she asked.

"Why don't you sit down for a minute here, Mrs. Owens?" Ramos suggested.

She gave him an inquisitive look with her china blue eyes and slowly sat down. "What's this all about, Enrique?"

"It's about Jennifer, Mrs. Owens."

"Jennifer? My Jennifer?"

He nodded.

"My God, she's dead. She's dead, isn't she?"

"I'm sorry, we believe so, yes."

She began to cry. She got up from the table and stumbled back into a bedroom and shut the door, which didn't muffle the rising wail of grief. We sat immobilized, none of us looking at the other. After a while we heard water running. She stepped out, drying her face on a pink towel.

"I'm sorry," she said to us. "You'd think after thirty-five years I wouldn't care if I ever saw her again. But I've always hoped—" She broke off.

"Of course, ma'am," Pete said, "that's only natural. And we are very sorry to have to be the ones to end those hopes."

"What about my grandchild?" she asked suddenly.

We were all startled.

"Grandchild?" repeated Ramos.

"Jennifer ran away because she was pregnant. She ran off to be with the father. Who is he? And what became of my grandchild?"

If I had doubts that Hannah and Jennifer were the same person, this last question ended them. Jennifer looked like the woman in the pictures, came from a Southwestern town with high levels of fluoride in the water, disappeared near the date Hannah was found, and she was pregnant.

We all exchanged looks. I went over to her and put an arm around her. "This is a very difficult story to tell, Mrs. Owens. Please sit down."

For a moment it seemed she would resist this idea, but then she meekly allowed me to lead her back to the chair.

I sat back down, across from her.

"Tell me," she said quietly.

"On June 17, 1955," I began, "a woman's body was found on the beach in Las Piernas. We now believe that woman was Jennifer."

"1955! Dead since 1955!" she exclaimed, but then fell silent.

"The woman was guessed to be about twenty years old. She was two months pregnant when she died. She was murdered."

"Murdered! Why? Why would anyone want to kill Jennifer?"

"That's one of the reasons we're here, Mrs. Owens. We don't know. Whoever killed her—" I tried to find the right words. "Whoever killed her took steps to make it hard to identify Jennifer." I rushed on. "A friend and co-worker of mine was a reporter on our local paper. His own sister had been killed and hadn't been found for five years. That happened a few years before Jennifer was found. He sort of adopted the case of this unidentified woman and tried to learn all he could. He ran a column about it every year. He used to tell me that he knew somewhere someone worried about her, the way his family had worried about his sister.

"Not long ago, a new coroner came to work in our city; he found new evidence about Jennifer. He got help from a forensic dentist. Did Jennifer have stains on her teeth?"

"Yes, poor dear," she said, glancing up at the photographs. "She was always so self-conscious about them. From the water here, you know. Too much fluoride."

"More than anything, those stains led us to Gila Bend. Unfortunately, my friend died before he could learn your daughter's identity. He knew that this would be very sad news to you, but I know he hoped it would be better than always wondering what became of her."

She was quiet for a while, then said, "It's true. At least now I know. Thirty-five years of hell. I've sat here and wondered why she hated us so much that she could never write so much as a postcard. I wondered if she was married, if the baby was a boy or a girl. I wondered why she wouldn't at least let the child see his grandmother. I wondered if she was dead. I wondered if she was being tortured. I wondered if she had amnesia. You wouldn't even believe some of the things I've wondered. At least that's over."

"How did you learn she was pregnant?" I asked.

"Oh, I nearly beat that information out of a cousin of hers. The weekend before she left, Jennifer had gone up to Phoenix to see her cousin Elaine. Elaine Owens—she's the daughter of my husband's brother. My husband was never more than a cattleman, and God rest his soul, not a very good one at that. But his brother did real good for himself. Made some money up in Jerome on copper, and sold out long before the bottom dropped out of the market. Went on to invest in God knows what all, but he certainly had the Midas touch.

"Elaine and Jennifer were about the same age, and even though they never paid much attention to us, the family was fond of Jennifer, and she got invited up to Phoenix pretty regular. I don't know. Looking back on it, it seems that was the cause of a lot of trouble."

"In what way?" I asked.

"Jennifer was always so unhappy when she came back. Who could blame her? She lived high on the hog the whole time she was there. Elaine would loan her clothes and they would go to parties with rich kids and so on. Then she'd come back here to little old Gila Bend and the feed store and this tiny little trailer.

"Anyway, this last time she went up to see Elaine, she came back in a real state. She would cry for no reason. Next thing I know, she's taken a bus to San Diego."

"Did you know anyone there?" Pete asked.

"Not a soul. So I drove up to Phoenix and just about skinned Elaine alive. She finally told me that Jennifer was pregnant and had gone off to California to find the father. I always figured that little snot knew who the father was, but she swore up and down that Jennifer didn't tell her his name and I couldn't get it out of her. Needless to say, we never had much to do with that side of the family after that."

"Do you still have their address?" Pete asked.

"Well, I've got one from back then. They might still be there, but I don't know. It's been a long time. Let me see." She got up and pulled open a kitchen drawer full of papers, and picked out a little address book. She put on a pair of reading glasses and read off a Phoenix address as Pete wrote it down.

She looked up over the rim of the glasses. "Did you find a little gold ring? Her daddy's mother gave her a gold ring with a little ruby in it. Was she wearing it?"

Pete and I looked at one another.

"No, ma'am," he said quietly, "we didn't find a ring."

25

Nobody said a word on the ride back to Gila Bend. When we reached the station, Pete looked up at Ramos. "You gonna tell her?" he asked.

"About the body? Yeah, I'll tell her. But not right away. Let this sink in first. Hell, she's over seventy years old. But she's made of strong stuff, you know?"

We nodded. Pete asked if he could make some calls. I told him I was going to walk around a little, but would meet him back at the station for lunch in about twenty minutes. Ramos accepted our invitation to join us.

They went into the station and I walked across the street to one of the motels. This one was done up in a flying-saucer and rocket ship motif. Outdoors, it was like walking around inside a clothes dryer. But once I was back indoors, I got gooseflesh from the chill. I kept thinking that the local people must adapt to rapid temperature changes like nobody else on earth. I looked around and found a pay phone. I called the paper and asked for Lydia.

"City Desk," came the response.

"Lydia? It's Irene. I'm calling from Gila Bend."

"Are you okay?"

"Fine. Listen, are you near an open terminal? Or can you connect me to someone who is? I'm out here without a laptop or modem but I think I've got something that shouldn't wait until I get back tonight. Can I give it to you over the phone?"

"Sure," she said, "hang on." She covered the receiver and I could hear her shooing people away from her desk. "Okay," she said at last, "I'm all set."

I gave her the story the best I could. I figured Wrigley would love touting the fact that largely through the efforts of O'Connor, a thirty-five-year old mystery had been solved. We had found Hannah's hometown just three days before the anniversay of her death. I briefly went over the work done by O'Connor, Hernandez, MacPherson, and law-enforcement officials in both cities that had led to the tentative identification.

More gingerly than I should have, I told as much as I could bear to tell about Mrs. Owens, trying to avoid feeling that I had taken advantage of being there at a time when she was vulnerable.

I also recapped the local angle: O'Connor's death, his son's beating, the deadly car chase and the sidewalk hit-and-run killing, all possibly linked to the old case. I wound up with the standard "investigations-are-proceeding" lines.

"That's it, Lydia," I said when I finished.

"Whew!" she said, "you've had a busy morning."

"Yeah, I've got pretty mixed feelings about it, too."

"You liked her mother, didn't you?"

"Yes, I did. I guess I went too soft there. Hell's bells, Lydia, you should have been there. I feel lousy about it. I haven't gotten my hide thickened up enough yet. Give me another two or three interviews with parents of dead children and I'll be able to do this kind of story without batting an eye." I took a deep breath. I realized I was getting defensive. "I guess I can't trade on anybody else's misery right now. I'm too rocky myself."

"Believe me, Irene, I understand. You know how I hate that 'invasive-but-it-sells-papers' stuff that Wrigley's so in love with. Besides, Phoenix is less than an hour's flight away, so if Big Bad John doesn't like the way you wrote it, I'm sure he'll send somebody out there tonight to steal a photo of Jennifer off that shelf and take a few pictures of Mrs. Owens crying. By the way—he put your piece from yesterday on A-one."

"Slow news day, huh?"

"Where is this modesty coming from?"

"Must be the heat out here. Anyway, got a couple of other loose ends to take care of before I head back. Everything going okay with you?"

"Nervous about my hot date tonight, but okay otherwise."

"You'll be fine."

"Hmm. I hope so. Well, I better flag John Walters down. I think he'll be pleased, kiddo."

"Hope you're right."

We hung up and I fished the number of the downtown branch of the Bank of Las Piernas out of my purse. I dialed and got through to the switchboard. "Ann Marchenko, please," I said.

There was a pause. "May I ask who is calling?"

"Irene Kelly," I said.

There was another pause and then a couple of rings. I was surprised when a man's voice answered. "Irene?"

"Guy?"

"Yes, hello! Why didn't you tell me you were a famous newspaper reporter? I saw your byline on the front page today. How are you doing?"

"I'm fine. And I'm not at all famous, but thanks for noticing the byline. I was trying to reach Ann Marchenko."

"Yes, I thought you might call today, so I asked the switchboard to give your call to me. Irene, I'm sorry, Ann Marchenko phoned in this morning and quit her job."

"Quit? Without notice? Why?"

"She wouldn't say why, she just told us she wouldn't be in again. It leaves us in quite a fix, I'm afraid. But as for you—perhaps someone else can help? Really, if there is anything I can do, please allow me to help. The bank isn't about to receive some bad publicity, is it?"

"No, no, I doubt that's the case. It was something else. Really, Guy, I can't think of anything you can help me with right now. I really didn't have anything specific to ask her. I'll let you know, though." I thought of Ramona Ralston. "Guy, I'm very sorry about—yesterday."

"That was not your fault, Irene. It was terrible, I agree. A horrible, horrible thing that happened. But it was not your fault."

"Thanks."

"And now I have a special favor to ask of you—perhaps it will provide a small distraction."

"Yes?"

"I would be honored if you would be my guest at a rather boring affair—I am invited to a political fund-raising banquet for one of our major depositors, Andrew Hollingsworth, the district attorney. If you would not mind being my guest, I'm sure the evening would pass less painfully. I'm giving you short notice, I'm afraid—it's tomorrow night. As an added attraction, you can enter the hallowed Sheffield Estate overlooking the beautiful Pacific. All this and the polite attentions of a former hockey player with a charming accent. What do you say?"

I laughed. "It's the best offer I've had all day. But I must warn you that I probably would have been sent along by the paper, so in turn you must warn the Hollingsworths that your guest is there as a working journalist."

"Oh, so I have invited you somewhere you would already have gone on your own. That's not so fun. Still, I think you are saying yes."

"I am."

"Can I pick you up about seven, then?"

"Fine."

"Where?"

This posed a problem. I didn't feel comfortable giving out Lydia's address, even to people who probably weren't at all involved in this mess. I was running low on clean clothes over at Lydia's, and anything fancy enough to wear to a political fund-raiser would be back at my house. I hadn't been there to collect my mail either. I gave Guy my address.

"*Bien*. I'll see you tomorrow."

"Guy, I do have a favor to ask. Would you please call Ann Marchenko at home and ask her to give me a call at the paper?"

"The bank is not involved?"

"I doubt it very much."

"Well, I will ask her to call you then."

I gave him the number at the paper and hung up. My twenty minutes were up, so I walked back to the sheriff's station. Pete and Enrique Ramos were standing in the lobby.

"So," Pete said, "think it will make page one?"

"Have you got that motel pay phone tapped?" I asked Ramos.

"Come on, old Pete here would be a pretty lousy detective if he couldn't guess what phone calls a reporter would run off to make on a story like this."

"Yeah, give me a break, Irene. Besides, I promised Frank I'd keep an eye on you. So who was the second call to?"

"Never mind the second call."

"Oooh, aren't we touchy?" he said.

I felt like bashing him one, but I figured he probably knew how to bash back. Besides, I was in a sheriff's station.

He smirked. "I made four calls myself. One to the department, the second to Phoenix Homicide, and the third to St. Anne's. Frank's not there anymore."

"Not there?"

"Nope, so I guess that eliminates St. Anne's as *your* second call. Too bad. Anyway, they sent him home. That was the fourth call. They sent Mike Sorenson over to keep an eye on him, and the big lout answered the phone when I called over to Frank's house. Almost wouldn't put me through—can you imagine? Frank sounds a hell of lot better than he did yesterday. Says hello to you and wants to know if we'll stop in if we get the chance—he's already got cabin fever, I guess."

"That would be great. I can't believe he's home already."

"Pretty standard for his type of injuries, I guess. If it's just a matter of hurting, they send you home to heal—better that way, you don't have to keep eating hospital food. Speaking of food—Enrique here is going to show us where we can find genuine Mexican food. Right?"

We ate lunch at one of those hole-in-the-wall cafes that are always the best for Mexican. Pete offered to drive back to Phoenix, so I had a cold *cerveza* with my enchiladas. Just knowing how hot it was outside made the beer taste better. The spicy sauce made it mandatory.

After a brief tussle over who would treat whom to lunch, Las Piernas hosted Gila Bend, and we thanked Enrique for all his help. With assurances that we'd keep each other informed, we drove off.

"Now," said Pete, turning up the road to Phoenix, "we'll go visit the City Mouse."

26

It was about 2 P.M. when we got back to Phoenix. We had four hours before our flight back. Pete got talkative again, this time about an ex-wife who could have doubled as any of your basic shrews. He wound down on it pretty quickly, though, ending up on a long spiel about how tough it is to be married to a cop. Again meaningful looks.

"Pete, do you like being single?" I asked, thinking I could get him to see the possibility that I might enjoy it as well.

"Sure I do. I mean, once in a while I wish there was somebody special, but I keep busy. And I've got friends. I'm not such a lonely guy. But I get you. You think I'm nagging you about being single at your age. Well, you know, they say you got a better chance of being hit by an A-bomb than gettin' married at *your* age."

"I don't think they call them A-bombs anymore, Pete."

He went on as if I hadn't spoken. "I mean, especially if you've *never* even been married *once*. Hell, if I were you, I'd run around telling people I was divorced. At least it would sound like somebody took an interest at one time, if you know what I mean."

"I know exactly what you mean. I just listened to a half-hour speech on what a crappy marriage you had. Gee, is this the great kinda stuff I've been missing all my life? And to think I've been such a wallflower the whole time, never knowing so much as the blush of romance! You got a date Friday night, oh, man-in-whom-someone-once-took-an-interest?"

"So what if I don't. You don't either."

"Like hell I don't. I'm going out to Sheffield Estates to see how the other half lives, on the arm of a tall dark stranger."

"Who the hell are you talking about? Frank's laid up, I know for damn sure he's not going out to the Hollingsworths'. Probably some nerd from the paper, going with you to cover some political powwow."

"Ha! Some detective."

"So who is it?"

"Figure it out for yourself."

We were in downtown Phoenix at this juncture, and the temperature outside the car could not have been any hotter than the one inside. We pulled up to the headquarters of the Phoenix Public Safety Department in silence.

"Pete—"

"Aw, forget it. We got work to do. We can fight all the way home on the plane."

"Truce then?"

"Okay, truce."

We shook on it.

I followed him into the tall building. His call from Gila Bend had prepared the Phoenix police for our visit. We were escorted down a long hallway to a little room with burgundy couches and chairs. We sat there for a minute, fidgeting as if we were in church, when a statuesque beauty opened the door. She was tall and thin and had a single streak of gray that came out of one side of her long raven hair. She was a knockout.

A heavyset man stopped behind her and said, "You using this room, Pazzi?"

She told him she was, then turned back to us.

"Pete Baird, Las Piernas Homicide?" she asked in a husky voice. "I'm Detective Rachel Giocopazzi, Phoenix Homicide. Or, as you've heard, 'Pazzi' around here. But that's because Italian and words of more than two syllables are too much for these guys."

"Not for me," said Pete, "my mother's maiden name was Gigliotti."

"*Ah, paesano!*" she said with a smile that apparently came close to rendering Pete unconscious, as he just grinned back shyly. I couldn't believe it. She looked over at me.

"Irene Kelly," I said, extending a hand. "Not half-Italian, not even a cop. But happy to meet you."

"Same here. I hear you're following up a very cold trail?"

"It's heated up." I gave her a brief version of the story of Jennifer Owens and the last few days in Las Piernas.

"I'd say you've had a rough week, lady. So you want to talk to the cousin?"

"Right," Pete managed to say.

"I think that can be arranged without much trouble," Rachel said. "The family's fairly prominent, but you're not thinking of bringing charges against anyone in the family, are you?"

"No, ma'am," he said, "strictly trying to figure out what might have happened to the Owens girl."

"You're going to have to stop calling me 'ma'am.' If I ever introduce you to my mother, call her ma'am. Meanwhile, I'm Rachel."

"Rachel."

"*Buono!* Shall we call first? She's Elaine Owens Tannehill now. Her parents still live in the area, but they're out near a country club in the desert. She and her husband live in the old family mansion."

"If you don't mind, I'd like to drop in unannounced," Pete said.

Rachel looked at him. "Why not? The maid will just give us the heave-ho if the lady of the house doesn't want to talk to us."

She took us out through a blast of heat to a white police car and we drove off to a ritzy section of Phoenix. We wound our way up a road to a hilltop that overlooked the city. A long wrought-iron fence covered with vines ran for some distance. We came to a break in the fence where two brick pillars stood. I could see a similar set a little ways down the road. We turned right and drove up a sloping circular drive to the front of a place that could have been used to film *Gone with the Wind,* a white Georgian-style mansion that commanded a magnificent view in every direction. I found myself looking down at my simple outfit and immediately felt out of place. How had young Jennifer felt, coming here from the silver trailer?

We went to the front door, a massive carved affair. Rachel seemed perfectly at ease. She rang the doorbell. As we waited I turned around and looked out across the perfect lawn to the road. I grabbed Pete's arm in panic when I noticed a car at the entrance we had just come through. The driver was staring at me, grinning. As Pete turned around, the car peeled out, but not before I'd recognized the driver. "Hawkeyes," I said aloud.

"Who?" asked Pete.

"Sorry. Name I made up for the guy on the plane—the last one on."

"Shit." Pete pounded on the door.

"Am I not clued in on something?" Rachel asked.

"Irene just saw someone watching the front of the house—he may be someone who was on our flight from Las Piernas," Pete explained. He looked around anxiously. "You know if there's any other way in? This Elaine Owens could be in danger."

"You think he's alone?"

"Couldn't be positive, but I think so. Irene, stay here."

"And let him come back and find me standing out here by myself? Forget it."

"*Capa tosta!*" Pete exclaimed and ran around to the back of the house.

"Hardhead," Rachel explained, and we started to run after him. I tried to keep up with her long strides as she followed Pete through a small gate. We rounded the corner of the house just as he made his way through an open sliding glass door. He ran back out almost immediately. "Rachel! Call for an ambulance!"

He ran back in and Rachel went full speed back to the car. I followed Pete to a room nearer the front of the house, but I followed slowly, afraid of what I would find there. As I came through the doorway of the room, I saw a woman tied to a chair. An ornate dining-room chair. Her shoes were off and her head was bent forward. On the top of her head a dark-red patch matted her platinum-blond hair. Pete grabbed a beautiful lace napkin from a formal table setting and pressed it to her head. "Mrs. Tannehill!" he shouted. "Elaine!" again and again.

I stared, suddenly realizing that this woman in her fifties was Elaine Owens Tannehill. Unlike her cousin, she had aged.

Pete stopped shouting. Elaine Tannehill was no longer breathing. We both heard her make a gurgling noise. He looked at her with alarm. She coughed once, and as I watched in horror, blood gushed out of her mouth and down the front of her elegant suit.

Pete frantically looked at the back of the chair. "Goddamn-son-of-a-whore! He shot her in the back! Her lungs have been filling up with blood the whole time I shouted at her like a dumb son-of-a-bitch!" He held his face in his hands for a few moments, calming himself. "Stay here," he said. "And don't touch anything."

He ran out of the room. I tried to look anywhere but at the dead woman. That was how I noticed something odd. An iron was plugged into the wall. In the dining room. Near Elaine Owens Tannehill's feet.

From a distance I heard Pete say, "Oh, sweet Jesus Christ." It was not a prayer.

27

Rachel came in carrying a blanket, and stopped cold when she saw the lifeless figure in the chair. She walked over and stooped down to look at the face. "Is it Elaine Tannehill?" I asked.

She nodded.

"She's dead," I said, realizing as I said it that Rachel knew that already.

Just then, Pete came back. "Bastard tortured her with the iron, then shot her in the back. I didn't even see the wound till after she coughed."

"Nothing you could've done if you'd seen it, Pete, and you know it," Rachel said. "Her lungs had probably been filling up with blood the whole time we were out knocking on the door. What about the maid?"

Pete shook his head.

"Irene," Rachel said, bringing me out of a fog that kept trying to settle over me. "Do you think you can describe the guy you saw? I put out a call on the car, but I didn't get a look at him."

I told her all I could remember about him.

She started to go back out to the car when Pete called to her. "Rachel, can you get somebody over to the parents' house? And maybe check on anybody else in the family? Who knows what the hell he wanted."

She nodded and left.

Pete looked over at me. "Let's get you out of here," he said. I didn't argue. He led me into another room, where we sat on a couch, not saying anything.

The wail of sirens soon reached us. Pete pulled back a curtain and from the window behind the couch we could see the police cars and ambulance beginning their climb up the road. "Son of a bitch probably watched us coming," he said angrily.

Soon the house was a swarming hive of activity and uniforms. I tried to stay out of the way of police, paramedics, and other officials who seemed to arrive in an endless stream. I overheard Pete telling someone the maid was downstairs, her throat cut. Rachel walked over to me. "Come on outside. You've had enough of this kind of stuff." She walked me out to the large veranda and sat me down in a shady spot. "You gonna be okay?" she asked.

"Sure, thanks." She hurried back inside. I fought down that now familiar set of sensations: queasiness, shakiness, weepiness. I forced myself to concentrate on the scenery around me. Before long I could feel my fears giving way before the view of city and farmland below, the distant mesas and muted red and sandy colors of the desert stretching beyond the city boundaries. The sun was hot and bright. Just below the veranda a beautiful garden was laid out in bright splashes of color. Birds and insects chirped as a hot breeze blew my hair around my face. I felt a welcome numbness gradually come over me. Then another siren would go up or down the hill, and I would have to start all over again.

I sat there for a couple of hours, I guess; I'm not really sure how long it was I waited. Eventually Pete and Rachel came walking across the stonework toward me. I noticed they seemed to be quite chummy, gesturing and smiling as they spoke in Italian to one another. They both grew circumspect as they drew nearer.

"Ready to go?" Pete asked. "I called the airline and changed our flight out. Leaves about seven. That okay with you?"

I nodded. "Did they find him?"

They exchanged looks. "Not yet," Rachel said. "But I doubt he'll use the airport. He'll know we're watching for him. We've got people on both the state line and the Mexican border watching for him and the car. The airport too, but I doubt he'll fly out of here—too risky. You gave us a good description. A guy like this has to have a sheet a mile long."

"She's right," Pete said. "In fact, I remember an old case in Las Piernas where somebody used an iron like that. I wasn't on that one, though. I'll have to look up one of the guys that worked it when we get back."

I stood up, reluctant to leave my little refuge. But I was anxious to get back home to Las Piernas as well.

"I'll take you back to your car," Rachel said. "We can talk on the way."

Pete told me that Mr. Tannehill and the Owenses had been contacted. Everybody was safe and nobody knew why anyone would want to kill Elaine Tannehill or her maid.

"Did you mention Jennifer Owens to them?" I asked.

"Yes," Rachel said. "At first they were kind of high and mighty about her, but when I told them what had become of her, they changed their tune. They even talked about getting in touch with Jennifer's mother. They didn't have any ideas about who got Jennifer pregnant. Maybe this guy you call 'Hawkeyes' was just trying to find out what Elaine knew."

"It obviously isn't a problem for him to go around murdering people on the off chance they know something about this case," I said.

"That's what's bugging me," Pete said. "I think Irene's right. We need to keep searching the Tannehill place, looking for something that connects Elaine to the guy who got Jennifer pregnant. Son of a bitch is really stupid. You know, if he had left things alone, we probably wouldn't have been able to get much farther than identifying the Jane Doe. It's an old case; nobody would have spent much time on it."

"Maybe he has a lot to lose," I said. "And maybe he got worried about people who might be persistent enough to figure it out, like O'Connor. You know he never would have let it rest. Well, I won't either. Maybe he knows that."

"He's going too far, too fast. He's bound to screw up."

"I hope you're right," I said, looking out the car window. I wondered if this Mr. X would screw up before I got killed or had my feet ironed. I didn't feel like talking about it and tried not to think about it. I let my mind go away from it all again. Sensing my mood, Pete and Rachel chatted about other subjects.

When we pulled in at the police department, I decided to give them some time by themselves, and myself some time to myself, so I offered to follow them back to the airport in the rental. Pete immediately approved of this idea, thanking me as he handed over the keys. Subtle guy, Pete.

I drove like a zombie, just keeping the back of the police car in front of me at a polite distance. If another police car had come along, I might have followed it anywhere. Before long we were back at the airport.

We checked Pete's gun in again and made our way over to the gate, stopping to buy him a pack of gum at the gift shop. Rachel sat with us until they called our flight. I noticed Pete wasn't powering down any gum.

I went over to a pay phone and called the paper. Lydia was gone by then, but Morry, the city editor, was still on the desk. I gave him what I could by way of an update.

Pete didn't have to tell me this time to wait to get on, even though none of us believed Hawkeyes would be taking a flight out of Arizona.

When they made the final boarding call, Rachel stood up and gave me a big hug. "You can handle it, Irene. Anyone who can survive a day with this meatball can handle anything."

"Hey, don't I get a hug?" Pete asked.

Rachel walked over and grabbed his face, pinching his cheeks and shaking them. "No, you don't," she said, laughing, and walked off with a wave.

"Nobody's done that since I was nine," he said, watching her go.

We boarded the plane. I fell asleep before Pete had his first stick of gum, and slept all the way to Las Piernas.

28

"Yo, **Rip Van Winkle!** They're gonna want to clean this plane. Come on, wake up, I'll buy you a cup of coffee." Pete was nudging me. Drowsily, I sat up and followed him off into the terminal. He led me into the airport coffee shop, sat me down and ordered two cups of coffee. I looked out the window into the dark until the waitress brought it. He watched me take a few sips, then said, "Are you ever going to speak to me again?"

"Sure I will. I'm sorry. I'm just . . . I don't know, Pete. I don't even know how to describe it anymore."

"Then don't try. Just drink your coffee. You up for a visit to Frank? Or do you want me to take you straight home?"

I thought about it. "I'm tired, but I'd like to see Frank."

He smiled at this, so I thought I'd do a little prying of my own. "So what's with you and Rachel?" I asked.

"Ah, she is gorgeous, isn't she? I admit it, I like her. But she's in Phoenix and I'm in Las Piernas."

"At least for now."

"You done with that coffee?"

"Hey, don't dish it out if you can't take it."

"All right, all right, I get you. How 'bout we make a pact—we'll avoid the subject of—for want of a better term, I'll say 'romantic interests'?"

"Sounds good to me."

We left for Frank's place. I realized that I had no idea where he lived. He had looked me up when he first moved down this way, but I had never been to his place. Pete drove us down near the beach, along a crowded row of little bungalows. He parked in front of one that was about a block from the water. I couldn't see much of it in the dark, but it looked fairly typical of the small wood-frame houses that were built along the beaches in the late 1930s.

It was about eight-thirty by the time we got there, and I wondered if Frank would still be awake. The lights were on, but that could be Sorenson, the officer who would be guarding Frank while he re-covered. We pushed open the gate of a low white picket fence and walked up to the front porch. We knocked and waited. The porch light came on. A large shadow came up to the glass at the top of the door, and we saw Sorenson peering down at us. He let us in, and told me that Frank was in the living room, which was toward the back of the house. Pete and Sorenson stayed behind to trade insults with one another in a manner that made it seem to be a long-standing tradition between them; I was anxious to see Frank, and made my way down the hallway.

I was surprised to see him sitting up on the couch, dressed in a gray sweat suit and white running shoes. "Don't tell me you've been out jogging," I said, "I wasn't expecting to see you up and around."

He grinned. "Good to see you. No, I haven't been jogging. These were just the most comfortable things I could find to wear." As I got closer I could see that the swelling had gone down from his lip, and his face was less puffy, though he still had the two black eyes and plenty of other bruises. He was pale, but all in all he looked a thousand times better than the day before. He started to stand up, and winced in pain.

"Don't push yourself," I said. "Go ahead, sit down, you almost had me convinced you'd been to Lourdes before you tried to stand up." He didn't argue and I took a seat on the other end of the couch.

"Ribs and head are still sore, and I look like I lost a fight, but at least I don't feel like I'm in a fog."

"I'm glad to see you looking so much better," I said, and smiled.

Pete and Sorenson came noisily into the room. "Hey, will you look at this guy?" Pete said, seeing Frank. "Hercules, I tell you. Why, he has the strength of ten men!"

"Shut up, Baird," Frank said, grinning up at Pete.

"Goddamn, Frank, I can't believe it. And here I was, all set to inherit," he said, looking around. The room was simply furnished, but felt very livable, not Spartan in any sense. The house had lots of windows, woodwork and built-in cabinets and shelves of the type so common in houses built in its time. In that way, it was not very different from my own.

Mike Sorenson turned to me and said, "Would you like something to drink, Miss Kelly? How about a beer or a Coke?"

"I'll opt for the caffeine, thanks."

He turned to Frank. "You doin' okay there, buddy?"

"Fine, Mike, thanks."

He started to walk off when Pete said, "Aren't you forgetting somebody?"

Sorenson stopped at the kitchen door and turned around, saying, "Why, yes, I believe I am." He flipped Pete the bird. Pete returned the favor with a gesture of his own.

Pete turned to Frank. "You supposed to watch him, or is he supposed to watch you?"

"Baird, you are a professional pain in his ass and you know it."

Pete laughed. "He makes it so easy."

Sorenson came out with a glass of Coke and ice, and sat down in a chair next to my end of the couch. Pete, giving up on being waited upon, went in to get a beer. He came back out and sat in a chair opposite Sorenson, near Frank. He lifted the beer toward Sorenson and said, "Thanks, pal."

"It was nothing," Sorenson said.

"So bring me up-to-date," Frank said. "I read about what happened in front of the bank yesterday." He looked over at me. "You didn't tell me, Irene," he chided.

"Sorry, Frank. You weren't feeling so hot and I was tired of thinking about it all."

"What happened in Gila Bend?"

Pete jumped in and told the story of our day in Arizona. As I was reminded of it, I could feel myself getting depressed, ebbing away from the excitement of seeing Frank doing so well and back into a sense of numbness. Pete was quite animated in his telling; but I felt myself becoming more withdrawn as he went on. By the time he got to the Tannehill part of the story, all I could see before me was Elaine Tanehill's last moments replayed again and again.

"Irene?" I vaguely heard Frank next to me and turned toward him. I tried a smile, but couldn't manage it.

"Mike," Frank said to Sorenson, "why don't you and Pete take a walk on the beach?"

I thought we were in for more banter, but he just said, "Sure. Let's go, Pete." And the two of them left without another word.

When they were gone, Frank patted the place next to him on the couch. "Scoot over here," he said.

I moved over.

He put an arm around me and I gingerly put my head on his shoulder, trying to avoid his ribs.

"The ribs aren't so bad," he said, reading my intentions. "It's the other side anyway."

I relaxed a little. He didn't say anything for a long while, just stroked my hair and held me.

"You must feel like your whole life has been turned upside down," he said quietly. "But it won't stay like this. Just keep telling yourself that. You've got to keep being a fighter, Irene. Don't let it beat you."

"I feel like it already has, Frank."

He reached over and took my hand. He ran his thumb gently along the backs of my fingers, not saying anything more.

I looked up at him. "I'll be okay," I said, and put my head back down on his shoulder. "How are you feeling?"

"Right now," he said with a grin, "I feel pretty damn good."

This mood was broken when we heard the front door open and Pete and Mike Sorenson came trooping back in.

"Uh-oh," Pete said, looking at us, "I told you we would interrupt something."

"Sorry, Frank," Sorenson said, "but I was freezing my nuts off out there."

"Hey, look," said Pete, "why don't Mike and I go out for a bite to eat or something?"

"Never mind, Pete," I said, "I need to be getting home. And I'm sure the Unsinkable Frank Harriman here could use some rest, too. Not to mention that Officer Sorenson is supposed to be keeping an eye on him. Okay if I come back tomorrow afternoon, Frank?"

"Sure," he said, "I'm probably not going into work until Monday."

"Thanks for the pep talk," I said.

"No problem. Take care of yourself."

We said our good-byes and Pete took me over to Lydia's. The house was dark when we pulled up. I had forgotten that she would be off on her big date.

"You gonna be here alone?" Pete asked, sounding a little worried.

"I'll be okay; there's a ferocious cat in there."

"Yeah, that cat's kind of famous in the department. We gave Frank hell about those scratches."

"Well, then you know I'm safe. Thanks for everything, Pete."

"See you later, Irene. I'll just wait out here for a while."

"I'm okay, really. If you're going to wait around until Lydia comes in, you may have a long wait. Might as well come in."

He shrugged. "Tell you what. Could I use your phone?"

As we walked in, Cody bit me on the ankle and then ran off down the hallway, apparently unhappy about having been abandoned. Pete called in to the department and arranged for a patrol car to make a few extra passes down our street.

"So long, Irene," he said as he walked out.

I locked up and climbed into bed. Cody joined me a few minutes later, acting as if nothing had happened. I pulled back the bedroom-window curtain and wasn't entirely surprised to see Pete still sitting out in his car at the curb.

I knew he was tired, but he wasn't going to break his pledge to Frank to watch over me.

I lay awake a long time, petting Cody, listening to him purr. "Cat, you miss me?" I asked him. He gave me a sandpaper kiss. I heard Lydia come in, but didn't get up to talk to her—I was afraid she'd think I'd stayed up waiting for her. I heard Pete's car drive off, and still I couldn't sleep. I decided to think of some pleasant memory. I put myself back on my grandmother's farm in Kansas. I was standing in a wheat field, watching the wind move the wheat in undulating waves of gold. Somehow the memory became a dream, and I was dancing through the wheat, feeling it brush against me while I held my face to the sun. I held my arms out to its warmth and whirled in slow, lazy circles, laughing as I turned. My grandmother, still alive in the dream, called to me, and I ran to her. I felt her soft apron and the smell of cinnamon as she hugged me with her thin old arms, and she said, "Child, what am I going to do with you?"

I woke up feeling fine.

29

"Hmm—something smells great. You making breakfast?"
Lydia called out to me as she made her way to the kitchen.

"Yeah, cinnamon toast. Here, have some."

"You always cut it up in little strips like this?"

"My grandmother did. I had a dream about her last night."

"I haven't had this in ages."

"Me neither." I sat down next to her, dishing out some scrambled
eggs and bacon. "A country breakfast. Hardens your arteries, but we
all got to live on the edge sometimes."

"This is great, Irene."

"Thanks. How was the date with Michael?"

"Eh."

" 'Eh?' "

"There was all this animal magnetism between us, but we couldn't
make much conversation. We just didn't have anything much to talk
about. We saw a movie, or it would have been the longest evening
of my life. After the movie, it was either make out all night or come
home alone and get a good night's sleep. God knows I've been horny
lately, but this is the nineties, not our college days, so Michael and
I left it at a goodnight kiss."

"You went that far on a first date?" I said with mock horror.

"First and last, I'm afraid," she said, shoving the morning edition
toward me. "You see the paper yet? People are going to get jealous."

Good old John Walters had given me another page one. The story
of Jennifer Owens was as public as it was going to be.

There were a pile of messages and O'Connor's mail waiting for
me at work. The mail made me think of the second envelope from

Wednesday, which I had completely forgotten. I opened my purse and found it.

It contained a note from MacPherson dated last week, saying he had found someone to do the computer drawings of the woman's face, and he would call when they were ready. I felt a great sense of relief. I hadn't been walking around for two days with some big clue stashed in my purse.

I sat down and began to go through the mail and messages. Yesterday, a note from Barbara, asking me to give her a call at the hospital when I got back. A call from MacPherson with "Says it's not urgent" written at the bottom of the message slip. Some calls from people I recognized as political organizers, probably about various people and issues in our upcoming election.

The mail was much the same, with the exception of one envelope. A scrawling, shaky hand was addressed to me, care of the *Express*, but marked "Personal & Confidential" in one corner. The return address was unfamiliar. Inside was a sheet of paper with a handwritten message:

Miss Kelly,

I understand you are now back at the newspaper. I tried calling you at Malloy & Marlowe to tell you I am deeply sorry about Mr. O'Connor. I have a few things to say, and no one left to say them to. I thought of you because I know you were his friend and co-worker, and I imagine you are now pursuing matters he left unfinished. This much I know of you.

As for Mr. O'Connor, it is important to me that you know that I always respected him. Had I known things would go so far, I would have told the truth long ago. But now I am tangled in a web I helped to weave. I cannot bear to live to see my forty-three years of service to this community overshadowed by what will undoubtedly follow. I ask you to forgive me for the unforgivable.

Emmet Woolsey

I re-read Emmet Woolsey's letter a half a dozen times. I felt uneasy holding this letter from a man who could not live with himself, who had been dead for three days. I knew it was evidence of a sort and should be turned over to the police; I also knew I should show it to John; but both actions seemed a violation of some kind of trust Woolsey had placed in me. I thought about how unwelcome an apology may sometimes be. I wasn't in a forgiving kind of mood.

I called Frank. It was early, but Sorenson answered on the second ring and told me they were both up and about. He handed the phone over to Frank.

"Good morning!"

His voice said he was in a cheerful frame of mind, and I immediately felt bad about calling. Maybe I wouldn't tell him about the letter after all.

"Good morning, Frank," I said, trying to lighten my tone.

"What's wrong?"

I wondered if I was ever going to be able to fool anybody about anything.

"Emmet Woolsey mailed a letter to me; I guess it's sort of a suicide note." I read it to him.

"Hmm."

I waited.

"They're going to want to take it as evidence," he said. "Do you have any problems with that?"

"None that I can't live with, but I should show the note to John. Okay?"

"Okay. I'll call in and ask someone to come by your offices." He paused, then asked, "Are you upset that Woolsey picked you to tell it to?"

"A little. I feel awkward. I can't forgive him. Not without knowing more than he's told me here. I feel sorry for him, but that's different."

"Somebody apparently had something on him. Guess we better try to find out why he was keeping things hidden about this case. I'll have somebody look into his background. Could you try back issues of the *Express* from around June and July 1955?"

"Sure, I'll go downstairs to the morgue and see what I can find out."

We said good-bye, and I got up and took the letter over to John Walters. He read it, grunted, walked over to a copier and ran off a couple of copies. "Here," he said, shoving the original and one copy toward me. "I don't even want to touch it. Goddamn coward worried about his fucking reputation. Makes me want to puke. You gonna find out who had his nuts in a vise?"

"Ooohwee. And I thought I was being stingy with him. Yeah, I want to know what he was afraid of. Must have been pretty bad if he stuck by his story through over thirty years of pestering by O'Connor."

"Don't tell me you're going soft on me, Irene. Are you forgetting what's happened because this bastard didn't have the balls to speak up?"

"No, I'm not likely to forget it."

"Hummph. Well, he's not getting a dime's worth of sympathy from me. You just think about Jennifer Owens's mother not knowing what happened to her daughter for thirty-five years. Go on, get back to work."

I went back to my desk and called MacPherson to bring him up to date and thank him for his help. Next I tried to call Barbara, but ended up just leaving a message for her at the nurse's station; apparently she had stepped out of Kenny's room for a moment. They wouldn't tell me anything about Kenny over the phone, except that he was still in intensive care.

I gathered the mail into a neat stack, and threw away the out-and-out junk. As I cleared off O'Connor's desk, I thought to myself that it was unnatural for it to be so clean. He never would have left it so orderly. I still felt like Goldilocks sitting in Papa Bear's chair, but I wasn't as uncomfortable as I had been a few days before.

I grabbed a notebook and headed down to the place where all the back issues of the *Express* were on file, as back issues were at any newspaper, in that place where dead news remains unburied—the morgue. And now, I thought, we'll see if Lazarus will rise.

30

The papers from the fifties were on microfilm, and so I used one of the aging machines down in that darkened area of the morgue to check the reels for the first two months of summer in 1955. The same thing happened this time that happens to me every time I go down to the morgue. I got hung up reading old articles and advertisements that caught my eye. The first one I came across was for a 1955 Packard—"The Patrician."

"One phone call delivers a new Packard to your door," the ad said.

Then I started wondering if porterhouse and T-bone steaks really were eighty-five cents a pound, like the "women's-pages" ads said. If they were, I supposed I could believe that a quart of ice cream was forty-five cents, too. There was a dress offered by a department store for $10.95, and it looked pretty snazzy. The models all wore gloves, hats, and pearl chokers. But what I really wanted was the "Davy Crockett Study Lamp" with six action scenes from his adventures.

I started paying more attention to news items. Neither the paper nor the town were as big in the 1950s as they were now, but there was still enough print to make me feel dizzy as the pages flashed across the screen.

Some of the headlines in mid-June 1955 looked sort of familiar, such as "Middle East Peace Talks Proposed," "County Budget Proposal Is Largest Ever," and "Soviet Minister Visits U.S.," while others caught my attention because I knew how they turned out: "Peron Claims Argentine Rebellion Finished," "Salk and Sabin Testify on Polio Vaccine," and a much smaller article, "South Vietnam Reds Tell U.S. 'Go Home.'" The local news included items such as "Downey Women's Club Honors HUAC Members" and "Committee Studies Fire-Department Integration."

Marilyn Monroe could be seen in *The Seven Year Itch* if you were willing to drive into L.A. to watch it at Grauman's Chinese. Locally, it was easier to catch *Jungle Jim and the Moon Men* or *The Creature with the Atom Brain*.

I don't know why I should have been startled by the large-type headlines that proclaimed "Woman's Mutilated Body Found Under Pier" on the front page of the June 18, 1955, issue. It was big local news, and there wasn't a chance that it would have received less sensational coverage. But now, knowing the future of this case—and having met the mother of the victim—I couldn't help but feel disturbed. O'Connor might have felt compassion for this anonymous victim and her family, but he had not been the only writer on the story; the other coverage was unflinching in its detail.

In issues over the next few days, the story had died down. With no clue to her identity surfacing, and little other progress being made, there was not much to feed to the public. Las Piernas City Councilman Richard Longren rallied his fellow council members to invest in better lighting by the pier and an expansion of the police force to increase beach patrols. I sat back thinking that our current mayor never missed a political trick, even then.

I rewound the microfilm to the date of Hannah's murder and went more slowly through each issue for that week. Page after page of reports that ranged from Congressional hearings to meetings of the Fuchsia Society. Then, in the local news section for Tuesday, June 21, 1955, I found my Lazarus:

Eyewitness to Fatal Accident Found
Coroner's Wife Will Not be Charged

Police announced today that no charges will be filed against Mrs. Blanche Woolsey, wife of Las Piernas Coroner Dr. Emmet Woolsey, in an accident that killed two last Sunday. A witness, whose identity was not revealed by police, saw the car of Mr. and Mrs. Henry Decker cross over a double yellow line and hit Mrs. Woolsey's vehicle at a curve on Hampsted Road before going over a cliff.

While other witnesses had earlier identified Mrs. Woolsey's car as the one seen weaving down the same road in a reckless fashion, this witness is apparently the only person to see the accident itself. Police refused to comment on why the witness might have delayed stepping forward until now.

Mrs. Woolsey remains hospitalized for injuries received in the accident.

So Woolsey's wife was saved from charges in what looked to be a felony drunk-driving case. But who had provided the witness? Could Frank find the witness's name in police records?

I kept looking through the issues for that week to see if anything more had been written on the accident, when I came across the society pages for Sunday, June 26. Over two different pages, large photographs, and lavish detail were given to what must have been the major wedding of the last half century in Las Piernas: the marriage of Elinor Sheffield to a young man who had been recently appointed to the staff of the district attorney's office—a young Harvard Law School graduate by the name of Andrew Hollingsworth—on the previous day.

Thinking of the Hollingsworths reminded me of Guy St. Germain and our plans for that evening. I was starting to wonder if it had been a mistake to accept his invitation. I kept asking myself why I had this urge to confess to Frank that I was going out with another man. Then I asked myself why I thought of it as confessing. It wasn't as if we were involved with one another in some exclusive arrangement. We really hadn't dated or anything. All we had done was have a picnic together. And been shot at and nearly killed in a car chase.

I rewound the microfilm and put it back in its box. I turned off the machine and sat there in the dark for a minute.

I didn't want to tell Frank, and I wasn't sure why. But I knew for damn sure that I didn't want him to hear about it from Pete Baird. Hell, considering Pete's basic buttinsky nature, I might already be too late to be the one to tell Frank about it. If I decided to tell him.

Nuts.

31

I went back upstairs and called Frank and told him what I had learned about Woolsey. He said he'd ask if Pete could spare some time to go through old files to find more information on the Decker accident and the shy witness. Hearing that he was going to be talking to Pete, I arranged to have lunch with Frank, thinking maybe I'd get a chance to talk to him about my plans for the evening. Since I had only been there once, I asked for directions to his place and told him I'd bring some sandwiches from his favorite deli, the Galley.

That settled, I spent the next few hours looking over some of the political stuff O'Connor had been covering, writing up a couple of brief pieces about events scheduled for the upcoming week. I went back through some of the computer notes, but I still couldn't make much out of the references to the mayor's race.

I did start to notice that almost every reference to the mayor's race had some connection to the one for the DA's office. I skimmed back over them a few more times. The notes on Hollingsworth were at least as plentiful as those on Mayor Longren. Most really weren't very revealing; they either seemed to chronicle fund-raisers held for the two races or contain general political background on the two men.

Both had held power in Las Piernas for decades, so there was little that was new in the background information. They were basically conservative, "law-and-order" types. Hollingsworth had a high conviction rate and Longren was an astute year-round grandstander. Running for city-wide office in Las Piernas was an expensive proposition, so incumbents never had too many problems getting re-elected.

It was easier for Hollingsworth to pay his campaign bills; he had married into the Sheffield fortunes. Longren struggled harder, but always seemed to manage reelection. There was some decline in his campaign war chest after the California campaign funding reporting laws went into effect in the mid-1970s, especially as the laws were made stronger over a series of later initiatives.

Those laws require candidates to file public reports which state the full name, address, occupation, and employer of anyone who contributes over ninety-nine dollars to a campaign in any one-year period. The idea is to give voters a chance to see who is backing whom and how much a candidate is dependent on a given supporter or company or political action committee. Longren's funding problems probably meant that before the laws were passed, his big money had come from people who didn't care to be identified.

While I was in the midst of all these political and legal musings, the phone rang. It was Barbara, calling me back. I asked how Kenny was feeling.

"Oh, he's doing a lot better. He's conscious and able to talk a little. He doesn't remember anything about being beaten, but the doctor says that isn't uncommon with head injuries."

"Maybe it will come back to him later."

"Maybe."

"You sound kind of down," I said. "Are you okay?"

"What? Oh, yeah, I'm okay. Just tired, I guess. He still seems happy that I'm here with him. I was kind of worried that things would go back to—well, go back to the way they were before."

"You've been great for him, Barbara, sitting there all those hours. Any chance of getting away for a while tomorrow?"

"I don't know. For how long?"

"Oh, how about lunch? Maybe we could go sit on the beach for a while. Whatever you want. I could use a change of pace myself."

"What the heck. Okay, let's go out together tomorrow afternoon. I've been reading about all the things that have been happening. Are you sure it's safe for you to be out in the open?"

"No, and if you're afraid to be with me, I don't blame you."

"Oh, I don't mind that part of it. I just keep wondering if you wouldn't be happier working for Kevin Malloy again."

"Probably safer, definitely not happier—no reflection on Kevin."

We said good-bye and hung up. I closed out the computer files and turned in what I had written. I called in the deli order, then took off for Frank's house.

In June, almost every day's weather forecast is the same: "Late-night and early-morning low clouds, burning off to hazy sunshine in the afternoon." The hazy-sunshine part was in progress when I drove out of the parking lot. When I reached the corner of Shoreline and Hermosa, I stopped off at the Galley and picked up the sandwiches I had ordered—a couple of pastramis with hot mustard.

I rode the long stretch past the marina and the mansions on the bluff, finally turning down one of the small avenues that led to the beach. I made a few more turns and looked for a parking place.

School wasn't out for the summer yet, so street parking was not too bad, but I took advantage of the fact that Frank had the ultimate beach-house luxury: a driveway and garage. I got out of the car and stood there for a moment, feeling the contrast of sun and ocean breeze on my face. Seeing the house by daylight for the first time, I noticed it was neatly painted and the small front yard was well cared for. Frank was no slouch.

I entered the fenced yard from a side gate and made my way to the front door. I was surprised when Frank answered the door himself.

"Where's your baby-sitter?" I asked.

"The department can't keep somebody on a duty like that forever. I don't think I was the target anyway. You're the one we need to keep an eye on. Come on in."

He was moving a little slowly as he led me toward the back of the house, but his steps weren't those of someone feeling weak or pain-ridden.

"You're really making progress," I said.

"Getting damned impatient with it all."

"Hey, a few days ago you scared the hell out of me. You could use a little boredom."

"Life has been anything but dull around you, Irene."

"Thanks, I think."

He took me out the back door onto a wooden deck. The yard was very private, another rarity in houses near the beach. Latticework over the deck was covered with honeysuckle vines. Beyond the deck was a winding brick pathway cheerfully bordered by poppies and other colorful flowers. In one corner, another deck began, shielded from view between the garage and back fence, where a willow grew. Tall plants of various kinds grew along the side fences. It was a green and peaceful place. Somehow I had not pictured Frank having this kind of yard.

As if reading my mind, he said, "I like working out here. It's where I spend a lot of my spare time. A little world of my own, I guess."

"It's great," I said.

We sat down in a couple of redwood chairs. He had put out a small cooler with some white wine in it. He poured out a couple of glasses and we drank and ate our sandwiches. Again there was that comfortable silence between us, and I felt my anxiety about talking to him about my plans for the evening ebbing.

"I'm going to the Hollingsworth fund-raiser tonight," I began.

He looked up over his wineglass, but didn't say anything.

"I'm going with Guy St. Germain."

Suddenly he put the glass down and started laughing, holding the side with the cracked ribs and saying, "Oh, God, that hurts." But still laughing.

"I don't suppose you'd mind letting me in on the joke?"

"Oh, I'm sorry. I can't tell you unless you promise not to be mad."

"Anything given an introduction like that is bound to infuriate me, so I won't make a promise I can't keep."

"Not worth any fury. Pete told me you were going out with someone tonight."

I could feel my temperature rising, even though I had half-expected Pete would talk. "And?" I said, trying to control my temper.

"Well, he told me he didn't think you'd tell me that you were going out, and that if you did, you wouldn't tell me who you were going out with or where."

"And what did you tell Pete?"

"It's not important. Thanks for telling me."

"What do you mean, it's not important? What the hell did you tell him? I know there's more to this than you've told me so far."

"Well," he said, hesitating, "we made sort of a bet."

"Sort of a bet, or a bet?"

"A bet, sort of."

"And the bet was?"

"He bet that you wouldn't tell me. I bet that you would."

I could feel my face flushing with anger.

"You're a cocky son of a bitch, you know that?"

"I can't believe you're angry over this. I just stated my trust in your openness."

"What kind of a simpleminded bimbo do you take me for? I didn't just fall off the turnip truck, Frank. You weren't betting on my openness. You were betting on—shall we say, your degree of influence over me?"

"Excuse me, Irene, but nobody can have a damn dime's worth of influence over you. *Goddamn*, you are stubborn. I've never met a more hardheaded woman in my entire life."

We were silent again, only this time we weren't at all at ease. An explosive tension hung between us. We stopped looking one another in the eye. I didn't just want to stomp off, and I didn't want to stay there avoiding eye contact. It would have been nice to have been able to vanish into thin air. It was a standoff, all right.

"I'd better be getting back to the paper," I said, but regretted the words as I spoke them.

"Fine."

The Arctic Circle was warmer in December than that one word in June. I decided to try again.

"Frank, I'm sorry if I lost my temper. I just wish every cop in Las Piernas wasn't briefed on our every move. I don't want this to be some kind of game."

"And you think I do?"

This steamed me. He was not cooperating. I decided I would get up and leave. Any minute, I was really going to do it. I was going to stand up and walk out and—and then what? Go to a political bash with Guy St. Germain? I didn't want to leave things like this with Frank.

"I apologize," I said, speaking two words I find very hard to say in these situations. "I know you don't think of this as a game either."

I could see the mollification process going on, and wasn't going to step in and screw it up. I waited.

"Who is this Guy St. Germain, anyway?" he said gruffly, then softened his tone a little when he added, "I mean, do you know him very well?"

"Not really. He's a former hockey player who's now a vice president at the Bank of Las Piernas. I met him the other day when I went into the bank to follow up on something in O'Connor's computer notes."

"How does a hockey player get into banking?"

"I don't know. We talked hockey, not banking."

"You're a hockey fan? Isn't it kind of a violent sport?"

I counted to ten. In between numbers, I told myself: He is just like the zillion or so other people you run into all the time, Irene. Probably a football or boxing fan who has never watched any part of a hockey game except a ten-second clip of a fight on a television newscast. He doesn't know hockey. Yes, it did feel like a cheap shot. Keep cool.

What I said was, "Yes, I'm an avid hockey fan."

Quiet again. Not as bad as the previous silence. I heard him exhale. Good, he was still breathing.

"Well, I guess I'm out of sorts," he said at last. "I'm not trying to pry about Mr. St. Germain. I just want to make sure you're safe. I don't trust strangers around you right now."

"I'm going to this dinner as a reporter, Frank. Guy St. Germain and I had a friendly conversation about hockey and a brief talk about one of the employees at the bank, and he followed it up with an invitation to sit next to him at this dinner. Neither one of us is really looking forward to the fund-raiser, and we each thought it would be nice to sit next to someone we would enjoy talking to."

"You have every right to go out with anyone you care to go out with. I'm not jealous," he said, "just concerned."

Yeah, right, I thought, looking skyward to see if pigs could fly after all. Aloud I said, "I'm glad you're concerned, Frank. But I don't think you need to worry."

"When is hockey season?"

I thought it was a weird question, but decided to roll with it. "The pros will start up again in the fall. You can find amateur games around here all year long."

He was quiet for a minute.

"Well, maybe you can take me to a game sometime and try to explain it to me."

"Sure, I'd like that," I said, feeling relieved.

All the same, he looked a little down. And tired. I decided to let him work through it on his own. Sometimes I actually do know when to shut up.

"I guess I better let you get some rest," I said. I gathered up the paper wrappers and other odds and ends from lunch, and stood up.

His ribs made it a little hard for him to stand up again, but I didn't want to fuss over him, so I tried to act like I didn't see him wince when he rose from the chair.

As we slowly walked away from the garden, I felt bad, as if we had somehow ruined it that day. It was like having an argument with somebody in a church.

We made our way to the front door.

"Thanks for lunch—and thanks for coming by."

"No problem. Look, Frank—" I stopped myself from bringing up the subject again.

His bruised face turned to me in a questioning look. I thought about how he got those bruises, and felt like a complete jerk. He must have seen the guilt on my face. He reached up and brushed some loose strands of hair away from my eyes.

"Give me a call later? If you get a chance?" he said.

"Sure. How late will you be up?"

"Don't worry about it. If I'm asleep, the machine will get it. I never know when I'm going to be asleep or awake anymore."

We said our good-byes.

"Irene?" He called to me as I went down the walk.

I turned around. "Yeah?"

"Have a good time tonight. I mean it."

"I'll try. Don't worry about me, okay?"

"Can't promise that."

"You better work on it Frank, or I'll drive you nuts."

"Too late for that warning."

That comment had me smiling to myself all the way back to the paper.

32

That afternoon, I studied up on current politics. I had kept up with most of it through O'Connor, but having the responsibility of covering it made me look at it in finer detail. At about five-thirty, Lydia stopped by my desk. "Ready to go home?" she said.

"Yeah, I'll drop you off and then I'm going to my place—I'm going to the Hollingsworth fund-raiser and someone's picking me up there."

A look of concern came over her face. "I don't think being at your house is such a terrific idea, Irene."

"And I don't think it's smart for anyone to know I'm staying over at your place—I'm going with Guy St. Germain, from the bank, and even though I'm sure he's not involved in any of this, someone else at the bank might be. So I'd rather not reveal the fact that I'm staying at your house—it might put you in danger, and I'd never forgive myself for that."

"Yeah? Well, how do you think I'm going to feel if something happens to you over there tonight? I think you're crazy to go anywhere near your house. Couldn't you have met Guy somewhere else?"

"I have to go over there to get clothes for tonight anyway. I need some time to get dressed and ready. I won't be there very long."

"I don't know, Irene. It just doesn't seem wise for you to be over there."

"I'll be okay. It won't even be dark by the time Guy picks me up."

Twenty minutes later, she was standing in her driveway, still protesting, while I closed the car door and drove off.

As I made the turn down my block, I felt growing apprehension. Lydia's nervousness was apparently contagious. I tried to convince myself that this was my own home, and that sooner or later I was going to have to return to it. Whatever bravado I had worked up came crashing down when I saw the large piece of plywood over the front window.

When Frank and I had left the house, it was dark out and I was too preoccupied to notice what the boarded-up window did to the look of the place. Now, in daylight, it looked stark and forbidding, a testament to the violence of this past week. It sealed off the house, made it look like abandoned, damaged goods. I wondered if Lydia was right after all. Too bad I didn't have the bucks just to go out shopping for new clothes.

But then I smiled to myself thinking of how pissed off the neighbors must be at me for not having replaced the window yet. It did add a sordid touch to the gentrification process. I'd have to make a call to a glass company.

I walked up the front steps, the nervousness creeping back over me. I opened the door and was met by a smell that made me realize I hadn't taken the trash out when I left.

The front room was very dark, owing to the fact that a major source of light was now covered in plywood. I found the switch, and my eyes immediately went to Granddad's chair. I had known it would be there, but the actual sight of the gaping hole in its back froze me in place. In my mind I could feel Frank tackling me to the floor, hear the glass shattering and the booming of the gun. Images of O'Connor's house, Frank slumped over the steering wheel, Miss Ralston on the sidewalk, and Elaine Tannehill tied to a chair quickly followed. I pushed the door shut behind me and locked it.

I was trembling and suddenly overwhelmed with doubt. I tried to shake it off, took some deep breaths. "This is my house, goddamn it!" I shouted at the top of my lungs. "And you bastards are NOT going to make me afraid of my own home." My own voice echoed through the empty house. I smiled to myself, thinking the neighbors really would think they had moved in next to a lunatic.

I picked up the pile of mail that had gathered beneath the front-door slot, and sorted through it quickly. Four bills and thirty-eight pieces of junk mail.

As I walked through the house, I turned on lights everywhere. I went into the kitchen and got the trash can, going around to the bedroom and bathroom to gather the trash from those rooms as well. I unlocked the back door and walked out into the yard. It was a poor cousin to Frank's, but it had its charm for me. The jasmine from my neighbor's yard was in the air again. My own yard's patch of grass was looking a little dried out, but it was comforting to see. The rosebushes I had planted along the back fence had scattered colorful petals all over the ground and had mostly bare hips and a few buds at this point, although one or two brave blossoms still held on here and there. I opened the back gate and set the trash out in the alley. All clear. No one lurking, waiting to kill me.

I shut the gate and started to walk back in, when I heard a car coming down the alley. I froze in my tracks, listening. It drove on without stopping. Nothing to be afraid of, I told myself. I went into the house and locked the back door. I went around to all the windows, checking the latches. As much as I had an urge to let air circulate through the house, I also was aware that my courage was wavering, that more and more I wanted just to hurry up and get dressed and get the hell out of the house.

I went back into my bedroom and pulled out my formal-but-not-too-formal blue dress. I liked the way it made my eyes look. I also found a slip, a pair of heels, and stockings. My clothes for the evening set out, I went into the bathroom and locked the door.

Somehow, being in the confined space of the bathroom made me feel safer. I started the shower going. I took off my watch and earrings, set them on the sink. Closed the toilet lid, undressed and set the folded clothes on top of the lid. Ah, routine.

I got in the shower and started to relax a little, although I was still pretty jittery. I felt as if I were on a pendulum, swinging between anxiety and anger. I didn't have time for a very long shower, but I made the most of it. I tried to lose myself in the steam and rushing water, the fragrances of my soap, shampoo and conditioner. As I rinsed the conditioner out of my hair, I stood listening to the roar of the water over my ears. I turned the water off. Suddenly I was paralyzed by fear.

There was a noise outside the bathroom.

I stood there, afraid even to reach for my towel, shivering and dripping wet. There it was again, muffled, but definitely a noise. On the other side of the bathroom wall? In the kitchen? Or was it the hallway?

I tried to open the shower door as quietly as possible. It made a creaking sound that I was sure could be heard in New Jersey. Cursing under my breath, I grabbed my towel and wrapped it around me. I looked at my watch—six-fifteen. Too early for Guy. I looked around to see what I could use for a weapon. Other than a nail file and a bottle of hair spray, not much. It wasn't even aerosol hair spray. So this was going to be my reward for being concerned about the ozone.

Suddenly there was a different noise. I waited. It was someone knocking loudly on the front door. I got on the bathroom floor and looked through the space under the door. No feet in the bedroom. I made myself open the bathroom door a crack. Closet still open, no one in there. I grabbed a robe, rearmed myself with the nail file, and crept to the bedroom door. I slowly opened it a couple of inches and peered nervously up and down the hallway. No one. The knocking came again, more insistent.

I heard a muffled shout through the door that sounded like my name. I made a run for the front door and stood to one side.

"Who is it?" I shouted.

"It's Pete Baird. Are you okay?"

I opened the door. He was standing there red-faced, with gun drawn. "Irene, are you all right?"

I nodded, standing back to let him in.

"Jesus Christ, lady, you really make my goddamn job tough, you know it? Do you have a fucking death wish or something? What the hell possessed you to come over here?"

"I might ask the same of you," I said, trying to slip the nail file inconspicuously into the pocket of my robe.

"What brings me over here? A good thing you've got friends, or you woulda been a stiff about a week ago, you know that? Your friend Lydia called Frank. Told him your great plan for coming over here. He got in touch with me just before I was leaving the office. Now, Miss Reporter, I've answered your questions, so you want to tell me what in God's name you're doing here?"

"It's my home," I said, trying to regain my composure.

"Oh, for Chrissakes."

Five minutes ago I was too scared to step outside my bathroom, or I would have been miffed at Lydia. As it was, I was damn glad Pete was here. "Look," I said, "it probably was a dumb idea, but my clothes are here, and I didn't want someone I don't know very well finding out about Lydia's house."

"Well, that might make a little bit of sense, but you should have had somebody come over here with you."

"You're right, I admit it. I just don't want to have someone hold my hand all the time. I'm not used to all this protection. I feel like I'm being a damned nuisance to everybody. I want to be able to take care of myself."

"I'll tell you what's a nuisance. Not getting an answer when I'm pounding on your front door, but seeing your car outside. I was about one minute away from calling for backup."

"Sorry, I was in the shower. I didn't realize it was the door at first, and I guess I was kind of spooked—I wasn't expecting anyone yet."

"You're aging me rapidly, Irene. If you don't mind, I'll wait here until your new boyfriend shows up."

"I'll ignore that last remark. I appreciate your coming by to watch over me. I'll feel better knowing you're here."

"Well, what do you know? The Queen of the Amazons will let me stay. If Frank wasn't such a good friend—"

"If a Mr. St. Germain comes to the door while I'm getting ready, would you be so good as to not try to scare him off? It's really none of your business if I'm going somewhere with somebody besides your pal Frank."

I went back to get dressed. The process was much faster without the fear slowing me down; another kind of fear, the fear of Pete's giving Guy a lot of bull, made me speed up. I managed to get dressed and put my hair up on top of my head in what I thought of as some kind of semi-prissy fashion.

Guy knocked on the door just as I was coming down the hallway, a little wobbly in the heels. Pete motioned me to stay back and carefully answered the door himself. Guy stood there in a tux, an absolute hunk. He seemed a little surprised to see Pete, and I saw him looking first at the window, then at the chair, and hesitating.

"Come on in, Guy," I called out from behind Pete. "This is Detective Pete Baird of the Las Piernas Police Department." They shook hands.

"Glad to meet you," Guy said with a smile. "You look very nice tonight, Irene. The blue in the dress looks good with your eyes."

"You from France?" Pete asked in a not-quite-nasty tone.

"Montreal, Canada."

"Hey, wait, I know you—Guy St. Germain—you play with the Sabres?"

"At one time, yes."

"Hell, I didn't recognize you without all the equipment on. I'm an old Sabres fan. Come on in."

Before I knew it, another hockey discussion began. I should have remembered that Pete came from upstate New York. Almost all those boys from cold country knew something about hockey. They sat on the couch, and Pete was chattering away.

"I'll be right back," I said, apparently to myself.

As I started down the hallway to the bedroom, I felt a cool breeze. It made me stand stock-still. The back door was open.

33

"**Pete!**" I shouted. He was by my side in an instant, Guy right behind him. "I locked that back door," I said, fear grabbing hold of me.

"Stay here with her," he said to Guy.

Guy moved me away from the door of the hallway. Pete cautiously made his way outside. We waited while he looked around the backyard and alley and along the sides of the house. He came back shaking his head.

"You sure you locked it?" he asked, inspecting the doorjamb.

"Positive. I was scared, being here by myself. Oh, God, just before you knocked, I thought I heard someone in the house."

"Let me use your phone. Where is it?"

I led the two of them into the kitchen. Pete called in to the department.

"Boyd? Yeah, Pete Baird. Tell the captain our boy might be back in the area. Yeah, there's a possibility he was over at the Kelly house just now. Yeah, I'm in the house with her. She's okay." He looked up at me. "No, it's a long story. Anyway, I stopped by to check on her. Back door was open, she says she locked it before I came by. No, I hadn't been in that part of the house. Yeah, well, tell him anyway. Thanks."

"They don't believe me?"

"Irene, when you've been a reporter as long as Boyd has been a cop, you won't believe an angel of God. But you'll investigate whatever he tells you anyway. You ready to get out of this place?"

"Yes, we need to get going." They both witnessed the routine of locking up this time, never leaving me alone, one or the other double-checking each window and door.

We walked out front. Guy was driving a sporty blue Mercedes 560 SL convertible. He opened the passenger door and helped me into the car—I tried not to be too clumsy about it.

As we drove off, I saw Pete following us. I knew it wasn't because he was a hockey groupie.

Guy looked up into the rearview mirror, and noticed it too. "Is this Mr. Baird a friend?"

"More like a friend of a friend. I've been working with Pete and another detective on the case you've read about in the paper. They're convinced—and at this point, I am too—that someone would like to see me out of the way. I'm probably a pretty scary person to go out with right now."

He laughed. "You're not so scary. And with your friend following us everywhere, I feel quite safe, even if we lack a little privacy. Does it bother you to be 'shadowed' so? I could probably lose him if it does."

"He'd find us sooner or later and he'd just be mad about it, so if you don't mind, we'd better let him keep an eye on us. He's a good friend of the man I've been working with on this case—the man who was injured in the car chase. I think Pete feels honor-bound to protect me while his friend recovers."

"Well, there is nothing wrong with loyalty. All right, we will not make his job more difficult."

We drove along toward the beach, where the gold and pink hues of the sunset colored the sky above darkened water.

"So," he said, "how did you become a reporter?"

"Went to college during the days when Woodward and Bernstein were covering Watergate. The school was flooded with journalism majors. I guess I was bitten by the same bug. Found out I really liked it. And how does a hockey player become a banker?" I suddenly remembered Frank asking this same question.

"It's not as strange as it seems. My family was in banking in Montreal. I wanted to play professional hockey right after high school, but my parents begged me to go to college, and so I majored in business while going to school on an athletic scholarship. My parents were right. All players someday have a life outside of hockey. But nothing will ever compare to the thrill of being in the NHL. If I could have, I would have played until I fell over dead on the ice. I wouldn't trade my hockey years for any amount of money."

"So how did you end up here in Las Piernas?"

"I married a woman from southern California. We settled in Newport Beach. My attraction to the ocean and the warm weather lasted longer than her attraction to me, I'm afraid."

"I'm sorry."

"No need to be. That was years ago. I moved here to get away from old memories and was pleasantly surprised. Las Piernas made me feel more at home. I've been quite happy here."

By then we were on the long road that led out to the cliffs. There were no other houses now, just trees towering above the two-lane blacktop. About three-hundred yards from the house, we came to a guardhouse and a gate. A yawning guard took a look at Guy's invitation and lifted the gate arm. Pete pulled over to one side, as if undecided about following us further. We drove in and pulled into a graveled parking area. I didn't see Pete's car come down the drive and assumed he had felt I would be safe for the time being.

We got out of the car and walked toward the house. The Sheffield Estate was huge. A three-story Victorian painted in bright colors, it had been the Sheffield home in the earliest years of their reign over Las Piernas. Elinor Sheffield spent vast sums to ensure that it was kept in top condition. The plumbing, heating, and utilities had been modernized, but in most other respects the original portion of the house was much as her great-great-grandfather had left it.

A butler directed us around a corner to the back of the house, which faced the ocean. Here the effects of modernization were more clearly seen. A large open room had been added, as well as a sweeping veranda. The second story of the addition held a sun deck, shielded from cold winds by tall Plexiglas panels. The portion of the original house which stood sentry over these additions was a high tower that stood at one corner. The tower's curving windows faced both the sea and the woods.

It was a warm night. Dozens of people chattered and glasses clinked; the cocktail hour was well underway. Guy managed to nab a couple of glasses of wine and we walked out to the far railing of the veranda, which came out nearly to the cliff's edge, commanding an almost 180-degree view of the beach and surrounding cliffsides. The lights of downtown Las Piernas and the marina glimmered to our right; to our left, the slowly sloping coastline was outlined by the lights of other cities. Below us waves fell in white rolling succession, booming at beach level but from this far above more like distant thunder.

From all around us came the sound of inconsequential conversation, small talk from bigwigs. Several times Guy was approached by someone who knew him from the bank. He would introduce me, a certain amount of chitchat would ensue, and then he would break off with a polite "Excuse-me-a-moment". I turned to watch the ocean.

"Don't get too near the edge, my dear, it's not as solid as it looks."

I turned and found myself facing a lioness. Elinor Sheffield Hollingsworth was no less than five-eleven, and with her high heels on she must have climbed to the neighborhood of six-one. At five-eight I'm no shrimp myself, but there was something more than height at work here. The woman had presence.

She smiled and extended a hand, giving me one of the firmest handshakes I've ever had from a woman. She had to be in her mid-fifties, but looked a dozen years younger. She moved with slinky grace, her long shapely legs carrying her without any of the awkwardness one might have expected with her height. She was tanned and athletic-looking without being leathery; she obviously spent time working out. She had short platinum-blond hair and eyes that were such a pale blue they were almost colorless. Until now I had thought her nickname referred to the family fortunes. But I could see why someone had long ago named her "the Ice Queen." From her proud bearing to her firm handshake, everything about her breathed power. Her eyes riveted one's attention. Here was a woman who wasn't afraid of anyone or anything. And yet, both her smile and the handshake were warm, welcoming.

"Irene Kelly," I said. "I'm with the *Express*."

"Yes, I know," she said. She arched one perfect brow. "Well, looking at you, my dear, I see we'll have to keep you at arm's length from your editor, Mr. Wrigley. He's right over there, so watch your stern if you go sailing past him. An unnecessary bit of advice to give any woman who has worked for him, I know. Of course, you have our dear Mr. St. Germain, who has always been an excellent defenseman—am I right, Guy?"

"If you say so," Guy said with a smile. "You look lovely tonight, Elinor."

"Oh, Guy—you are such an obvious flatterer. But I'll forgive you, bankers can't help it when it comes to dealing with the filthy rich. Come along, Miss Kelly. I'll introduce you to the people you've come here to meet."

I looked helplessly at Guy, who merely smiled and said, "No one refuses Elinor, I'm afraid. Perhaps later she will take pity on me and return my date to me."

"You'll do fine, Guy," she said, "Run along and hobnob with the hoi polloi." She led me off toward a small group. I caught Wrigley looking at me with mouth agape. I only hoped I wouldn't stumble as I tried to keep up with her in my heels. As we walked, she said, "If you want the truth, Miss Kelly, I'm bored silly by these affairs. I decided you might liven up my evening considerably. You're the most exciting person in Las Piernas right now."

"Me?"

"Why, of course. I'm rich, not illiterate. I read the papers. You've had quite a week." She stopped and turned to me with a worried look. "Oh, dear, I don't mean to sound so unsympathetic. To you it's not excitement. Mr. O'Connor was a close friend of yours, wasn't he?"

"Yes. He meant a great deal to me."

"Nothing can replace such a loss," she said. "I'm sorry. I see I've upset you. What can I do to change that? Let's get these introductions over with and I'll think of something."

She broke off our conversation to say loudly to the people in the circle, "Watch your tongues, ladies and gentlemen, I bring a member of the fourth estate within earshot of you." They looked up all at once, like grazing deer that have heard a twig snap. I had met some of the political figures that were in the group—the mayor, Richard Longren, and several council members. Most of them, experts at remembering names, greeted me at once.

Elinor introduced her husband, Andrew Hollingsworth. He was a good-looking man with a tan equal to his wife's and a hundred-watt smile. As powerful as I knew he was, standing next to Elinor he couldn't help but be eclipsed. And yet I could see he used this as an asset, letting her charm the crowd while he rode on her coattails.

Some general small talk and coos of sympathy were made about the events of the last week, and I saw Elinor pulling her husband aside and directing him over to another cluster of people. He excused himself and walked over to the other group, leaving our own circle quite distracted, until she stepped in to call their attention back to herself. After a few moments she said, "I promised Irene a quick tour of the house before dinner. Please excuse us."

Of course there had been no such promise, but I was as much under her spell as they were, and I followed her into the house. As soon as we were a little distance from them, she said, "I must keep an eye on Andrew or he'll spend all of his time with his friends from the city. But they see each other every day and he needs to keep our other guests happy too." I knew, though, that what I had seen was not a man playing the congenial host. I had seen a man directed to someone who could be of political help. Elinor was his spotter, apparently, picking important people out of the crowd for Andrew to schmooze with.

We entered the house. I'm not the kind of person who has a background that would make me a good appraiser for a place like Sotheby's, so I can't do justice to the Sheffield Estate's art collection. I can say that the effect of the decorating style was one that was pleasing and spare. A painting here, a small sculpture there; walls painted in muted colors; furniture with simple but elegant lines. The art objects were placed carefully and in such a way as to attract attention gently without being obtrusive.

She took me through the hall and into the older part of the house. We came into a room that had served as a large entry; a grand curving staircase and balcony overlooked its marbled floor. Elinor was recounting bits and pieces of the family history associated with various parts of the house. We came to a large dining room that had paintings of her ancestors adorning the walls. "Terribly old-fashioned of me, I know, to have the old curmudgeons staring down at us over dinner. They don't look a very happy lot, do they?"

She was right. Most of the people in the paintings looked like their underwear was on too tight. But my Irish ancestors probably would have looked even less comfortable—if anyone had ever wanted peasants to sit for portraits.

"I make up for this room in Andrew's office," she went on, "which is quite modern. We'll skip the kitchen, which is over there to the right, as the chef will never forgive me if I interrupt his preparations. The house even has a basement, can you believe it? There's a small storage room and a pantry. We'll skip all of that; the only entry is through the kitchen. Do you exercise?"

I shifted conversational gears and said, "Yes, I try to. This last week hasn't been very normal in terms of those kinds of routines."

"Well, I just wanted to make sure you could manage the stairs. They're rather steep. You should do all right if you've stayed in shape." As we wandered through a maze of hallways she asked me about being a reporter, where I had worked, how long I had known O'Connor, and so on. When we reached a doorway at the end of a hall, she said, "It will be easier if we take off our shoes." And, to my shock, she reached down and took off her heels. I took mine off as well, quite happy to be out of them for a few minutes, and smiling at the idea that Elinor and I were about to run around the Sheffield Estate in our stocking feet. She saw me smile and said, "I know, can you imagine how fast my grandmother is spinning in her grave?" She laughed and opened the door. We were in the tower. A long spiral staircase wound its way overhead. We set our shoes down at the bottom of the stairs and started our climb.

Now, I'm in pretty good shape, but this woman, who was about fifteen years older than me, was hauling her buns up the stairs at a good clip. She was enjoying watching me try to keep up with her. I didn't want to work up a sweat in my formal wear. Fortunately, she stopped between the second and third floors to allow me to admire the view.

It was magnificent. The ocean, the lights, the party below. "It's beautiful," I said. "I appreciate your taking time out from your other guests to show me around."

"Nonsense. I'm enjoying this immensely, hearing all about the newspaper. And I seldom meet women who can keep up with me on the staircase." She laughed softly. "Are you ready to continue?"

"Lead on," I said, and we made our way up the last flight. Here the stairway came into a large room that took up the entire top floor, with the exception of a small bathroom at the back. That shows foresight, I thought. I could hardly imagine what it would be like if you had to run down those stairs to relieve yourself. The room had close to a 360-degree view. It put the one from one flight below to shame.

"Wow," I said. "Your grandfather knew what he was doing with this room."

"Yes, it isn't easy to get to, but it's so lovely once you're here, it's hard to leave. Andrew uses this portion of it as an office," she said, as we strolled past a desk with a computer on it. On the wall near the desk were framed degrees. There was the fine scroll of the Harvard Law School degree. I was interested to see that Elinor had gone to Stanford and had a degree in biology.

"You went to Stanford?" I asked.

"Yes," she said distractedly, moving toward the windows.

I had just glanced at the degree below hers, Andrew's undergraduate degree, when Elinor said, "Now who on earth could that be?"

I went over to the window and stood next to her. I could see the road, a chain of lights with dark patches between. Below us and to the right was the guardhouse, and a car had pulled up in front of it. "Well, I'll be," I muttered.

"You know the car?" she asked.

"Yes, it belongs to a homicide detective on the Las Piernas Police Department. His name is Pete Baird. He's keeping an eye on me."

"Really?" She smiled. "You're not a suspect, are you?"

"Oh, no, I mean that he's trying to make sure I'm safe. Protecting me."

"You don't strike me as someone who needs protecting, Irene. Am I wrong?"

"Until this week, the answer would have been, 'No, I don't need to be looked after by anyone.' But I have to admit my confidence has been shaken. I don't know. I'm trying to be realistic, and after all that's happened, I guess I have to say nothing is as it was a week ago."

"No, I suppose not," she said. There was a chirping from the telephone on the desk. "Excuse me."

She lifted the receiver. "Yes, Markham?"

She listened for a moment. "Yes," she said, looking over at me, "I know. A message for Miss Kelly? Well, certainly, let him in. Tell Detective Baird to meet us on the side patio."

She pressed the receiver down and then pressed a couple of buttons on the phone. "Mary? Would it possible for you to get a couple of sandwiches and a thermos of coffee together without sending Henri into a fit? Thank you my dear, I know you're taking your life into your hands on my behalf."

She hung up. "Shall we go downstairs? Mr. Baird has told my guard that he would like to speak to you."

"I'm sorry to cause you all of this trouble."

"You must learn to stop apologizing to me, my dear. It's unbecoming. Besides, I never do anything I don't want to do." She smiled, and moved to the stairway.

We made our way down the stairs in silence. I couldn't figure out what Pete was up to. If this was his idea of a way to keep tabs on me for Frank's sake, I was going to be pissed.

At the bottom of the stairs, Elinor said, "I suppose we should put our shoes back on. Detective Baird may wonder why we are running around in our stocking feet." I reluctantly got back into my heels. When I've gone a few months without wearing high heels, the next time I get into them I look like someone who's on ice skates for the first time. She beckoned me to follow her through a different door from the one we had entered by and I wobbled out after her.

The door opened onto a short hallway that ran between the kitchen and the stairs to the basement. I peered down into the basement while we waited there a moment. From what I could see, it was a small room that housed some gardening equipment, old newspapers, and a couple of spare propane tanks of the kind used for barbecues.

A stout, elderly lady in a blue housecoat opened a door opposite the one to the basement. Behind her, I caught a glimpse of the enormous kitchen, a hive of activity in which tonight's banquet was being prepared. She closed the door behind her and winked at Elinor as she stepped into the hall. "There you are, Miss Elinor," she said, handing over a thermos and two large wrapped sandwiches. "And don't you worry about Henri. He knows better than to fuss at me."

"You're a wonder, Mary. This is Irene Kelly. Irene, this is Mary O'Brien, who has been with our family for many years."

"Kelly," said Mary, "that's a good name."

"O'Brien's not half bad either," I said, and we smiled and shook hands.

Elinor thanked her and we stepped outside onto a small lighted patio. The patio held two large gas barbecues and some white patio furniture. It was surrounded by a low hedge. Pete was standing to one side, pulling nervously at his collar. I shot him a "this-had-better-be-good" look.

"Elinor Sheffield Hollingsworth, this is Detective Pete Baird."

"Pleased to meet you, Mr. Baird. I've brought you some sandwiches and coffee. It's not quite the fare Miss Kelly will be dining on this evening, but I supposed it would be better than waiting for her on an empty stomach."

"That's very kind of you, ma'am. I know you're very busy here tonight and I appreciate your letting me speak with Miss Kelly."

"Think nothing of it. Do you wish this to be a private conversation?"

"Oh, no, ma'am. It's nothing like that." He turned to me. "I just wanted to let you know that you don't need to worry about Hawk-eyes anymore. I got a call on my radio a little while ago. He's dead."

34

"**Who on earth** is Hawkeyes?" asked Elinor.

"A man who seems to have followed us from Las Piernas to Phoenix. We think he killed two women there," I explained. Again, that image of Elaine Tannehill came haunting me.

"Oh, yes, the story in today's paper. What happened to him, Mr. Baird?"

"Department got a tip he was holed up in a little hotel down on Fifty-sixth. When they checked it out, he was dead. I don't have any details yet. We might need for you to come in later and identify him as the guy you saw leaving the Tannehill place, Irene. But mainly, I just wanted you to know. Figured you'd be a little relieved."

"A little." In truth, I was wondering who was so thoroughly cleaning up after himself. "Thanks for telling me, Pete. I guess I'll feel better when we know who's really behind all of this." I looked at him, standing there with his thermos and sandwiches. I never saw anyone look so out of place. "Aren't you off duty?"

"Officially, yes. But I told Frank I'd keep an eye on you, and that's what I'm gonna do."

"I'm fine. Why don't you go home and relax?"

"You'll find out I can be just as hardheaded as you are. Go on and enjoy your party. Thanks for the sandwiches, Mrs. Hollingsworth. Sorry to disturb you."

"Not at all, Mr. Baird. Good evening."

He walked off across the gravel parking area. Elinor and I watched him in silence.

"What an amusing man," she said after a moment. "I don't think he came up here to tell you about this Hawkeyes fellow at all. I believe he was simply concerned about your safety."

"I doubt that he worried I was in any danger in this crowd. He may have been checking up on me for other reasons—it's a long story. Anyway, I suppose we should rejoin the others? Guy is probably wondering what happened to me, and I'm sure you want to spend some time with your other guests."

"Yes," she sighed, "I suppose so. But I've enjoyed myself. You must come out here sometime when there isn't such a crowd."

"I'd like that."

We went back to the veranda. The others were just starting to move toward the hall, where dinner was about to be served. Elinor walked me over to Guy, who was talking with a local business-man.

"Thank you for loaning Miss Kelly to me, Guy, I've enjoyed her company."

"I won't say I haven't missed her, but I'm sure the two of you got along famously."

She left to go to her husband's side and we moved to our table, which was shared by four other couples, all of them business leaders in Las Piernas. As I half-listened to their chatter about the effects of redevelopment on our downtown business district, I wondered at the net worth of the table (a fantastic sum, I'm sure), about what drew these people to these events (in a nutshell, power and influence) and if they really enjoyed them (highly doubtful).

Guy and I chatted amiably through dinner. I told him of my tour through the house. He remarked that Elinor showed very few people more than this modernized area, and that such a tour was a sign that she'd taken a great liking to me. One of the guests at our table said, "You're Kenny O'Connor's sister-in-law, aren't you? I thought he mentioned his sister-in-law worked with his dad on the paper."

Rather than going through the business about ex-sister-in-law and on-and-off reporter, I simply said yes, I was.

"Kind of surprised he's not here tonight," the man said. "He's a regular booster of Hollingsworth."

"He's had an accident, I'm afraid. He may be out of commission for a while."

Coos of sympathy all around while I tried to count how many lies I had just told. I hadn't figured Kenny for having any political interest. He had a construction business, so maybe he needed to grease some wheels at City Hall. But I couldn't figure out what a district attorney could do for him.

Dessert and coffee were served, then Andrew Hollingsworth rose and made a brief speech of thanks to his guests. As he spoke, I thought of how easy it must be for him to win over a jury. He had a way of mixing enthusiasm and forceful persuasion that made you feel as if he must be right about whatever he had to say. Perhaps only later would you realize that, unlike the warning on cereal boxes, the package had been sold by volume, not by weight.

The party gradually wound down. We took our leave, and I thanked Elinor again for the special treatment. Her husband and the mayor broke off a tête-à-tête when we approached to say our good-byes, and seemed quite happy that we didn't linger.

As we walked out to Guy's car he said, "Oh, I almost forgot to tell you. I tried calling Ann Marchenko. I'm not sure what's happened to her. Her phone is disconnected and she seems to have gone out of town. I'm afraid it may be quite difficult to get in touch with her anytime soon."

"Nuts," I said. "She knows something, and now I may never find out what it is."

"Yes, it's all very strange, isn't it?" he said. He paused as we got into the car. He started the engine and we drove out of the parking area and past the guardhouse. Pete had turned his car around and was waiting for us. I looked in the rearview mirror; sure enough, he was following us.

"I see we still have our shadow, eh?" said Guy. "Anyway, as I was saying, I thought there was something very strange about what had happened with Mrs. Marchenko. As I'm sure you know, bank employees who quit suddenly and then disappear from view raise our suspicions, so I did a little investigating of my own."

I looked toward him. He had a grin of self-satisfaction.

"And?" I said.

"And I am convinced that she herself is not guilty of embezzlement or anything of that nature. But I think she saw something. As you know, she worked in our safe-deposit area. Do you know much about safe-deposit boxes?"

"I've never had much of anything worth keeping in one."

"Then I'll tell you something about how it works. The bank has one key; the customer has another. The customer must sign in, and the signature is compared to a signature card. The customer and a bank official walk into the vault, and the customer hands over his or her key to the bank official only long enough to open the small door behind which the box is kept. The two keys are inserted, and the box removed and handed to the customer; the customer's key is returned. Usually, the customer is shown to a private viewing area. Under no circumstances are we allowed to see what the customer has in the deposit box, or to watch as he or she opens it."

"That doesn't sound so great when you stop and think about it. The bank has no idea what people are storing in its vault?"

"That is the policy of every bank I have ever worked for. They do not want to have liability for what is in the boxes. There are certain laws, though, which make us pay attention to patterns of use of safe-deposit boxes—laws which concern money laundering."

I perked up, remembering the computer notes. LDY?VS. "Maybe that was what O'Connor had been referring to in his notes—something about money laundering."

"Really? That's very interesting." He was quiet for a moment, as if thinking over what I had told him, then he went on. "Let me try to explain how a safe-deposit box might be used for money laundering. Drug dealing and other illegal activities often produce large amounts of cash. There are federal reporting laws which require us to have a customer fill out a form whenever more than ten thousand dollars in cash is deposited."

"What if they just launder it in slightly smaller amounts?"

"The law also requires that the bank report what are known as 'suspicious transactions.' Say someone always deposits $9999, staying just under the limit—the bank is required to report these transactions to the IRS. We must file a Currency Transaction Report.

"And so anyone who has some reason to hide cash or movements of cash must find ways to do it without attracting the bank's attention."

"But someone attracted Ann Marchenko's attention?"

"Exactly. Safe-deposit boxes can be used in a number of ways to launder money. One method is to put two people on the signature card, and use the safe-deposit box itself as a way of transferring funds. Person X goes into the vault and deposits a certain sum in the safe-deposit box. Person Y shows up sometime later and takes the cash out. Who will know?"

"Do you think Ann Marchenko suspected something like that?"

"Until you came by asking for her, I really had no idea. But I did a little snooping around and found that she has a very close friend at the bank, another employee that she often went to lunch with. I talked to this woman, and she told me, after a time, that Ann had noticed something suspicious in the safe-deposit area. She had reported it to her supervisor, Ramona Ralston. Apparently Miss Ralston told Ann not to mention it to anyone else, and said she would take care of it. This was some weeks ago. As far as I can tell, Miss Ralston never mentioned it to any other person in bank management. I am one of the people who should have heard of this."

"Any idea what she learned?"

"No, but at least we have something to go on. I will be going over our records of movements in and out of the safe-deposit area to see if I can discover anything, find any patterns."

"Guy, this is great. Please let me know if you find out anything more."

"Certainly. I've sort of enjoyed being an amateur detective," he said.

We arrived at my house. He pulled over to the curb and shut off the engine. He turned toward me. I was a little uncomfortable. Pete had pulled over some distance behind us and discreetly turned out his lights. But more than that, I was afraid of what Guy's expectations might be at this point.

"Irene, I am concerned about your staying here tonight."

"I have a confession to make, Guy. I haven't been staying here for a few days. I trust you, but I owe it to the person who took me in not to publicize where I am staying now. I hope you don't mind."

"No, not at all. I understand. It is wise, really. We should not have met here, though."

"In hindsight, I think you're right."

"And now, as an amateur detective, may I make another observation?"

"Sure." Uh-oh, I thought, here it comes.

"You are not really interested in—well, shall we say, seeing me again?"

"Oh, I don't know, Guy," I said, flustered at his directness. "This is such a mixed up time for me—I don't know."

How lame can you get, I chided myself—why don't you be as direct as he is? "The truth is," I went on, "I've recently met up again with someone that I knew a long time ago. There has always been some spark between us. We probably don't have a prayer of ever making it work out—he's a cop, and that creates some problems in itself—but the spark is there. I guess I'd like to see what happens. I should probably have my head examined for not forgetting the whole thing. And for disappointing someone like you—you're an attractive and interesting man. And I enjoy your company."

"Oh, Irene, stop. Next you'll tell me I'm a nice guy, and every man hates to hear a woman say that." He laughed. "Well, do you have any sisters? Any more like you at home?"

This brought on an idea. "I wouldn't dare introduce you to my sister—as I said, I like you, Guy. But there are more at home, you might say. Let me think about it. I may have a friend you would like. In fact, I think you would like her very much."

"Well, Irene, if your old flame turns out to have burned out after all, then keep me in mind. And I'm game to meet your friend. But I hope you will let me continue to help on this story you are working on?"

"More than that, Guy. I really need your help—and I would hope we could be friends." I paused, looking at him and thinking I really *was* crazy. "I appreciate your being so understanding," I said. "I feel kind of bad about not being able to respond the way you would have liked me to."

"Don't trouble yourself over it, *chère*. I'm always glad to have a friend. When I was twenty, this would have been a disaster. But at this point in life, friends are very important to me. Now, go home, and get a good night's sleep. I'll call you when I've learned more about whatever it was that frightened Mrs. Marchenko away from the bank."

"Goodnight, Guy." I leaned over and kissed his cheek. He smiled and said goodnight, and I got out of the car. I waited until he drove away, then waved to Pete, got in my own car, and drove off to Lydia's, Pete right behind me.

When I got to Lydia's, he got out of his car and came over to me. He looked at his watch. "Well, it's midnight. How does it feel to have had a day when nobody tried to kill you?" he asked.

"Pretty good, really. The business at the house scared me, but I've learned my lesson there."

"Yeah, well, I hope so."

"You finally going home now, or am I going to see your car parked out front all night?"

"Going home. You take care, Irene."

"You too, Pete."

I crept into the house, only to find Lydia and Cody watching television together. At least, Cody was giving the impression of watching it.

"Well, hello there," she called.

"Hi. How are you doing?"

"Fine, but I'm worried that you're mad at me."

"For calling Frank? No, I guess I should thank you for that. You were right—I was being stupid."

"I don't know, Irene. Later I thought about it and I figured you were just getting sick of having all of us hovering over you all the time."

"The jury is still out on that one. Anyway—change of subject— how would you like to meet someone tall, dark, and handsome?"

"This, I take it, is a rhetorical question?"

"Let's have lunch together on Monday. I'd like to have you meet somebody."

"Gonna make me wait until Monday, huh? Okay, you're on."

"Well, I'm turning in. I'll let you sleep with that whore of a cat of mine."

"He is sort of like a living teddy bear, isn't he?"

"At nineteen pounds, he could be mistaken for a bear."

Cody gave me a look that said he understood perfectly well what I was saying, and didn't appreciate it much. He snorted. We laughed. That really made him mad, and he jumped off her lap and trotted off to the kitchen to sniff at his food bowl.

"Well, I guess he's going to stop sleeping with me for good now," I said. "Goodnight."

" 'Night."

I was in bed with the lights out when I remembered that I'd told Frank I'd call him. It was after midnight. I decided he would be more upset if I didn't call than if I did and woke him up. I reached over and picked up the phone by the bed. It had one of those light-up dials, so I called him in the dark. He answered on the second ring.

"Harriman."

"How official-sounding you are, even after hours."

"Irene? Thanks for calling. Are you okay?"

"I'm safe and sound. How about you? Did I wake you?"

"No, I was lying here awake, wondering about you, to tell the truth."

So he was in bed, too. Something nice about that. "Hmm. Well, what did you wonder? I had Pete following me around all evening, so you couldn't have wondered if I was safe."

"I did anyway."

"How are you feeling?"

"Better. Restless, but not so sore. What are you up to tomorrow?"

"Going to have lunch with Barbara, but nothing else planned."

"Want to get together later?"

"Yes, I'd like that."

"Stop by after lunch, okay?"

"Sure."

"How was the fund-raiser?"

"Well, for some reason Mrs. Hollingsworth took a shine to me and decided to give me a personal tour of the place. It's really something. And she's really something."

"Yeah, that's what I hear. Don't they call her the Ice Queen?"

"Yeah, I guess because she sort of overwhelms you at first. But I don't know, I kind of like her. She can be abrupt and opinionated, and I wouldn't want to get in her way if she wanted something. But she has a sense of humor. And she did things she didn't need to do— she even fixed Pete up with some sandwiches and coffee when she found out he was out there watching over me."

"Well, you're right, that doesn't sound too coldhearted. Poor Pete. He's put in a long day."

"He's devoted to you. I don't kid myself that he's really there for my sake."

"Pete's a good man. And he likes you. He'd probably keep an eye on you anyway."

"Are you kidding? I make him mad all the time."

"You'd be surprised how many people you have that effect on."

"Very funny. I'd better get some sleep if this is the kind of humor I'm going to have to put up with tomorrow."

"Goodnight. Sweet dreams."

"Thanks. You too."

I hung up and lay awake for a little while. Something was nagging at me, something that had come up in the course of the day, but I couldn't figure out what it was. I was tired and distracted by thinking about the conversation with Frank.

I fell asleep, and as ordered, had sweet dreams. Amazingly sweet for a good Catholic girl.

35

Saturday morning I awoke when a big tomcat jumped up on my shins.

"Ouch! Cody, you did that on purpose!" He looked at me with all the innocence he could muster in his ornery cat face, and purred loudly. I reached out sleepily and scratched his ears. He came padding up along my body, stepping on a number of major organs that didn't need to be poked about by a cat's paw, and came to rest between my breasts. He started purring and kneading, then lifted his chin, just in case I had an urge to scratch it. I stretched and looked at the clock. It was 11 A.M. This startled me fully awake. "Thanks for coming in, Cody. I might have slept until noon. Damn near did anyway."

He wasn't too happy when I rolled out of bed, but he followed me around as I got ready for lunch with Barbara. I took a quick shower and put on a pair of jeans and a soft gray T-shirt that I'm rather fond of. Lydia had left a note saying she had some errands to run and might catch me later on. I looked down at Cody with suspicion. "How soon after she left did you get lonely?"

He responded by rubbing up against my legs. " 'Love the One You're With,' is that it? Just like the old song." I picked him up under his front legs and made him dance while I sang the chorus to him. He wasn't nuts about this and scurried off when I set him down again.

This little exercise filled my head up with songs from my junior-high and high school days, starting with "Suite: Judy Blue Eyes." As I drove toward St. Anne's, I was singing the "Do-do-do-do" part of it at the top of my lungs. It was a warm, sunny day and I had the top down on my old Karmann Ghia, which is not much younger than the song. I stopped at a light and a guy who looked to be about my age leaned out the window of his pickup truck. I thought he was going to ask me if I was some kind of maniac, but he started singing the harmony. The light changed and we nodded and smiled, but I must admit I was a little more subdued after that.

I pulled into the visitors' parking lot at St. Anne's in a fine mood. On my way into the front entrance, I stopped by a newsstand and plunked in a quarter for the *Express*. I gave a start when I unfolded it and saw a picture of Hawkeyes on the front page. Near it an article entitled "Suspect Found Dead" told about police finding him after an anonymous tip. It said the cause of death was not known, which seemed odd to me. I guess I had assumed he would have been shot or knifed or something obvious. Identification pending.

As I made my way to Kenny's room, the article and the hospital atmosphere got to me and I was downright somber by the time I got there.

Barbara smiled at me as I walked in.

"Look who's here, Kenny. It's Irene."

So he was awake. He had fewer bandages, although his face was a mass of deep-purple bruises. His eyes were less swollen. His upper body was still immobilized by bandages and splints. "Hi, Kenny," I said, wondering why I felt a knot in my stomach.

He didn't say anything, but he looked toward me.

Barbara talked on as if he had given me a warm greeting. "Irene has been asking about you, Kenny. She's been by here and she's really helped me out a lot."

Nothing. He turned his eyes away from me.

"Shall we go?" I said to Barbara.

She was staring at Kenny, who, in turn, was staring at some place on the wall.

"Yes, I suppose so," she said after a minute. We got up and left.

"There's a burger joint on the corner that makes terrific strawberry shakes—you up for that?"

"Sounds great," she said. "Hospital meals have all the charm of a well-balanced diet. I'd love to eat something sinful for lunch."

"Okay, we'll split a big order of fries, too."

"Sorry about Kenny. He's been very moody today. He's feeling frustrated and uncomfortable. It's just a guess, but I think the fact that his dad is dead is starting to sink in."

"I understand," I said. Oh, O'Connor. Are you really gone?

"Remember how it was when Dad died?"

"Sure." In the silence that followed, I thought to myself, sure I do, Barbara. I watched him ebb away from himself day by day. I sat there with him, watching the guy I always thought of as the strongest man on earth become a fragile reed—while you hid out in the frenzy of your courtship with Kenny.

But this subsided. I couldn't blame Barbara for dealing with Dad's. illness in some way other than the way I dealt with it. We just were and probably always would be very different people. And as painful as those days with Dad were, at least he and I had them together, and I was richer for it.

"I hate myself," she said suddenly.

"Why?"

"I'm so selfish sometimes. You stayed with him. I didn't."

Had I spoken my thoughts aloud? No, I knew I hadn't. I recovered my composure and said, "It's over, Barbara. It doesn't matter who stayed with him. Right now all that matters is that we stick by each other."

"I've thought a lot about Dad lately," she said quietly. "I ask myself why I can stay with Kenny, but never could stay with Dad. I don't know. Maybe it's because Kenny has always been so dependent on me, so it's not so scary that he needs me now. With Dad it was the other way around."

"Like I said, it's over—it was years ago. You need to take a break from Kenny every now and then, Barbara. Sitting around in that hospital room with him, looking at him all beat to hell—that's bound to make you feel a little morose."

"I guess you're right."

We grabbed a booth at the burger place and ordered our All-American lunch. She lightened up a little and we ate in a companionable way, mainly because I was trying out a new way of communicating with her. It involved a lot of biting of my tongue and redirecting the conversation if she started to get critical. I have to give her credit, too; I think she was pretty much trying to do the same thing.

I walked back to the hospital with her, but decided I didn't need another trip through the halls today. "Thanks for doing this, Barbara. I know you don't like to leave Kenny."

"Thanks for coming by. It was nice to get away for a while."

I started to leave, and she said, "Irene?"

"Yes?"

"I just was wondering how things are going for you."

"What things?"

"I mean, I guess I forgot to ask earlier how you are doing with—you know—everything that has happened to you."

"It got to me for a few days, but I think I'm doing a lot better now. It was hard for me to keep my balance, you might say. Friends help. You help."

"I do?"

"Yeah, sure you do."

She started to cry.

"Oh, for pity's sakes, Barbara," I said, putting an arm around her. "I didn't say that to make you cry."

She bit her lower lip and sniffed, wiping the tears away in a really ladylike way. I was proud of her. I would have used the cuff of a sweatshirt or something.

"I'm a mess," she said.

"You just need some rest and an occasional change of scenery."

"I'll try to take your advice."

That will be a first, I thought. I gave her shoulders a squeeze. I looked around and saw a pay phone. "If you're okay now, I'm going to go make a phone call."

"Why not come in and make your call from Kenny's room?"

From Barbara, this was an exceptionally generous offer. But she instantly read my hesitation.

"Oh, this is a *private* call, isn't it?" she said, breaking into a grin. "Are you calling that detective?"

"Yes," I said, wondering why I didn't lie.

"That's great!"

"Barbara, I said 'I'm calling him,' not 'I'm marrying him.'"

"I know, I know," she said, but she still had that grin. Better than tears, I guess. "Well," she said with a girlish giggle, "I'll see you later."

She practically skipped into the hospital. Barbara is a charter member—nay, the founder—of that club that's worried about my marital status. It was sad that the club was so desperate for any glimmer of hope. I could see the minutes of the next meeting: "We are happy to say Irene called an eligible male for other than business purposes." Applause thunders in the meeting hall. For a moment, it made me think of just spending the rest of the day by myself.

But then there were those dreams from the night before. I made the call.

Frank answered with his last name again.

"Kelly," I said back.

"Hi. Coming over?"

"Leaving St. Anne's right now. See you in a few."

"I'll be waiting."

I hung up and allowed myself the same kind of grin I had just seen on Barbara.

36

I turned on the radio and listened to rock and roll from the modern world so that I wouldn't sing oldies all day. It was a good day for a drive down to the beach. I pulled up in Frank's driveway and went to the door. He opened it, and I must confess to giving him a very unladylike stare. Barbara would have been appalled. But she wasn't looking at Frank's legs for the first time.

He was wearing a pair of shorts and some sandals, and his legs were tanned and muscular. He had on a T-shirt that didn't make the top half look so bad either. Yowza.

By the time I got up to his broken nose and bruised eyes, I realized that I was being pretty obvious in my assessment of him.

"Hi," I said, feeling the color rise in my cheeks. "Been out in the sun?"

"Just out back for a few minutes. Are you up for a walk on the beach? If I don't get out of the house for a little while, I'm going to start climbing the walls."

"A walk sounds great."

He closed up the house and we made our way down to the beach at an easy pace. Frank walked a little slow and still seemed a little stiff because of the ribs, but he was moving around a lot better than the day before.

We reached the boardwalk, where a double stream of humanity strolled in each direction past food vendors, street musicians, and little booths offering sunglasses, beachwear, jewelry, sandals, and every kind of T-shirt imaginable. We forded the stream without getting jostled, a real accomplishment. Of course, Frank looked as if he had just stepped out of a boxing ring, so people tended to back off from him.

"Are you embarrassed to be seen with me?" he asked, noticing their reactions. "Once I've shaved, I tend to forget that I look like this."

"Not embarrassed in the least. Besides, I figure you earned some of those bruises on my behalf."

"Just the way things happened."

"No sale, but the modesty does make you more charming."

"You are impossible."

"No, but I'm not easy either."

He shook his head as if to say he gave up, and we started walking again, this time winding our way between bodies tanning on towels. The soft sand was harder for him to manage. I could see he was relieved when we made it to the wet, firm sand near the waves. I stopped to tie my shoes. He watched me, and smiled.

"I can't believe it. You still don't know how to tie your shoes."

"What are you talking about?" I said, though I knew exactly what he meant.

"I just remember that in Bakersfield, you always had trouble keeping your shoes tied. I remember figuring out that you tied them backward—you're the only person I know with shoestring dyslexia."

"Blame my father. I learned to tie shoes by tying his for him in the morning before he went to work. So I still tie them as if they were on someone else's feet."

"Yeah, but how long ago was that?"

"Never mind how long ago. Besides, they come untied because I step on my own laces."

"I can see how it would make you feel better to believe that," he laughed.

"You'd better quit it, Frank, you'll make your ribs sore again."

"Tell you what—let's take our shoes off—then we won't be interrupted all the time while we walk." He eased himself down on to the sand, and we took off our shoes. It felt good, sitting there in the warm sand, a few feet out of the reach of the waves.

"Seems like I spent whole summers running around barefoot," I said.

"I can see why."

"Enough about the shoelaces, already."

"Okay, okay. I spent whole summers barefoot, too. Drove my mother nuts. 'You'll step on a piece of glass!' she'd say, or 'People will think I don't buy you shoes.' But after the first week or so, my feet were so tough I could have walked on razor blades."

"My mother used to say the same things to me. Barbara would be inside, trying on my mother's high heels, and I'd be barefoot, climbing the tree in the front yard."

"You had lunch with Barbara, didn't you? How's she doing?"

"Other than the fact that she spends too much time sitting there staring at four walls and trying to cheer Kenny up, she seems all right. We actually got along with one another today. I don't know. We've never been real close, but we were okay until my father's illness; then Dad died and she got married to Kenny, and except for a brief spell after Kenny dumped her, we haven't had much to do with each other. We always seem to get on each other's nerves."

"I didn't know your dad had died," he said.

"It was before you moved down here, about seven years ago. He had a long fight with cancer."

"I'm sorry." He was quiet for a minute, watching the waves. "My dad died three years ago."

I looked over at him.

"I guess I should be grateful," he said. "It was quick. He had a heart attack."

"Not any easier on you."

He was quiet for a long time, but then said, "Maybe not."

"How's your sister?"

"Cassie? She's doing great. She and my mom still live in Bakersfield. She's married and has two kids."

"Two kids? Your little sister has two kids?"

"Two boys, four and six—Brian and Michael Junior—hellions, both of them. But I'm crazy about them. Her husband is with the Highway Patrol. Cassie did okay by marrying Mike—he's good to her. We've turned out to be one of those real cop families: my dad, Mike, and me."

For a long while, we didn't say anything.

"You know what's crazy?" I asked.

"Yeah—the fact that we didn't get in touch with each other more often."

"Right."

We watched a big black dog dive into the waves, swimming after a Frisbee. He returned soaked and sandy, but carrying his trophy proudly, prancing back to his owner, whom he showered with ocean water as he shook his dripping coat.

"I guess we could have tried harder," Frank said.

"I don't know. Timing was bad, I guess. We get to know each other, I move down here. You move down here, but you're with somebody. You get in touch with me, but by then I'm with somebody."

"What happened to that guy?"

"Greg?" I asked, grimacing. Greg, the man I was seeing around the time Frank returned to Las Piernas, was part of my Dating Hall of Shame. "In a word, nothing. I got tired of nothing and we broke it off. He just never got his act together. I think I was going through one of my desperate periods when I hooked up with him."

"I can't imagine you being desperate."

I laughed. "Believe me, Frank, I have. And I ended up with some real doozies. True disaster cases. I pride myself on the fact that it has been a while since it happened. Maybe I matured enough to figure out that it was better to just ride out any panic I was feeling about being alone."

"I know what you mean."

"You do?"

"You think that only happens to women or something? I think it's almost a universal experience for anyone who's single long enough."

"I guess you're right. You were pretty serious about somebody for a while, weren't you?" Of course, I was pretending Pete hadn't already given me the salient details about the woman who lured Frank to Las Piernas.

"Yeah. Her name was Cecila. She was with the Highway Patrol. I transferred down here to be with her, then she decided to go back to Bakersfield. It was just as well."

"I suppose I should be grateful to her."

He looked at me. "You don't have to be grateful to anybody." He looked back out at the water, suddenly self-conscious. "I should have looked you up again. I've thought about it lots of times."

"Yeah, I thought about you, too. Guess I didn't want to find out you were married or in some steamy romance with somebody."

He laughed. "I've come close to being a monk."

I decided not to reply that close only counts in horseshoes. I also decided I'd be better off not recounting the details of my last decade.

A big wave hit the shore and came within inches of soaking our behinds.

"Time to move on?" I asked.

"Sure."

We started an easy stroll toward the pier. It took a while, but we made it there just as the afternoon winds were starting to come up. I could see that his ribs were bothering him by the way he walked, and that he was starting to wear down.

"Let's take the boardwalk back," I suggested, seeing that the afternoon crowd had thinned out.

"Okay," he said, and took my hand. We walked like that all the way back to the house, not saying a word, just watching people. I had noticed earlier that Frank had the cop's habit of casually but constantly taking in all that was happening around him.

When we got to the house, I followed him into the kitchen, where he opened a fairly empty refrigerator, then asked me if I had plans for dinner.

"No, but you look tired. Why don't I run to the store and pick up some groceries—I'll make something for us here."

"I'll go with you. I'm enjoying being out."

He looked pretty beat to me, but I said, "Okay."

"If you won't call me a yuppie, I'll invite you to sit in the hot tub later on."

"So that's what's in the corner of your yard. Yuppie, huh? You're not exactly in one of those lines of work they classify as 'yuppie.' I'll have to stop at my house and get my suit."

"Okay, great. Hang on a second." He walked down the hall into one of the bedrooms while I waited. It took him a while to come back out.

When he did, he had his shoulder holster and gun on. I have to admit that it took my mood down a notch.

He caught the change and said, "I just want to make sure you're safe while we're over there."

"It makes sense, I just wasn't thinking along those lines."

He put on a windbreaker and we walked out to the car. He had a hard time lowering himself into my little convertible. He managed it, though, and said, "God, I miss my old Volvo."

"Sorry, Frank. You're at the mercy of those of us who still have their wheels." I backed out as gently as I could, not wanting to jar him around any more than I had to. But he seemed so glad to be out of the house, I don't think he would have noticed.

"You're not supposed to be doing this yet, are you?" I asked.

"That just makes it more fun," he said.

When we got to my house, I was worried about him trying to get in and out of the car again.

"Why don't you stay here—I'll only be a minute."

"Get real," he said, and shoved himself up out of the seat. Except for a kind of exhaling noise he made when he stood outside the car, he wasn't going to show me that it bothered him. I decided not to comment on it.

I wasn't so shocked by the appearance of the house this time. I unlocked the door, but Frank made me wait while he checked the house. "It's okay," he said at last. He walked to the back of the house with me, and I thought he was going to follow me around, but he was going toward the back door. He opened it and checked out the door and lock. "The guy was smooth, I'll say that for him."

"Pete told you what happened?"

"Yeah." He was looking out at the backyard. "Roses," he said, as if he were a thousand miles away.

"Isn't that supposed to be 'Rosebud'?"

"Huh? Oh, no. Sorry. I was just thinking about pesticides."

"You think there's some kind of bug in my roses? I know my garden doesn't look half as snazzy as yours, so I'm open to suggestions."

"No, it's something that Hernandez told me today. They've identified what killed the guy you saw in Phoenix—the one you call Hawkeyes. It was nicotine poisoning."

"He died from smoking?"

"No, he didn't smoke. Nicotine is very toxic. Someone put it in his after-shave—it's been done before. If you absorb nicotine into your skin at a high-enough dosage—and it doesn't have to be very high—you're a goner."

"Someone poisoned his after-shave?"

"Yeah. Weird. But like I said, it's been done before. Hernandez said there was a famous case in England—woman did her husband in the same way."

"So where do you get nicotine? Boil cigarettes?"

"I suppose you could, but I'm not sure. Hernandez said it's sometimes used as a pesticide—especially on roses. I was just thinking that it would be easier to trace if it was a pesticide for something a little rarer than roses."

"So he knew whoever killed him?"

"Most victims know their killers."

"Hard for me to think of him as a victim."

"I know what you mean. I'd say he probably did know the poisoner. This wasn't a spur-of-the-moment kind of murder. It would take planning, knowledge of Hawkeyes's habits, where he lived, when he'd be away long enough to gain access to his house to poison the aftershave. Maybe it was given as a gift, knowing sooner or later he'd use it. I don't know what the level of nicotine was, but someone would probably not try it with a smoker except in a heavy dose—smokers sometimes develop a level of tolerance to nicotine. The poisoner also had to have some idea of his taste in after-shave. No use dosing something he'd never use."

"Do you know who Hawkeyes was?" I asked.

"Yeah, they've identified him. He had a record. Even had a conviction on a prior use of the trick with the hot iron on the feet. His name was Alf Bryant. Very twisted kind of guy. Apparently somebody didn't want him talking about his recent work on their behalf."

He looked out the back-door screen, making me think about the possibility that this 'twisted guy' had been in my house while I was taking a shower.

Frank looked over at me. "Don't think about it anymore. Not today—I'll quit bringing it up."

"I'm okay. I'll get my suit."

We locked up and drove over to the store. There was some fresh swordfish on sale, so we picked up a couple of steaks of it, a cold bottle of fumé blanc, and salad fixings. After a brief hassle at the checkout stand, we agreed to split the bill.

It was starting to get dark by the time we got back to his house. While Frank opened the wine, I made a call to the paper to make sure the story about the nicotine poisoning had gotten out of the coroner's office. They had heard about it and already had someone working on it.

We let the swordfish cook on the grill while we made the salad.

We ate outside on the patio. The warm evening air was redolent with honeysuckle.

"Great dinner," he said.

"My compliments to the co-chef."

We finished the wine and cleaned up.

"We should wait awhile before sitting in that hot tub," he said. He turned the radio on to a classical station. "This okay?"

"Fine." I don't know what it was, but it was gentle and soothing. I sat down on the couch next to him. He was rubbing his forehead. "Headache?" I asked.

"Yeah."

"Lie down with your head in my lap."

He gave me a look that said "What are you up to?" but he did it. A long time ago, a friend of mine taught me a few things about massage—the genuine article. One type of massage is great for headaches. Keeping in mind that he had some tender spots from the accident and that his concussion was probably causing the headaches, I very gently started rubbing his forehead, his neck and shoulders, and the area behind his ears.

"That feels great," he said.

"Good. Let me know if I hurt you—I'm trying to avoid the bruises."

"You're doing fine."

He closed his eyes, and within about two minutes was fast asleep.

"I knew you were worn out," I whispered.

I watched him for a long time. After a while my feet started to tingle from lack of circulation, but I held off waking him.

He moved a little and I guess that woke him up. He seemed a little startled at first, then relaxed. "Well, I'm an exciting kind of guy to be around. You've probably spent more time around me asleep than awake this week."

"You're a guy who was in the hospital a couple of days ago. Why don't you call it a night? The concussion, wine, and hot tub might not be such a great combination right now anyway."

He reached up and traced my brow. "You'll take a rain check?"

"It's a deal."

He dropped his hand to cover a yawn.

"In that case," he said, "I'll admit to being dead tired and a little achy and thank you for being understanding."

We said goodnight and I left.

As I crawled into bed later that night, I thought about how I had made it through two days in a row in a fairly peaceful fashion. Cody jumped in with me and I snuggled close to him. I felt good all over. I don't know how I could go from feeling so good to the nightmare, but that night I dreamed that someone was trying to cut off my hands and feet.

37

I **woke up in darkness,** startled and drenched in sweat, after hearing myself cry out in my sleep. In those first few seconds, bordering between being asleep and awake, I wasn't sure my hands and feet were still attached. As I reassured myself that the faceless villain of my dreams had not succeeded, I became aware that my heart was racing. I took some deep breaths and tried to calm down.

I looked at the clock radio. Three in the morning. The dream still seemed close to me, and I felt some small fear of its return should I fall asleep too soon. I decided to get up for a few minutes, hoping that if I left the room, the dream would quit hovering over me, and leave by the time I got back to bed.

Cody made some fussing noises as I turned on the light and sat up, and was throughly displeased when I got out of bed. He seemed to waver between following me to see what I was up to and staying in bed. In the end, his curiosity won out and I heard him thump to the floor behind me.

We went into the kitchen, where I cut a few pieces of salami as a treat for Cody and poured a glass of milk for myself. Now that I was awake, I reflected on the fact that this was really my favorite time of day, when the coolness of the air combined with a kind of stillness. Distractions were at a minimum. No one was going to call or drop by, few if any cars would be on the streets. There were enclaves of activity here and there, but most of the city was asleep. "Just you, me, a few night owls and certain members of the criminal element are up and about," I said softly to Cody, who was washing up after his meal. He looked at me as if I should hear some reply he had made, then went back to work on his front paw.

The paper I had bought earlier at the hospital lay on the kitchen counter, and I began to browse through it. When I reached the front page of our local news section, I saw something that triggered a memory that had been itching at me since the night before.

It was an announcement of a graduation ceremony for Las Piernas College. The memory it triggered was that of the moment just before Elinor Hollingsworth had noticed Pete's car at the gate. We were up in the tower, and I was looking at Andrew Hollingsworth's undergraduate diploma. It was from Arizona State University.

In itself, it might not mean anything. Lots of people had graduated from there. As far as I knew, Hollingsworth had always been thought of as a "clean" candidate. Other than O'Connor's suspicions about some funding irregularities between the DA and the mayor, I had no recollection of any scandals associated with him. And in Las Piernas, anyone married to a Sheffield would be under lots of public scrutiny.

I thought about the microfilm article on the Hollingsworth wedding, which had been so close to the date of Jennifer Owen's murder. I would have to look at the microfilm for those dates again. He had been a recent graduate of Harvard Law School, so he would have been older than Jennifer by some years. He also would have been away from Arizona for a while. I didn't know if he was from Arizona originally, or if he had just gone to undergraduate school there.

No use suspecting everybody who had ever been in the state of Arizona, I told myself. All the same, I knew that whoever was involved was powerful, and few men in Las Piernas were more powerful than Andrew Hollingsworth. What if on the eve of his wedding, a young woman had suddenly shown up to tell him she was pregnant with his child? Would he kill her? Mutilate her body? Why not just pay her to keep quiet?

Who would have better access than a district attorney to a rogue's gallery like the one that had been involved in the dirty work so far? I tried to picture Andrew Hollingsworth in this role. It was not impossible, but I had a long way to go before I was out of the realm of speculation.

I picked Cody up and lugged him back to the bedroom. "You weigh a ton, old boy," I whispered to him, and got a purr in response. I flopped down on the bed with him, and we got settled in. I turned the light out and lay in the dark, thinking of Frank. I wondered if he was still asleep. I wondered if we would start driving each other crazy if we got any closer to each other. He could irritate me so easily, and I knew I could return the favor. Yet, paradoxically, there was something so comfortable about him, so easy to be with.

I wondered if I felt drawn to him because of the circumstances, if I had reached out to him as some kind of refuge. I was vulnerable, and I knew it. O'Connor's death alone was enough to make me feel I had lost my footing. Was I getting close to Frank just because of the situation we were in? Could I have any kind of perspective on anything in a week like the last one? Was I just grateful to him for protecting me? Guilty because he had been injured?

I thought of him standing there in his shorts and smiled in the darkness. I didn't know if Frank and I would be able to be more than good friends, but I did know that something more than dependence and guilt was involved.

"I like the guy," I said aloud, and Cody looked up at me. I scratched him between the ears. Before long I was fast asleep. Morning came so quickly, I'm not sure I had time to dream.

38

I woke up with the lousy awareness that exactly one week ago, my whole world had blown apart. O'Connor dead a week. I lay in bed, feeling the spike of painful, hopeless longing for his company run through me. I wanted so much to hear his voice, his laugh, his lousy Irish jokes. I wanted him to come back, to be alive again. I knew I wasn't going to get what I wanted, but I wanted it anyway.

I made myself get up and get dressed. It didn't help. Lydia was scheduled to work a half-day at the paper; I asked if I could ride in with her.

"Sure," she said, studying me. "What's wrong?"

I shrugged, not wanting to open a Pandora's box of emotion by talking about how much I missed O'Connor. I was afraid I'd spend the morning blubbering into my breakfast cereal. I tried to make an effort at light conversation; when I failed to carry that off, I settled for being quiet.

Throughout breakfast and the drive to work, Lydia didn't try to force me to confess my mood or the cause of it. If I had been on better emotional footing, I would have been grateful for it; as it was, I felt bad about not talking to her. I wondered if she regretted taking in such a brooding boarder.

"Lydia," I said as she pulled into a parking space at the newspaper, "I don't know how long all of this will go on. Maybe I should try to figure out some long-term arrangements."

"What are you talking about?"

"I don't want to put a strain on our friendship. Maybe I should look for a place of my own."

"Irene," she said, giving me the exact same look that Sister Joseph used to give me when I had misbehaved in third grade, "relax. We've been friends over a long period of time. We survived *both* Catholic school *and* being roommates in college, and we're still friends. So we'll be okay. Not another word on the subject."

"But if I start to bother you—"

"Irene."

Even Sister Joseph was never so exasperated with me. "Yes?" I asked meekly.

"I know what's wrong with you this morning. I don't like thinking back on it either. But there are fifty-two Sundays every year and we can't just fall apart on every one of them. So let's deal with it like good little workaholics. Get out of the car."

So I shut up and we walked into the building together. Once there, we went our separate ways; Lydia went to work at the City Desk, I went to the morgue. I checked out the same roll I had looked over before, and threaded it through the machine.

A little bleary-eyed from lack of sleep, I tried to concentrate on the microfilm images on the small screen before me. I found the June 18, 1955, issue again, with its story of Jennifer Owen's murder. It struck me that I was reading the article on the thirty-fifth anniversary of the night she was murdered.

The June 21, 1955, issue had the story of Blanche Woolsey's accident. Finally I came to the June 26 issue, with its coverage of the Sheffield-Hollingsworth wedding.

I paid closer attention to it now. Elinor wore an ornate wedding gown; the young woman in the photos looked as self-assured at twenty-two as she did today. The years had not done much to change her. Was it my imagination, or did Andrew Hollingsworth look nervous? Of course, many bridegrooms do.

The article talked of family, friends, and attendees. The guest list read like the blue book of Las Piernas. The groom's family had arrived from Boston, Massachusetts. So Andrew had merely chosen a warm climate for his undergraduate work, and returned to his local neighborhood for his law degree.

Suddenly, I came across a paragraph that riveted my attention. It told of how the bride and groom had met. "Richard Longren, Las Piernas City Councilman, proudly took credit for introducing the happy couple to one another." Apparently, Longren and Hollingsworth had been fraternity brothers at ASU. Longren was three years ahead of Hollingsworth, but they had been good friends. Hollingsworth came out to visit Longren in Las Piernas one summer vacation before law school.

I combined what I read on the microfilm with stories I had heard from O'Connor over the years, or knew from growing up in Las Piernas. The Longrens were in the same social circles as the Sheffields, at least on the outer orbits, since the Sheffields were a circle of their own. I remembered hearing that Richard Longren had all but ruined his father's once very successful lumber business. Evidently his political ambitions had taken precedence.

The gist of the microfilm story was that Longren had taken his old pal Andrew Hollingsworth out to some fancy to-do at the Sheffield place. Andrew met Elinor, and, as they say, the rest is history. She waited for his graduation from Harvard, but persuaded Daddy Sheffield to make sure Andrew could clerk wherever he wanted to during summer breaks. Andrew knew a good deal when he saw one.

I returned the microfilm. I walked upstairs to the newsroom and sat at O'Connor's desk. I needed time to think.

Both Richard Longren and Andrew Hollingsworth had gone to ASU. I wondered if Elaine Owens Tannehill had attended ASU as well. If she had, then that might provide some kind of connection between one or both of the two men and Jennifer Owens. I picked up the phone and called Arizona information. I asked for the number for the Owens, but it was unlisted. I hung up and thought for a while. I called information again, with success this time, when I asked for the numbers of Rachel Giocopazzi and the Phoenix Police.

I tried Rachel at home first. She answered on the second ring with a terse "Giocopazzi."

"Rachel? Irene Kelly."

"Oh, Irene! For a minute I thought those bastards were gonna call me in on a Sunday. First day off I've had in the last nine days. So how are you doing, kid?"

"I'm doing a lot better than the last time you saw me. I guess you know the guy who killed Elaine Tannehill is dead."

"Yeah, your pal Pete is coming out here again to tie up some loose ends on that one."

I found myself grinning into the phone. So old wily Pete had finagled at least one more trip to see Rachel. Good for him.

"You still there?"

"Yeah, sorry—got distracted here for a minute. I'm at the paper. I was looking at some old microfilm and started wondering about something, and I thought you might be willing to help me out."

"Sure, if I can."

"Any chance I could talk to Elaine Tannehill's mother? There are a couple of people here who might have known Elaine when she was younger."

"You have some idea on who hired Hawkeyes?"

"Too early to call it an idea. Just some pretty loose speculation."

"Hmm. Will you let me know if you turn up anything solid?"

"No problem. I just don't want to open a can of worms by guessing aloud at this point."

"Well, I tell you what. Even though it is a Sunday and my day off, I'll call in and get a number for old lady Owens. I'll ask her if she's willing to talk to you; if she is, I'll have her call you. I couldn't get much out of her this week—she's been pretty upset—so no guarantees. But I'll try. That good enough?"

"That would be great. I really appreciate it, Rachel, and I'm sorry to bother you on your day off."

"Ah, I make noise about it, but what else do I have to do?"

"Well, I still appreciate it." I gave her the numbers for the paper and Lydia's house.

I hung up and sat there brooding over the bits and pieces of information I had. I reached over and turned the computer terminal on, and went back to the sections of O'Connor's notes on the mayor's race. The election would be held in November. The primary had just been held during the first week of June, and for the first time in years, Longren had failed to take enough of a majority to avoid a runoff.

I looked over the two pieces of code that had caught my eye the last time I went through the files:

RCC—DA + MYR =o=. LDY? $ VS $ BLP AM W/C.

>>>MYR PD FR DA RCC $? CK W/AM @ BLP

Ann Marchenko and the Bank of Las Piernas. Now that I had talked to Guy about her job in the safe-deposit area of the bank, maybe I could see a new way of reading the messages on the screen.

In the first line of code, a question had come up in O'Connor's mind about fund-raising moneys that concerned the district attorney and the mayor. After the rat nose, "LDY?" might stand for "laundry" or "laundering." "$ VS $" might mean that the moneys accounted for in the campaign funding report didn't match what one or both of the candidates had received. Somewhere, something didn't balance out.

The second line of code was easier to figure out. "Mayor paid from district attorney's fund-raiser money? Check with Ann Marchenko at the Bank of Las Piernas."

Together, the two lines suggested that the district attorney might be laundering funds he raised and feeding them to the mayor through some kind of system that used Bank of Las Piernas's safe-deposit boxes.

I looked at a section of the screen just below the second line of code and saw a group of initials I hadn't paid much attention to before:

A H
R M
E N
R L

I had originally thought them to be names of people O'Connor planned to call or interview. They weren't phrases or anything I could make sense of. He would often put a person's initials here or there. But it was uncommon for him to put four sets in a row without some kind of intervening commentary.

AH might be Andrew Hollingsworth, and RL, Richard Longren. But who the heck were RM and EN? I stared at this list of initials until I had a headache that was pulsing in time with the cursor on the screen.

"Patience," I could hear O'Connor say. I snapped a pencil in half with my patience and shut the terminal down.

I walked over to Lydia. "I've got to get some air," I said testily.

"I'm off in an hour," she said. "Should I meet you somewhere for lunch?"

"Okay, how about the Tandoori?"

"Great. I haven't had Indian food in a long time."

By the time I stepped outside I was in a better mood. I decided that I would go by Kenny's room and see how he was doing; maybe say hello to Barbara if she was there.

It was getting to be a little easier to walk into St. Anne's. I strolled down the hall, but when I got to Kenny's room, it was empty. I felt my knees buckle. Had Kenny died? I shook myself as if I were trying to throw off a chill. Nonsense, I told myself. His condition was improving. Barbara would have called if he had taken a turn for the worse.

One of the nurses who had seen me come by before told me that Kenny had been moved out of ICU and into another room. She told me how to find it. I thanked her, and she looked at me curiously. "Are you all right?" she asked. "You look a little pale."

I told her I was fine, thanked her again and made my way to Kenny's new room.

When I got there, he was alone. "Barbara?" he called out.

"No, Kenny, it's Irene."

He didn't hide the disappointment. "Oh," he said.

"How are you feeling?"

No answer.

"Look, Kenny, I know you and I haven't always been bosom buddies, but maybe for Barbara's sake we could try to be civil to each other."

He looked over at me. "I feel lousy. What would you expect?"

"That you'd feel lousy, I guess."

"Well, I do."

I thought for a moment. Should I just leave? I decided I would at least give it one more try.

"Kenny, I know it's a really hard time for you. You've been through a lot. I'm very sorry about your dad."

"I'm not."

"What!" I felt myself go into a cold shock.

"I said, 'I'm not,' as in, 'I'm not sorry my father is dead.' "

The cold shock began to turn into a slow burn. I wanted to break a couple more of his lousy bones.

"You heartless, selfish little son of a bitch!"

"I'm just telling you the truth. You never could accept the truth about Dad. You idolized him. You worshiped him like some kind of god. You made him into something he wasn't."

"Oh, really." I was trying very hard to get back into control of my temper.

"Really. The truth is, my father was an alcoholic who never gave a tinker's damn about me because I couldn't and wouldn't be a newspaperman."

"That is pure bullshit."

"Is it?"

"He loved you, Kenny. You were his only son—his only child."

"I was a responsibility to fulfill. An obligation. You were his only son, Irene. You were the one he adopted as his child. You were the son I could never be."

"You are really one fucked-up individual."

"You even talk like a man. You were tougher than I was. You still are."

I held my tongue. My head was pounding. I took a lot of long slow breaths.

"You know, Kenny, maybe if I lived your life, I'd be as bitter as you are—but I doubt it."

This was met with stony silence.

"I can accept the fact that your dad drank too much. You're right. He did. But there was more to him than that, and you know it."

"Go away, Irene."

"He loved you, Kenny. He told me more than once how glad he was that you came to live with him. How a piece of him had been missing until you came back."

"I said, go away."

"He loved you. And if you don't know it, that is about the saddest thing I can think of—that he died unaware that you didn't believe in his love, and that you didn't love him back."

"I did love him," he said quietly, and shut his eyes to me.

I walked out, my face a big mess, tears rolling down my cheeks. People stared at me as I went by, then turned away in embarrassment if I caught them looking.

Out on the sidewalk I was given a wide berth. I stopped and I got out my handy Kleenex packet, which up until recently was only used when other people started crying or sneezing, and tried to get myself together. After a few minutes I was okay again. I allowed myself a king-sized sigh. I couldn't help Kenny. The old feeling I always had in connection with him.

As for my own sadness, I resolved that my love for O'Connor was not going to be my burden, but rather my strength.

39

I still had a little time to kill before meeting Lydia at the Tandoori, so I walked around downtown, window-shopping. There are all kinds of specialty shops in downtown Las Piernas. I walked past a place that repaired typewriters, another that sold boots—no shoes, just boots—a glassblower, a used-book store, an antiques dealer, and a place that sold and repaired electric razors. About every fifth door led into a little café or restaurant. Most shops were kept up pretty well, but a few looked as if no one had dusted out the display case since 1935.

Like every downtown of every city of any size, downtown Las Piernas had pawnshops, bail bondsmen, fleabag hotels, and places that had what my grandfather called "girlie shows." But that group of businesses was an endangered species in the wake of redevelopment. While 1930s-born Broadway still had many buildings with mythology-laden art-deco fronts and curving lines, they were fast becoming overshadowed by the shining, angular monoliths of glass and mirror that had recently grown up along Shoreline Drive. As soon as the ocean view had been walled off, I had no doubt the developers who spawned these architectural behemoths would trudge inland, and squash the griffins and centaurs and cherubs of Broadway. The Bank of Las Piernas and other more modern buildings had already taken the place of some admittedly funky predecessors.

Even with my browsing, I got to the Tandoori before Lydia. The Tandoori was one of the few downtown lunch spots that didn't close on Sundays. The air inside the restaurant was fragrant with curry and spices.

Lydia arrived and we were courteously guided to a booth near the back. There were about ten other people scattered around at the other tables, which just about made a full house.

We went about the business of studying the menu without saying much. Lydia chose a curried vegetable dish and I went for the murg sag and an order of garlic nan. The waiter left and Lydia looked over at me.

"Are you going to tell me about it, or should I pretend your eyelids aren't swollen and your nose isn't red?"

"Have you ever noticed that, in the movies, a woman can cry and neither her mascara nor her nose will ever run?"

"That's Hollywood."

"Yeah." I told her about my conversation with Kenny. She shook her head silently.

"He's lost his mind. Don't let him get to you."

"Too late. Maybe I'm the one who's crazy for even trying to talk to him. Double crazy for letting it bother me."

"Truth be told, I probably would have strangled him on the spot."

"What do you suppose brought him to say things like that?"

"You're kidding, right?"

"No, I'm not."

"Irene, if you haven't been able to see how threatening you are to Kenny, you ought to start learning Braille."

She had a point. Kenny had said as much to me.

Our food arrived, but my appetite had left. I picked at the soft thin bread covered with bits of garlic and made a stab or two into the spinach-and-lamb dish. But I couldn't force myself to do much more.

"You know what we need?" said Lydia, watching me. "We need to have a memorial service or something for O'Connor. I mean, he hasn't really been—I don't know—put to rest."

"Barbara wants to have an Irish wake. She wants to wait until Kenny is feeling better. I wonder if she's even mentioned the idea to him."

"What happens at a wake?"

"That's the problem. We don't really know except from hearsay and movies. But Barbara's going to talk to my grandfather's sister; Mary's from the old country."

"I'll bet Kevin could help out."

"You're right. Kevin's probably waiting to hear what we're going to do."

I thought of all the other friends of O'Connor, and felt a little better. For every Kenny, there were a hundred people like Kevin, who thought well of O'Connor and would not shun his memory.

"Ready to go?" Lydia asked. I felt bad about leaving so much food, so I asked to have the murg sag wrapped up to go.

When we got home, I was about to put the Styrofoam container into the refrigerator when Cody intercepted me, and I dished out some of the lamb for him. Lydia sat on one of the barstools at the kitchen counter and listened to the answering machine. Her mother had called to invite her over to a cousin's birthday party on Thursday. There was also a message from Frank. Lydia gave me a very meaningful look, although he had simply said, "It's Frank—Sunday morning. Give me a call if you get a minute."

Fortunately, Cody distracted her by having a sneezing fit after eating the murg sag.

I called Kevin, but he wasn't home, and his machine wasn't on. I tried Frank. He answered with the usual "Harriman."

"Hello, Harriman," I said.

"Hello, Kelly," he said warmly. "Sorry about conking out so early last night."

"It was kind of fun watching you sleep."

Lydia, hearing only my side of the conversation, raised her eyebrows. I grabbed a section of the Sunday paper from the counter and swatted her.

"What was that?" Frank asked.

"There's a fly in here." Lydia stuck her tongue out at me.

"Do you have plans for the afternoon?"

"Nothing special. Are you going stir-crazy again?"

"You guessed it. Would you mind going out for a drive? I just need to get out of the house for a while."

"I wouldn't mind at all. Give me about an hour, okay?"

"Great."

We hung up and I found myself being studied by Lydia.

"Okay, Irene. Give me all the details. What's going on with you two?"

"You've got it all wrong, Lydia."

"Oh, sure. 'It was fun watching you sleep.' "

"Last night he fell asleep on the couch, with his head on my lap. We were both fully clothed. You'll have to look elsewhere for your big romantic story."

"Who says that's not romantic?"

I was rescued from a reply by the ringing of the phone. I picked it up and said hello. A genteel, very controlled, voice came over the line.

"Hello. May I please speak to Miss Irene Kelly?"

"This is she."

"Miss Kelly, I am Alberta Owens, Elaine Owens's mother. Detective Giocopazzi suggested that I give you a call in connection with my daughter's murder."

Rachel had come through for me.

"Thank you for calling me, Mrs. Owens. I appreciate it very much."

"Detective Giocopazzi tells me that you were present when my daughter died, and helped to identify the person who killed her. I suppose I don't need to tell you how anxious I am to be of help. Justice won't bring Elaine back, but perhaps it will provide some comfort."

I hesitated. "I suppose she told you that the man who killed your daughter is dead?"

"Yes, and knowing that the man who murdered my only child is dead is some relief. But why was she killed? Why did he make her suffer so much?"

Her voice caught for a moment on this last question. What could be worse than losing a child in such a way? Somehow, knowing how hard she was trying to be calm while talking to me made hearing this little catch all the more painful.

"Mrs. Owens, I know you're aware that there is some possibility of a connection between your daughter's death—"

"Her murder. Dying is natural. This was not."

"—between your daughter's murder and the murder of her cousin thirty-five years ago."

"Jennifer. Yes. We've had many shocks in this week. I've tried to send word to her mother of our . . . our sympathy and regret. She hasn't a phone, so it has been difficult, but we managed to reach her yesterday. She will be coming here for Elaine's funeral on Monday."

There was a brief silence while I thought over something she had just said.

"Mrs. Owens, how did Elaine ask Jennifer up from Gila Bend for a visit? I mean, was there a phone in Jennifer's household then?"

"Oh, no, there's never been telephone service out to the trailer.

No, they were correspondents. They wrote to one another constantly. Mostly girlish fiddle-faddle."

"Would any of those letters still be in existence?"

"I doubt it. I wouldn't know where to begin to look for them in any case."

"Mrs. Owens, this is very important. Would you please look for anything resembling a letter? I believe Elaine was killed because she knew something or had something that incriminated someone here in the murder of her cousin."

"Well, if you think it's so important, certainly I will look for them."

"Did Elaine attend college?"

"Yes, for a time she attended Arizona State University, here in Phoenix."

I could feel my pulse quickening.

"Did you know any of the young men who came to the parties Elaine held while she was in college?"

"Certainly. I don't recall all of their names, of course. They were mainly young gentlemen from the university."

"Do the names Richard Longren or Andrew Hollingsworth mean anything to you?"

She thought for a moment. I pulled at my lower lip, then realized Lydia was watching me and stopped.

"No, I'm sorry. I can't say they do. Do you suspect them in some way?"

"Not necessarily," I said, willing any disappointment out of my voice. "How about the Theta Delta Chi fraternity?"

"Elaine's husband was a member of Theta Delta Chi. He would often bring his fraternity brothers to her parties."

"Could you find out from him if Richard Longren or Andrew Hollingsworth ever came along to any of the parties?"

"Yes, we will be seeing him this evening. He is quite devastated by all of this. I'm sure he'll want to be of help."

"You have my number here if anything turns up. If I'm not here, you can speak to Lydia Ames, my roommate."

"If I find the letters, shouldn't I contact the police?"

"By all means. Please give them to Rachel Giocopazzi and ask her to let me know."

"That would be fine. Mind you, Elaine wasn't much for saving mementos. I doubt she kept letters from her youth."

"Well, thanks for trying, anyway."

We said good-bye and hung up.

Lydia was full of questions.

"Look," I said, waving them off, "this could be completely innocent. And it may be that they knew Elaine but never met her cousin."

"You don't believe in that much coincidence, do you? Same school, same frat, same circle of friends, moving from Phoenix to Las Piernas?"

"Not even the slightest shred of evidence. Phoenix and Las Piernas are not small towns. There could be any number of people here who came to Las Piernas from Phoenix. I'm just exploring possibilities."

I excused myself to take a shower. I knew I hadn't been entirely honest with Lydia. Her questions about Frank had made me close off; when she asked about Hollingsworth and Longren I had denied my real suspicions. I decided to talk to her more about it later. Throughout the day, I had become more and more convinced that the mayor and Hollingsworth at least knew something about Jennifer Owens, and one of them may have killed her. I was certain that finding evidence was only a matter of time and effort.

40

I dressed quickly and headed out for Frank's house. The phone call from Alberta Owens had delayed me a little, so I decided I'd put off my talk with Lydia. Maybe we could get together this evening. When I got to Frank's house, there was already a car in the driveway—I recognized it as Pete's. Since it was another sunny beach weekend day, I had to park four blocks away, which made me even later.

I knocked on the door and Frank opened it, seeming relieved to see me. "Just starting to get worried about you."

"Well, I was running a little late anyway, but then I had to park in Timbuktu."

"Sorry, Irene!" Pete called out from the living room.

As we walked down the hallway, Frank said, "I'm sorry, too. I wasn't thinking. Pete's been good enough to loan me his car while he's in Phoenix. He's flying down there tonight."

"That's okay, Frank, I needed the exercise. And I know about the trip to Phoenix." I looked over at Pete, who sat on the couch with a suitbag next to him on the floor. "Hello, there, Pete. I talked to Rachel this morning. She told me you were going to be visiting there."

"Oh, yeah? So how come you were talking to Rachel? You had to call her at home—it's her day off."

"Pete—let her at least have a minute to get settled," Frank said. "Have a seat, Irene. You want something cold to drink?"

"Thanks—water would be great."

He walked off to the kitchen. Once again his powers of recovery amazed me. He was moving around much more easily, his facial bruises were fading and the swelling from the broken nose was way down.

Pete tapped his fingers impatiently while Frank was away.

"Excited about your trip?"

"Hey—I thought we declared a truce about this subject."

"My, aren't we touchy? That wasn't a question about Rachel."

"The answer is yes, and the reason is obviously Rachel and you know it. So don't try to weasel your way around me, lady. You broke the truce, so fair is fair—what's up with you and Frank?"

Just then Frank came back into the room and handed me a glass of ice water.

I smiled. "Thanks, Frank. Now what was that you were asking?"

Pete colored. "I asked how come you were calling Rachel on a Sunday at home?"

"Oh, is that what you wanted to know?" I took the longest sip of water I could without drowning.

"Must have been thirsty," Pete muttered.

"I was."

Frank looked between us, suspecting something but not able to figure out what was going on.

"Anyway," I continued, "I called Rachel to ask if she could convince Elaine Tannehill's mother to get in touch with me."

They both looked up with interest. Pete leaned forward. "And?"

"And she did." I turned to Frank. "That's partly why I was late."

"Never mind that," Pete said impatiently. "Why did you want to talk to her mother?"

"Because I had a little idea I wanted to follow up on. I wanted to know if she remembered any of the people who used to come to Elaine's parties when Jennifer was around. As I talked to her, I also remembered that there wasn't a phone out at Jennifer's mom's trailer. So I asked Alberta Owens—that's Elaine's mom—how the girls kept in touch. Turns out they were great letter writers."

"Why didn't I think of that!" Pete exclaimed. He looked over at Frank, who was grinning with satisfaction.

"What'd I tell you, Pete?"

"I never said she was dumb, Frank—just maybe too smart for her own good."

"I understand English, so you don't have to talk like I just left the room. Besides, it was a pretty useless idea, as it turns out. Alberta Owens said she doesn't think Elaine kept any of the letters."

Pete sat back. "I'm telling you, it's going to be hell trying to figure out who's behind this. I think we should stick with the more recent stuff. Someone is very good at tying up loose ends, and you can be damned sure they were just as neat and tidy thirty-five years ago."

"You ever find anything out about the accident Emmet Woolsey's wife was in? Who was the witness?"

Pete and Frank exchanged glances.

"What?" I asked.

"The file is missing," Pete said.

It really wasn't a surprise. As Pete said, the killer was good at cleaning up messes. How difficult would it be for someone on the DA's staff to remove a case file?

"I wonder if your brother-in-law has remembered anything."

"Ex-brother-in-law. You'd be surprised what he can forget," I said, unable to keep the bitterness out of my voice.

Frank and Pete both looked at me in mild surprise.

"I think I'll pay him a call when I get back from Phoenix," Pete said. "How's he doing?"

"He's out of intensive care," I said, managing this time to keep my tone more even.

"Hey, that's great." Pete said, grinning. "I'll bet your sister's happy."

The doorbell rang, saving me from making a response. It was Pete's taxi. He picked up his bag and said good-bye.

Frank and I walked back to the living room and sat next to one another on the couch.

"Are you going to tell me what's wrong?" he asked.

"What makes you think anything's wrong?"

"You're a little touchy, it seems."

If I hadn't been noticing the same thing all day, I would have denied it. But it was true.

"I thought you needed to get out for a while," I said.

"It can wait."

"It's been one of those days. I've only had about four hours of sleep. I woke up feeling sad about O'Connor, and all day I've either felt basically at peace with it or completely out of sorts. I keep thinking about standing there on O'Connor's front lawn. Then Kenny and I had a really awful conversation at the hospital. He basically dumped on O'Connor and said he wasn't sorry his father was dead. It was a bit much for me. I'm sorry, Frank. I'm just sort of frazzled right now."

"That's understandable. Do you need company, or would you rather get together some other time?"

I had mixed feelings. I wanted to spend time with him, but right at that moment I really wanted to be alone.

"You won't feel insulted?"

"Not at all. And that answers the question. I'll walk you back to your car."

He put his arm around me as we walked.

"Irene, you won't try to solve O'Connor's murder on your own, will you?"

"What's that supposed to mean?" I said, regretting my testiness as soon as I had spoken. But he acted as if I had been as pleasant as a spring morning.

"It means," he said, "that you're still not safe. I probably don't have to tell you that, but I just don't want your desire to find out who killed him to lead to your getting hurt—or worse."

"I can't just roll over and play dead, either, Frank."

"Well," he said, a little exasperation edging into his voice, "I guess you're going to do whatever you want to do anyway."

"Right."

He was quiet the rest of walk. I kept thinking of things to get a conversation going, but the problem was that I knew I was being difficult. And I didn't like to admit it. But as we reached the car, I turned to him.

"Don't pay attention to me today. In fact, if you could erase the last ten minutes from your memory tapes, I'd appreciate it."

"Don't worry about it."

I drove back to Lydia's. On the way, I remembered another one of those sayings O'Connor was always pulling out of his hat. "It never does any good to tell another person 'Don't worry,' " he said.

He was right. Frank's parting words aside, I was worried about the effect my emotional state might have on—on what? Hell, I didn't even know what—our friendship? Our relationship?

My mood did not improve.

41

Lydia was surprised to see me walk back into the house, but didn't say anything about the brevity of my visit with Frank. She may have been scared off by the dark scowl I found myself wearing as I came in. I realized I needed to smooth things over with her.

"Look, Lydia, about the Hollingsworth-Longren thing. I'm sorry I was so short with you this afternoon."

"You're just having a bad day, Irene. Besides, I've been sitting here thinking about it. I wondered how Jennifer could be pregnant by one of them, when Richard Longren had already been here for years and Andrew Hollingsworth was in his final year at Harvard."

I felt like my feet had been pulled out from under me. I had been so concerned with proving it was Hollingsworth that I hadn't asked myself the obvious questions about why it might not be him after all. Such as the fact that he was probably miles away from Jennifer when she got pregnant. "Lydia, you know how most people get wiser with age? I think I'm getting dumber."

"Oh, you hadn't thought of that?"

"No. Obvious as it is, I hadn't thought of that."

"Well, wait a minute, Irene, maybe there is some way it could have happened. Let's see. How far along was she?"

"Somewhere around two months."

She counted back on her fingers. "June to May, one month, May to April, two months. April. Maybe she traveled to Boston or Las Piernas in the spring of 1955."

"Not likely. She was poor. She didn't even have enough money to buy her bus fare all the way to Las Piernas in June."

"Hmm. Let's consider it the other way around then. Maybe one of them went to Arizona."

"I don't know."

"Well, why not at least look into what was going on in April of 1955? Maybe something will ring a bell."

"Maybe, but I can hardly go up to the two them and ask, 'Where were you in April of 1955?' Besides, it could have been late March as well. They only estimated that she was two months along. And the father and the killer might be different people altogether."

"What would make a young woman leave home like that unless she thought someone was going to take care of her when she arrived at her destination?"

"Yeah. And all they did was feed her a taco and kill her. I don't know. Maybe when she arrived here in June, she never even got together with the guy who got her pregnant. Maybe some homicidal maniac got to her before she even met up with the guy again."

"Oh sure, a homicidal maniac. After all that's happened, you can't possibly believe that. There's got to be a connection—Elaine Tannehill's murder would be proof enough."

"You're right. There is a connection. I just can't figure out who's holding the other end."

"Well, let's think about it. She got pregnant in March or April."

We sat and thought.

"Spring break," I said at last. "Andrew Hollingsworth could have spent his spring break in Phoenix."

"Right! And Longren could have come up with some reason to be in Phoenix for a few days, too. He was already on the council then, wasn't he?"

"Yes. I'll check the microfilm for March and April of 1955. Maybe it will mention some trip." I was excited again. If I could place either one of them in Phoenix during the time Jennifer would have become pregnant, I would have gone a long way toward building a case for at least linking them to all that had been going on.

"Have you talked to Frank about any of this?" Lydia asked.

"Sore subject."

"You two fight?"

"No, I was just real bitchy to him. You know what I need, Lydia? A nap. I think I'm going to try to get some sleep."

"Probably a good idea. But think about catching him up on all of this. I still worry that someone is after you, and I'd like the police to get to the killer before he gets to you."

I yawned and nodded. "Okay, I'll talk to Frank." I went back into the bedroom and peeled off my clothes. I was asleep almost as soon as my head hit the pillow.

I woke up in darkness. I was completely disoriented for a few minutes. Cody walked up to my face and nuzzled me, and I felt a little calmer. I looked over at the clock radio. Nine o'clock. I had slept over six hours. I wondered how much that was going to screw up my sleep patterns.

I sat up and stretched. I went out into the living room. Lydia was gone, but there was a note saying she was going to meet Kevin Malloy and some reporters from the *Express* down at Calhoun's and to join them if I felt like it. I considered it, but decided that I wasn't ready to go out to a place I associated so strongly with O'Connor. God knows when I'd ever go to Banyon's again.

I fidgeted around for a while and finally picked up the phone and called Frank. We did our now routine exchange of last names.

"What's up?" he asked.

"An apology. Sorry about this afternoon. I've had some sleep now, so I can probably talk to you without biting your head off."

"You had a rough morning."

"Yeah, well, it doesn't excuse my bad manners. Anyway, I apologize."

"Well, I've had some sleep myself. I knocked off not long after you left."

"Think you'll be up for a while?" I asked.

"All night, I'm afraid. And I've got to report in tomorrow."

"I'm in the same boat. If we don't make too late an evening of it, want to go out for a drink somewhere?"

"Sure—how about the Stowaway?"

The Stowaway is a small, quiet, and casual bar that has a terrific ocean view. It's not a place to go if you're in a rowdy mood or up for anything fancy, which suited me fine.

"Sounds great," I said. "You want me to drive?"

"I'll come by for you. I don't think I can handle the Karmann Ghia until my ribs heal a little more."

"Give me about half an hour."

I ran in and took a quick shower to wake myself up and changed into my favorite pair of jeans and a white blouse. I was just putting on my sandals when the doorbell rang.

Frank was wearing shorts again, and we spent a moment looking each other over. Cody came up to the entryway and gave him a yowl of greeting.

"Hey, there, Cody." He picked the big lug up and scratched him affectionately.

"You're brave," I said, noticing that he still had a thin line on his face where Cody had dug the deepest.

"So is Cody. I'm glad to see he's not afraid of me."

He set Cody down gently and we made our way out the door.

We drove in silence to the Stowaway. The bar is dark and plain on the inside, no attempt to compete with the scenery outside its one wall of long windows. It was built on three levels, so that anywhere you sat, you had an unobstructed view of the water.

They weren't crowded, so we were able to sit next to one of the windows, on the lowest level. Frank went up to the bar and brought back a Myers's and OJ for me, a beer for himself. We watched the waves rolling in on the moonlit beach below.

I drank about half my drink while he sipped at the beer.

"Frank."

He looked at me.

"I need to fill you in on a few things."

He didn't say anything, just sat up a little straighter. This was going to be business, and he subtly adopted a different posture. More distant. I didn't like it, but it was too late.

I told him about seeing the degree from ASU, about my suspicions of Hollingsworth and Longren, about the connection of the DA and the mayor in all of O'Connor's notes, about Ann Marchenko and Guy's discussion of the safe-deposit boxes and money laundering. He asked a question or two for clarification here and there, but otherwise made no comment.

When I had finished, he said, "I really appreciate your telling me all of this, Irene. When are you talking to Guy St. Germain again?"

"I'm going to try to have lunch with him on Monday."

He looked down into his beer. It seemed to me he was a little curt when he said, "Let me know what you learn, okay?"

"Okay, but I think we need to be cautious there, Frank. He's sticking his neck out for me. He doesn't want any negative publicity for the bank."

"Publicity is your department." Unmistakably curt.

I bristled at his tone for a moment, but suddenly it dawned on me that I hadn't told Frank anything about how I had left things with Guy, and that he might be jealous.

"By the way, I'm bringing Lydia along when I go to lunch with Guy. I'm hoping they'll hit it off with each other."

He looked up at me. "Really?"

"Really. I can only handle making one guy pissed off at me at a time."

"I'm not pissed off at you."

"Give it another five minutes."

He smiled briefly, then grew serious again. "Irene, look, let the department check Hollingsworth and Longren out. I'll let you know what we find out and you can write your story from there."

"I was wrong. It's going to be less than five minutes."

He took the hint and we sat there quietly for a while.

"I guess I'm a slow learner," he said. "I've known all along that you were going to keep poking your nose into things until you got hurt. Just try to understand that it isn't easy on me."

"I might not get hurt. I might be able to help prevent other people from getting hurt."

"That's my job."

"That's both of our jobs."

He shook his head.

"What?" I asked.

No reply. He looked out the windows, sighed and looked back at me.

"Please be careful," he said.

"I will."

He looked out the windows again. I couldn't read him at all. It bothered me. Maybe he had decided to stop mollycoddling me. But I worried that instead he was only distancing himself from me.

"Let's go," he said at last.

He drove me home, walked me to the front door, and said a polite goodnight.

I lay awake a long time, angry by turns with myself and then with Frank. Finally I fell asleep.

I dreamed a memory-dream of O'Connor that night. It was a mixture of two separate evenings we had actually spent together, interspliced into one in the dream. We were laughing and drinking and watching fat women dance. He turned to me and said, "Remember what Sister Kenny once said."

"Sister Kenny?" I said in the dream, just as I had the night he brought it up. "Is she someone who taught you in Catholic school?"

He laughed in the dream, as he had then. "No, my dear, I suppose you are too young to remember Sister Kenny. Elizabeth Kenny. She was an Australian nurse who developed a treatment for polio. And took a lot of guff along the way—but anyway, what she said was, 'Better to be a lion for a day than a sheep all your life.' "

"I like that."

"I knew you would"—he smiled in the dream—"I knew you would."

42

Lydia and I drove separately on Monday morning. I went back down to the morgue and checked out microfilm rolls for the last week in March and all of April 1955. Throughout both months Richard Longren was mentioned frequently. Nothing about his leaving town. And during Easter week, he was featured in an article almost every day, in connection with some special committee that was looking into the polio-vaccine controversy and which vaccine should be used by the health department in Las Piernas.

So that let Longren off the hook as far as an opportunity to get together with Jennifer Owens.

I looked up at the clock. I had spent over two hours looking at microfilm. I decided to go upstairs and call Guy.

Guy was his charming self and said that he would love to meet for lunch. "I also have something on that matter we discussed the other day," he said.

"What did you find out?"

"I think it would be better if we waited on that," he said, and I realized that someone must be standing near his desk. He went on. "By the way, why don't you have your friend with the spark join us? He may find it interesting as well."

"Okay, I'll meet you at the bank at about eleven. I'll bring both friends if I can."

"I think it would be better if I met you."

So someone *was* nearby.

"I take it we don't want to meet at some banker's hot spot."

"No."

"How about the Thai Royal down on Broadway and Pacific?"

"Good. See you there."

I stopped by Lydia's desk and filled her in on the lunch plans. "He wants me to invite Frank, too."

"Oh, no," she said.

"What do you mean, 'Oh, no'?"

"God, Irene, it will be like a double date."

"Relax. He's a mature person."

"What's that mean? Is this guy 109 years old or something?"

I laughed, realizing I really hadn't filled her in on Guy. So I told her a few details, and I could tell she was interested.

John Walters strode up to us. "This sounds very much like girl talk to me. You got anything useful to tell me today, Irene?"

"I think I might have something pretty big before the end of the day," I said.

His bushy brows lifted.

"Can we talk in your office?" I asked.

He motioned me to follow him as he waddled off.

"So what's the story?" he said as he seated himself at his desk.

I filled him in on what I had learned from Guy.

"Well, what do you know. Hollingsworth and Longren, eh?" He mulled this over for a moment. "Do you think O'Connor got killed over this?"

"I'm not sure. I still think that was in connection with Jennifer Owens—Hannah."

"Hmm." He studied me, a skeptical look on his face. But he said, "You watch your backside—understand? Now get out of here and get back to work."

"I understand they're taking up a collection in the newsroom—they want to pay your tuition for charm school."

"OUT!" he shouted, but I was already on my way.

I called Frank at police headquarters. I didn't know how he would respond to the idea of meeting Guy, but I was at least going to give him the invitation.

"Frank?"

"Irene? What's up?"

"Guy St. Germain has found something out down at the bank. He specifically asked if you could be there when he talks about it. We're going to meet at the Thai Royal at eleven o'clock. Can you make it?"

He didn't respond right away.

"I don't see why not," he said at last, and I felt a wave of relief.
"Great. See you there."

Sam was elated to see me. Naturally, when I told him a couple of
gentlemen would be joining us, he was beside himself with joy.

He showed us back to the same booth that I had been in the day
Frank had called to say Kenny had been hurt. It seemed like a long
time ago.

Guy arrived first, and as I had hoped, he and Lydia seemed to hit
it off from the word "go." Frank arrived a little late, apologizing as
he and Guy appraised one another. He had apparently been swamped
that morning, trying to catch up on all the loose ends from his days
spent recuperating. I introduced him to Guy, and they shook hands
as Frank sat next to me. Sam practically danced over and took our
order.

"Well, Detective Harriman—"

"Call me Frank."

"Very well, please call me Guy. I really appreciate your meeting
with us. When Irene told me her friend was with the police, I knew
it must be someone trustworthy, so I asked her to invite you to join
us.

"Irene, you have told Frank about the safe-deposit boxes and so
on?"

I nodded.

"*Ah bien*. What I have to say is—something happened this morning
which made me curious. It turned out to be a part of a pattern. A
man by the name of Robert Markham came into the bank carrying
a large briefcase and signed in to use his safe-deposit box."

"I've heard that name somewhere before," I said, sitting upright.
"And his initials are on the list on O'Connor's computer notes. There
were four sets of initials: AH, which I figured was Hollingsworth,
RM, which might be this Robert Markham, and then EN and RL.
RL for Richard Longren, but who is EN?"

"I believe I know. Robert Markham has entered the safe-deposit
area on several different occasions. Each time, three days later, someone named Elizabeth Nickerson came in. They share the same deposit
box."

"Elizabeth Nickerson?" said Lydia, "Mayor Longren's administra-
tive assistant?"

"The same."

"So who is Markham?" Frank asked.

"He works for Andrew Hollingsworth," Guy explained. "He performs a number of duties: chauffeur, guard; whatever is needed, I suppose."

"He was the guard at the gate when we were there," I said.

"Yes," Guy said. "We found the pattern by looking at the signature card and activity records for a safe-deposit box he rented; Miss Nickerson is authorized to use the same box. He comes into the bank on the morning after a fund-raiser for Hollingsworth. I believe he is putting some cash into the safe-deposit box, and Miss Nickerson is removing it. That way, nothing is reported to the Fair Political Practices Commission."

Our food arrived and we ate in silence, thinking over all Guy had told us.

"I'll have to report this to the U.S. Treasury Department and to my superiors at the bank," Guy said. "They will not be pleased, I am afraid. The Hollingsworths have several very healthy accounts with us."

"Is there anyone you can trust there?" I asked.

"Oh, don't misunderstand. They can be trusted. They know what the penalties for withholding the information can be, and when I tell them that the police and the newspaper have already been in contact with me on the matter, they will not really have a choice."

"It still takes guts," Frank said. "What can I do for you?"

I was happy to see he had warmed up a little.

"Can you contact the state attorney general's office?" Guy asked. "I believe they are the ones to talk to about getting subpoenas and warrants if need be—since we can hardly contact our own district attorney. If Mr. Markham has left the cash, we will need to enter the box before Miss Nickerson cleans it out.

"I am also worried that this is somehow connected to the attempt on Irene's life, since she was coming out of the bank when a car tried to run her down. And because her friend was killed and he was also investigating this same matter, I am quite concerned."

"I am too," Frank said, looking at me meaningfully. "As soon as I get back to the office I'll try to get a subpoena for the contents of the box and see what I can do about Markham and Nickerson as well. I'm not sure the attorney general will go for it unless you can provide me with the records of their movements."

Guy reached into his pocket and removed a set of neatly folded papers. "Will these do?"

It was a copy of the signature card, with both names on it, and copies of each time they signed in to use the box.

"Thanks," Frank said, "this should do it."

Guy paid for our lunches over our protests and we thanked Sam and left the restaurant. On the sidewalk outside, I stayed close to Frank, letting Guy and Lydia have a moment or two together. Just in case.

Frank turned to me when we reached Pete's car. "He's a nice guy. I can see why you like him."

"Sorry. I'm busy trying to win someone else's affections."

"Oh yeah? Maybe you've already won them."

I looked up at him. I felt the same reticence I had noticed the night before. "Still mad at me?"

"I haven't been angry, really. Just worried about you. Anyway, I better run."

I waved good-bye to him as he pulled away from the curb and turned around to see Lydia doing the same with Guy.

"Well?" I said, as I walked over to Lydia.

"We will be best friends for another twenty-five years, Irene."

"So you like him."

"I like him. We're going out to dinner tonight."

"Boy, not wasting any time, are you? Good thing I made you watch all those hockey games with me."

"No kidding. But he's pretty easy to talk to anyway. But we better get back to the paper before John bursts a blood vessel."

We drove back, each of us with our own thoughts and distractions.

43

I worked on pretty dull stuff the rest of the day. I'd look over at Lydia every once in a while; she looked like a regular bluebird of happiness. I kept thinking of Frank, pushing him out of my mind and thinking about him again. Lydia went off to a city editors' meeting at about five o'clock.

I decided I would take a run along the beach. I had some shorts, a tank top, and my running shoes in the cubbyhole of the car, so I went downstairs to get them. I changed up in the women's room and bundled up my work clothes. I was just stopping by the desk to put away a couple of pens I'd found in my pocket when the phone on my desk rang.

"Irene? Elinor Hollingsworth."

If she hadn't told me, I never would have recognized the frightened woman's voice on the phone as that of the cool, calm Ice Queen I had met a few days before.

"Elinor? What's wrong?"

"Oh, Irene, I'm so upset. It's Andrew. He's done something terrible."

"What?"

"I think he killed your friend, Mr. O'Connor."

I swallowed hard. "What makes you think that?"

"I found something he wrote to one of those men who died in the car crash. About a bomb."

"Elinor, get away from him. Call the police."

"No! I can't trust the police department. He owns Bredloe in Homicide and a dozen others. I have to get this to someone who can be trusted. And he can't see me doing it. I don't want him to suspect anything until someone honest can arrest him. No one is here now—he'll be gone for at least an hour. Can you come out here? I'm at the estate. I'll give the note to you and you can give it to your friend in Homicide. Maybe he'll know what to do."

My mind was whirling. Captain Bredloe—who knew I was staying with Lydia—on the take from Hollingsworth?

"Please, Irene! I don't know when I'll get another chance like this. He has Markham watching me all the time. This is the first time Markham has taken him somewhere without me."

"Okay, Elinor. Stay calm. I'll see what I can do."

I hung up and called the police department. I asked for Frank.

"He's not in," a voice said on the other end. "You want to leave a message?"

"Just tell him Irene called."

I scribbled a hasty note to Lydia telling her I was going out to the Sheffield Estate, to tell Frank if he called back.

I raced out of the building, jumped into the car and headed down to Shoreline Drive. Five-o'clock traffic was at its worst, and I felt myself break into a cold sweat as I inched my way out of downtown. Finally I reached a more open stretch of road, and drove like a mad-woman to make up for lost time. As I approached the road that ran along the woods, I slowed a little.

What the hell was I doing? I had to be crazy to be coming out here alone. On the other hand, I thought of Elinor's pleading. I couldn't let her down. I would try to get her to leave with me. Anything would be better than staying there with someone as ruthless as Hollingsworth.

I was down to a cautious creep as I approached the gate. Its arm was raised and the guardhouse empty. The whole place seemed de-serted. It was a spooky contrast to Friday night. I got out of my car and was locking the door when a voice not three feet away from me said, "What are you doing here?"

I turned to see Andrew Hollingsworth staring at me.

44

"**Where's Elinor?**" I asked.

"And I asked you what you are doing here."

It was then I noticed that he looked very peculiar. He was covered in sweat and his eyes were darting nervously between me and the house as he closed the distance between us. I started to move to the other side of the car. He lunged out to grab me, but I ducked his movement and he went sprawling.

I took off running. He got up and came after me, but I made it to the woods. I darted in and around the trees that bordered the road, not looking back but just going for all I was worth. At some point I slowed just long enough to glance back. I couldn't see him. I kept running.

I hid behind a large tree and caught my breath. I looked back, and this time I had a fairly clear view of the house. Andrew Hollingsworth was walking with his back to me, toward the house. My breath came in sharp, stabbing gulps. I felt dizzy. What had gone wrong? Hollingsworth must have come home unexpectedly. But I didn't see any sign of Markham anywhere. What had he done with Elinor? Or what would he do, now that he had seen me?

I started moving cautiously toward the road. I wanted to follow it out, but I didn't want to be out on it. I knew that the tower would afford Hollingsworth a perfect view of the road itself. If I stayed in the woods, he might not see me.

I tried to remember how far the road went before there was another house or building, and felt dismayed. By the time I got anywhere, even if I ran, Hollingsworth could be long gone. He might even be getting a car now, suspecting the direction I would be headed.

As if to confirm these thoughts, I heard the sound of a racing car engine. I lay down and looked out at the road. The sound came closer, and I realized that it was coming into the estate, not from it. My relief turned to horror when I saw that the car was Pete Baird's. Unaware of any danger to himself, Frank had come after me. The car flew by, and I helplessly watched him disappear from view. I had to try to get back to the house and warn him before Andrew Hollingsworth found out he was here. I ran back through the woods. My legs felt shaky but I forced them onward. As I came within view of the house, I froze and dropped to the ground.

A group of people was making its way into the house by the side door off the barbecue patio. Even from the back, I recognized them.

Frank was first, with his hands raised. Then Elinor.

Then Andrew, with a gun.

45

I felt sick. I was quivering with fear and exhaustion, but I had to think of something. Maybe I could get inside the house and use the phone. But would anyone get here fast enough to save Frank and Elinor?

I looked out at the cliffside. Could I be seen or heard by someone below on the beach? Not likely. I noticed some ships out on the water. Maybe I could do something to attract their attention. Something that would also distract Andrew Hollingsworth and give Frank and Elinor a chance to escape.

Suddenly I remembered the propane tanks and the newspapers in the basement. If no one was in the hallway, I could probably get down there long enough to start a good-sized fire, one that could be seen from the water. It would be risky for Frank and Elinor, but with luck it would provide enough of a distraction for them to get out safely.

I crouched low and made my way to the side patio. I leaned up against the wall of the house. The kitchen windows were closed, but I could hear voices—mainly Andrew's, but I couldn't make out what he was saying. If they were in the kitchen, it would be hard to sneak into the basement without being seen or heard. I couldn't think of any other way into the house that would be any more quiet, so I went ahead and slowly turned the knob on the door leading into the house.

I slowly pulled the door open and was relieved to see the door to the kitchen was closed. I opened the basement door and went softly down the stairs. It was dark, but a little light came through a small window. My eyes got used to it and I found the propane tanks. I looked around the room for items that would burn.

I found newspapers and some matches. I opened both propane tanks just a crack, so that the hissing would not be loud enough to attract attention. If I went upstairs and tossed a match down here as I left, I figured I would have the distraction I was looking for. I was on my way up the stairs when the door suddenly opened.

I saw the gun first. Then I realized Elinor Hollingsworth was the one pointing it at me.

"Thank God you're safe!" I said, feeling relieved.

"Oh, you're the one who's in danger. Come on up and join your friend. You've been making enough noise down here to wake the dead."

She laughed a strange laugh, still pointing the gun. I finally caught on.

"Don't try anything foolish, Irene. I'm an expert with firearms."

I walked up the stairs and she prodded me into the kitchen. Andrew held a gun on Frank. I guessed from Frank's empty shoulder holster that Elinor had his. Frank looked over at me, and for a moment we exchanged a look of mutual fear for one another. He forced a smile and said, "Come on in, Irene. We can wait here and watch the Hollingsworths get arrested."

"Shut up!" Andrew said.

"Now, now, Andrew," said Elinor, cool as ice. "There aren't going to be any arrests. And even if I believed for a moment that the police were on their way, I have the comfort of knowing that these two will not live to see their would-be rescuers. Stand a few feet away from Mr. Harriman, please, Irene. The two of you will be very much together soon."

"Let me guess," Frank said. "Looking at old Andrew quiver and quake here, I'd lay money you were the one who killed that girl."

"Of course I was. Do you think I was going to let some little white trash strumpet from Arizona spoil my wedding plans? And Andrew was going to marry her! Can you believe it?"

A pained look crossed Andrew's face. Elinor smiled and went on.

"She shows up in town one night, tells him that she's pregnant. She says it was from his visit to her on spring break. That was rather naughty of you, wasn't it, Andrew?"

Andrew's eyes glazed over, as if he had mentally withdrawn from us.

Elinor smirked. "She tells him she's written a letter to her cousin, naming the father-to-be. What does he do? He tells her he'll make an honest woman of her!"

Elinor hooted over this. "He came to tell me we would have to break off our engagement. I told him not to worry, to leave it all to me. And convinced the little whore that she should meet me under the pier and the rest has been history in this town for thirty-five years."

"Not exactly," I said, finding my voice.

She shot a hard look at me.

"What did you do with her hands and feet?"

Andrew blanched, but Elinor cackled.

"Oh, that was inspired. What better place for a pair of feet than at the end of a pair of legs?"

"She buried them under the Las Piernas cliffs," Andrew said quietly.

Frank and I looked at one another.

"As for the hands, well, I made a very special wedding present of them to my dear husband."

"Elinor! For God's sakes!"

"They want to hear the story, Andrew. You know, Andrew thought I had just paid her off to leave town until the story came out in the paper the next day. I called him to remind him that I knew where he had eaten dinner with her, that he was the last one to have been seen in public with her, and that I could easily provide the link between the two of them. Who in Las Piernas wouldn't take my word over his? Why, at that time, no one would have thought of a woman doing such a thing anyway."

Even now it was hard to believe. Elinor had great physical strength and an iron will. A lady who always got her own way. "Why not just pay her off?" I asked.

"Oh, I tried. And I would have been good for it. It's worked with our beloved mayor for years. But the cheap tart said she didn't want my money, she wanted Andrew. Well, she simply couldn't have him. I had come prepared in case she refused."

She eyed us warily.

"Andrew, get some rope from the basement. We don't want to take chances with these two."

"No," he said. "You know I won't go down there."

Elinor sighed. "His wedding present is in the freezer down there. He won't go near it." She laughed at him. "She's not going to reach up and grab you, Andrew." He turned red, but said nothing. She walked over to her husband. "Andrew has been very good to me over the years, so I put up with his little phobia about the basement."

"Why O'Connor?" I asked. "What did he ever do to you?"

"He was about to figure out who she was, that's what. I learned that from his son."

She smiled at the look of surprise on my face. "I had an affair with Kenny. Strictly for espionage purposes. The little blabbermouth told me every move his father made. Of course he was clueless as to my reasons for wanting to know. Kenny's not much of a lover. Nothing like Andrew. Andrew is a fantastic lover. I'm disappointed Kenny survived, but I understand he's not saying anything."

I looked at Andrew. He stood with a stony expression, not directly acknowledging our presence with anything other than the gun. If Elinor was embarrassing him, he didn't show it.

"I'm surprised Andrew can get it up for you after the way you treated his girlfriend," Frank said.

A look of cold fury passed over her face.

She walked up to Frank, put the gun to his temple, and cocked the trigger. "Raise your hands higher."

He did. She drew her other arm back and punched him hard in the ribs. He paled and exhaled loudly, but he didn't give her the satisfaction of hearing him crying out. She stepped away with a smile on her face.

Frank's forehead was covered with sweat, but he lowered his arms again and said nothing.

"Irene, I really like you. And he does seem to be quite a man. I'm rather sorry we didn't get to know one another better. Wouldn't cry out for me. Well, we'll see."

"Elinor, let's get this over with and get out of here," Andrew said. She looked at him.

"Very well, put them in the freezer. I'll get the rope."

She waited a moment to make sure he obeyed.

He motioned us over to a walk-in freezer not far from where we stood. He pointed the gun at me. "Open it."

I did as I was told. I yanked at the handle and pulled the heavy door open. It was a small meat freezer. Various cuts of meat hung in it, large containers of ice cream were stored on racks on one wall. I shivered as I stood behind the door. I'm not sure it was from the cold.

He turned the gun on Frank. "Go on, you first."

"Hollingsworth, this is your chance to get free of her," Frank said. "Why let her push you around? She's the murderer, not you."

For a moment Andrew Hollingsworth looked bewildered. He glanced back at Elinor, then back to us. He leveled the gun at Frank, his hands shaking. "Get in there," he said.

"You're a DA, you know how it works. We'll tell the attorney general you helped us out. He'll go easy on you."

He said nothing, just stood there quivering like a frightened animal.

"Let Irene go. She hasn't done you any harm."

"Andrew!" Elinor commanded.

It was only one word, but it cracked through the air like a whip. Hollingsworth grew wild-eyed. He turned the gun toward me and screamed at Frank. "Get in there! Do it now or she's dead! I'll do it! I'll blow her head off!"

Frank walked stiffly and slowly, the barrel of Andrew's gun now following his every move. He went into the freezer. I hated myself, knowing he was here because of me.

Elinor had walked over to the basement door.

"That's odd," she said.

All I heard after that was a loud explosion.

46

I felt myself ripped away from behind the door and hurtled hard into a wall. I lay there, flat on my back, stunned and unsure of what had happened. The air was hot. I felt my face covered with something sticky, something salty that was in my mouth. My ears felt as if they were filled with water. Next I became aware that there was smoke filling the room. I closed my eyes. It dawned on me that there was no sound.

Someone was lifting me. I opened my eyes and saw Frank looking down at me. He was trying to say something to me, but he wasn't making any noise. I smiled at him and closed my eyes.

When I opened them again, I was looking up at a smoky sky. I was coughing. Frank's face came into my field of vision again. I realized he was bending over me. We were on some grass. He held me. I felt sleepy.

I looked up into his face. What was wrong with his eyes? They were watery. He was trying to say something. I think it was my name. He wasn't making any sound. I moved my hand to his lips. I closed my eyes again.

47

The first sound I heard was snoring. I woke up in a strange room, hearing snoring. That and a hammering inside my skull. I slowly turned my head to see Frank sleeping in a chair behind bars. I gradually realized I was in a hospital bed, and the bars were the bed railing. My head hurt so bad, it was easier to shut my eyes. I fell back to sleep.

When I woke up again, there was a woman's face looking down at me. "I think she's coming around now," the voice said, and I realized it was Sister Theresa. Soon I saw Frank standing next to her.

"Hi," I said.

"Hi." He took my hand. That felt good.

"Your sister has been asking about you," Sister Theresa said. "I think I'll let her know you're awake."

Frank sat down, but kept hold of my hand. I let go and slipped my arm through the rails to make it easier on him.

I fell asleep.

Later that night, I finally managed to stay awake for more than five seconds at a time. Frank was still holding my hand.

"Frank?"

He sat up with a start. He looked exhausted.

"Irene? How do you feel?"

"Like hell. What happened?"

"Did you open those propane tanks in the basement?"

I was still a little foggy. Gradually I remembered where I had been just before the explosion.

"Yes. But I didn't light them."

"It filled the room up with propane. Elinor flipped the light switch and it sparked. It exploded. And burned."

"Are you okay?"

"Yeah. I guess they did me a real favor sticking me in that freezer."

I remembered seeing him put in there at gunpoint, remembered Elinor holding the gun to his head and striking his ribs hard. I felt the color drain from my cheeks.

"Irene? Are you okay? Do you want me to get the nurse?"

"No," I said. "I'm okay. I just remembered how they treated you. I was so afraid for you."

"Believe me, it was mutual. God, you gave me a scare. When I brought you outside—"

His voice broke and he was quiet, looking away.

"I'm okay," I said.

"Hello there!" Barbara called from the door.

She came over to the other side of the bed. "This guy is worse than I am. Even Sister Theresa couldn't get him to take a break."

The memory of hearing him snore came back to me and I smiled.

"Hi, Barbara. How's Kenny doing?"

"He'll be in here to apologize to you any day now," she said.

"What do you mean?"

"He told me what he said to you about O'Connor. I told him either he apologized or I wasn't ever going to have a thing to do with him. He started crying and going on about how he killed his father. I tell you, he's delirious. I told him you and Frank knew who killed his father, and that as far as I knew, his name hadn't come up. Do you know what he was talking about?"

Frank and I exchanged a brief look.

"No," I said. "He probably just feels bad about what he said to me. Tell him I said all is forgiven." I turned to Frank. "What happened to the Hollingsworths?"

He shook his head.

"Oh."

"Longren has confessed to the money laundering and providing a false alibi for Emmet Woolsey's wife; he claims he never knew about the other stuff, but nobody believes him. He's washed up anyway. Elaine's mother never found the letter. It was probably thrown away years ago. We called her to let her know what happened. Small consolation."

My head felt heavy and woozy. I shut my eyes and it cleared.

I looked up at Frank again; there was concern in his face.

"How did you know I was out there?" I asked.

"Lydia. She called me to say you had left her that note. But we can talk about all of that later. Just get better. They want to hold that wake for O'Connor and they're waiting for you to get out of here to do it."

"I owe you a lot," I said drowsily.

"Not a thing. Go to sleep."

I did.

48

It was a grand occasion. There was food and drink and joyful and tearful remembrances of the man we loved.

"Do you believe in ghosts?" I asked Frank.

"Only Casper."

"You should get to know O'Connor's—it's even friendlier."

I must have talked and laughed and cried with a hundred people. Barbara and Aunt Mary had set the whole thing up at Barbara's house. Sam and Roselynn had provided some of the food. Probably one of the first Irish wakes to serve Thai food.

I avoided the booze—I wanted to give my head a chance to stop aching from the blow I gave it when I hit that kitchen wall. Frank didn't drink either, telling me I should have one sober person to talk to.

Kenny was there, home but not really up and around. He and Barbara were going to make another go of it. I was happy to notice that she was being more assertive around him.

Kevin had brought the gang from Calhoun's, someone else had brought a group from Banyon's. There were reporters, cops—even Captain Bredloe, who of course had never been on anyone's payroll. Just another of Elinor's lies. I saw MacPherson and Global Guru Fred Barnes, and dozens of other people who had come into contact with O'Connor over the years.

Pete had shown up, and Rachel had come with him. They sparred with each other verbally. Pete had more than met his match with her. She hadn't moved from Phoenix, but something told me one of them was going to relocate before long.

Guy and Lydia were in the throes of new love, which can be boring to observe if you're not one of the parties involved. I was happy for them all the same.

Aunt Mary had located an Irish band, complete with fiddle, guitar, bodhrán, pipes, harp, tin whistle, and voices that lovingly sang the songs of Eire. They did a moving version of an old favorite of O'Connor's, "Bonnie Light Horseman." I felt the tears well up for the umpteenth time as it was played. I looked over to see John Walters himself getting misty-eyed.

After a great many pints had been downed and songs had been sung, Frank took me out to his car, another used Volvo he had picked up while I was in the hospital.

As he drove along, I realized that he wasn't taking me to Lydia's.

He brought the car to a halt in his driveway. He got out and opened the door for me. We walked inside, and he closed the door behind us.

He took me in his arms and gave me a long, slow, burning kiss. I kissed back for all I was worth. "Stay with me," he said softly.

I did. And later, as we lay holding one another in bed, warmed by love and ready at last to fall asleep, I heard him softly sing, "Goodnight, Irene."